Usborne Illustrated Originals

Around the
World
in Eighty Days

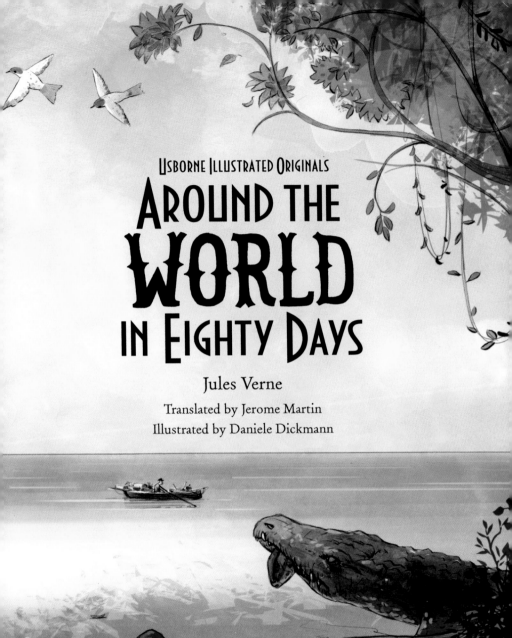

Usborne Illustrated Originals

Around the
World
in Eighty Days

Jules Verne

Translated by Jerome Martin
Illustrated by Daniele Dickmann

CONTENTS

1972

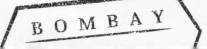

BOMBAY

Mr. Phileas Fogg, Esquire

CHAPTER I

IN WHICH PHILEAS FOGG AND PASSEPARTOUT
AGREE TO BECOME MASTER AND SERVANT

In the year 1872, the house at No. 7, Savile Row, Burlington Gardens – the house in which the playwright Sheridan died in 1814 – was inhabited by Mr. Phileas Fogg. He was one of the most singular and notable members of London's Reform Club: notable despite his apparent determination to do nothing at all that might attract attention. Nothing was known about this enigmatic person, except that he was a handsome and polished man of the world. It was said that he resembled the dashing poet Byron – but a bearded, impassive, irreproachable Byron who could have lived a thousand years without growing old.

Certainly an Englishman, it was more doubtful whether Phileas Fogg was a Londoner. He had never been seen at the Exchange, nor at the Bank, nor at any of the counting-rooms of the City. Neither the basins nor the docks of London had ever received a vessel chartered by Phileas Fogg. He didn't appear on any administrative committees. He had never been entered at the Inns of Court: not at the Temple, nor at Lincoln's Inn, nor at Gray's Inn. His voice had never rung out at the Court of Chancery, or at the Queen's Bench, or at the Exchequer, or in the Ecclesiastical Courts. He was not a manufacturer, nor a merchant, nor a gentleman farmer. He was a member of neither the Royal Institution, nor the London Institution, nor the Russell Institution, nor the Western Literary Institution, nor the Artisans' Association, nor that Institution of Arts and Sciences, which flourishes under the direct patronage of Her Majesty the Queen. He belonged, in fact, to none of the numerous societies that swarm the English capital, from the Harmonica Society to the Society of Entomologists, founded with the principal aim of destroying pernicious insects.

Phileas Fogg was a member of the Reform Club, and that was all.

Some, indeed, might wonder how so mysterious a gentleman should have joined that exclusive association. In fact, he was

recommended by the firm Baring Brothers – bankers with whom he had an open line of credit. His checks were regularly paid from his checking account, which was always swiftly replenished.

Was this Phileas Fogg rich? Undoubtedly. But the manner in which he had come by his fortune was unknown even to the best informed, and Mr. Fogg was the last person to whom one might apply for information. In any case, he was neither lavish nor miserly, and whenever support was needed for a noble, useful or benevolent cause, he supplied it quietly and sometimes anonymously.

He was, in short, the least communicative of men. He spoke as little as possible, and his silence made him appear even more mysterious. His daily habits were quite open to observation, but everything he did was so mathematically regular and repetitive that it only seemed to deepen the mystery surrounding him.

Had he traveled? It was likely, for no one seemed to know the world better than he. He appeared to be personally acquainted with every corner of the globe – however distant. Sometimes, with a few words, he corrected the thousand conjectures circulating in the Club with regard to lost or missing explorers. He pointed out the true probabilities – and so often did events confirm his predictions, that he seemed gifted with a

sort of second sight. He must have traveled everywhere, at least in spirit.

It was in any case certain that, for many years, Phileas Fogg hadn't stirred from London. Those privileged to know him slightly better than others declared that nobody had ever seen him anywhere else. His only pastimes were reading newspapers and playing whist. He often won at this card game which, as it was played in silence, suited his nature. However, his winnings never entered his accounts, and he used them instead to swell his charitable donations. What is more, Mr. Fogg evidently played not to win, but for the sake of playing. The game was in his eyes a struggle: a struggle against an obstacle, but a motionless, unwearying struggle that spoke to his character.

Phileas Fogg, it seemed, had neither wife nor children. This might be true of even the most honest gentleman – but it is equally true that Mr. Fogg had neither family nor friends, which is admittedly more unusual. He lived alone in his house on Savile Row, where no one ever visited. A single servant was all that he required. He lunched and dined at the Club at hours mathematically fixed – in the same room, at the same table – without inviting any guests or speaking to his fellow members. He returned home at precisely midnight, only to retire at once to bed. He never made use of those comfortable rooms the Reform

Club keeps for the convenience of its favored members.

Of every twenty-four hours, he spent just ten at his residence – either sleeping or readying himself for the day ahead. When he chose to take a walk it was, with a regular step, on the mosaic flooring of the Club's entrance hall, or in its circular gallery, where twenty Ionic columns of red porphyry supported a dome of clear blue glass. When he dined or lunched, the resources of the Club – its kitchens, pantries, buttery and dairy – crowded his table with their succulent stores. It was the Club's waiters, solemnly dressed in black and wearing noiseless, soft-soled shoes, who served each course in special porcelain and on the finest linen tablecloth. It was the Club's lost-mold crystal decanters that held his sherry, his port, or his claret spiced with vanilla and cinnamon. And finally, it was the Club's ice – ice transported at great cost from the American lakes – that kept his drinks at a suitably refreshing temperature.

If to live in this manner is to be an eccentric, one must admit that eccentricity has its advantages.

The house on Savile Row, without being sumptuous, was extremely comfortable. The unvarying habits of its occupant made light work for the single servant. Nevertheless, Phileas Fogg demanded of this servant a regularity and promptness that was altogether extraordinary. On this very 2nd of October,

he had dismissed James Forster because the unfortunate youth had committed the oversight of preparing shaving water at a temperature of eighty-four degrees Fahrenheit instead of the required eighty-six – and he now awaited James's successor, who was expected at the house between eleven o'clock and eleven thirty.

Phileas Fogg sat squarely in his armchair, his feet close together like those of a soldier on parade, his hands placed on his knees, his body straight and his head erect, and he watched the slowly moving hands of a complicated clock. It showed the hours, minutes, seconds, days, months, and years. At exactly half-past eleven, Mr. Fogg would, according to his daily habit, leave the house and repair to the Reform Club.

At that moment, someone knocked at the door of the parlor where Phileas Fogg was seated, and James Forster, the dismissed servant, appeared.

"The new servant," he said.

A young man of about thirty entered and bowed.

"You are a Frenchman, I believe, and your name is John?" inquired Phileas Fogg.

"Jean, if Monsieur pleases," replied the newcomer. "Jean Passepartout, a name that has stuck with me, and which fits my natural talent for getting out of various scrapes. I believe I'm an

honest fellow, Monsieur, but to be frank, I've had several trades. I've been a traveling singer, and I worked as a stable-hand in a circus, where I used to vault like Léotard, and dance on a tightrope like Blondin. I became a gymnastics teacher, so as to put my talents to better use, and then finally I was a sergeant in the Paris fire department. In fact, I have several notable fires in my dossier. But five years ago I left France and, wanting to try the pleasures of family life, entered into service as a valet here in England. Now, finding myself between jobs and hearing that Monsieur Phileas Fogg was the most exact and sedentary man in the United Kingdom, I have come to Monsieur in hopes of living with him a tranquil life, and forgetting even the name of Passepartout."

"Passepartout suits me," replied the gentleman. "You have been recommended to me. I have a good report of your character. You know my conditions?"

"Yes, Monsieur."

"Good. What time do you make it?"

"Twenty-two minutes past eleven," returned Passepartout, hauling an enormous silver watch from the depths of his pocket.

"You are running behind," said Mr. Fogg.

"Pardon me, Monsieur, but that's impossible."

"You are running behind by four minutes. No matter: it is

enough to note the discrepancy. So, as of this moment, twenty-nine minutes past eleven o'clock in the morning, on Wednesday, the 2nd of October, 1872, you are in my service."

With this, Phileas Fogg stood up, took his hat in his left hand, placed it on his head with the regular motion of an automaton, and went off without a word.

Passepartout heard the door to the street shut once: it was his new master going out. Then it shut a second time: it was his predecessor, James Forster, departing in turn. Passepartout remained alone in the house on Savile Row.

CHAPTER II

IN WHICH PASSEPARTOUT IS CONVINCED
HE HAS FINALLY FOUND HIS IDEAL

"Goodness me," said Passepartout, somewhat flustered by all this, "I've seen people at Madame Tussaud's as lively as my new master!"

It should be said that Madame Tussaud's 'people' are figures made of wax, much visited in London, and so lifelike that they might almost speak.

During his brief interview with Phileas Fogg, Passepartout had quickly and carefully assessed his future master. He appeared to be a man of about forty, with fine, handsome features, and a tall, well-shaped figure. His hair and beard

were fair, his brow unwrinkled, his face rather pale, his teeth magnificent. He seemed to possess to the highest degree what physiognomists call, 'repose in action', a quality shared by all those who prefer to act rather than talk. Calm, phlegmatic, clear-eyed, with unmoving eyelids, he was the very type of those poised and collected Englishmen whose slightly academic attitude is so marvelously captured by the paintbrush of Angelica Kauffmann. In all the phases of his daily life, this gentleman had the air of one whose every part was in perfect equilibrium – as perfect as a chronometer by Leroy or Earnshaw. Indeed, Phileas Fogg was exactitude personified, and this could be seen even in the expression of his very hands and feet, for in men, as in animals, the limbs themselves are expressive of the passions.

Phileas Fogg was one of those people who, mathematically exact, unrushed and always prepared, economize their every step and movement. He never took one step too many, going always by the shortest route. His gaze never wandered, nor would he permit a superfluous gesture. He was never seen to be agitated or moved. He never hurried, but he always arrived on time.

It is because of this that he lived alone and, so to speak, outside the course of normal social relations. He knew that, in society, one must rub elbows with people. But rubbing elbows

causes friction – and since friction slows the mechanism, he chose not to rub elbows at all.

As for Passepartout, he was a truly Parisian Parisian. He had spent the last five years in England as a valet, searching in vain for a master after his own heart. Passepartout was by no means one of the impudent Frontins or Mascarilles depicted in the plays of Molière, with their shoulders up and their noses held in the air, and with a bold stare for everyone. No. Passepartout was an honest fellow, with an agreeable physiognomy. His lips were slightly protruding, as if to taste or to caress. His very being was sweet and serviceable, and he had one of those fine, round heads that one likes to find on the shoulders of a friend. He had blue eyes, a ruddy complexion, and a face just plump enough for him to see the edges of his own cheeks. He had a broad chest and a strong, vigorously muscled frame, and the exercises of his youth had imbued him with Herculean strength. His brown hair was a bit unruly. Although the sculptors of antiquity had eighteen different ways of arranging Minerva's coiffure, Passepartout knew only one way to manage his own: it was done with three quick strokes of a large-toothed comb.

It would be imprudent at this stage to say whether Passepartout's lively nature would agree with Phileas Fogg. Would he turn out to be the perfectly methodical servant

As for Passepartout, he was a truly Parisian Parisian.

that his master required? Only time could tell. Having had, as we saw, a hectic and unsettled youth, Passepartout now longed for repose. And despite all he had heard about the frigid and phlegmatic English gentlemen, England had so far disappointed him. He had served in ten different households without being able to take root. To his great dismay, he found each of his masters to be whimsical and irregular, constantly running around the country or on the lookout for adventures. His most recent master, the young Lord Longsferry, Member of Parliament, having spent his nights in the 'oyster houses' of Haymarket, would return home all too frequently on the shoulders of policemen. Passepartout wanted above all to respect the gentleman he served, and he therefore ventured a few mild observations on this conduct. These were poorly received, and he took his leave. Then, learning that Phileas Fogg was looking for a servant, he made inquiries about the gentleman. A master with such a routine existence, who never traveled or slept away from home, and who never absented himself for even a day, could not fail to please him. He presented himself immediately and was accepted.

At half past eleven, Passepartout found himself alone in the house on Savile Row. He promptly began its inspection, examining every corner from the cellar to the attic. The house

pleased him. It was clean, tidy, solemn, and well-organized.
It reminded him of an elegant snail's shell – but one lighted and
warmed by gas, for indeed, carburetted hydrogen, or methane,
met all of the house's requirements in these respects. On the
second floor, Passepartout recognized at once the room that
was to be his. It suited him perfectly. Here, electric bells and
speaking tubes provided a connection with the rooms on the
first and the ground floor. On the mantelpiece stood an electric
clock that was synchronized with the clock in Phileas Fogg's
bedroom: each instrument beat the same second at the same
instant.

"Well, this is just fine!" said Passepartout to himself.

He also found, in his room, a card fixed above the clock. It
was the program of his daily duties. It listed all that would be
required of him, from eight o'clock in the morning, when Phileas
Fogg invariably rose, to half past eleven, when he left the house
to lunch at the Reform Club. Every one of his responsibilities
was set out: the tea and the toast of twenty-three past eight, the
shaving water of thirty-seven past nine, the coiffing of twenty
to ten. And so it continued. From half past eleven to midnight –
the hour at which the methodical gentlemen retired – everything
was regulated and foreseen. Passepartout happily reviewed the
document, committing each detail to memory.

As for Monsieur's wardrobe, it was well supplied and in the best taste. Each pair of trousers, each suit and waistcoat, was numbered and listed in a registry stating on what date, according to the season, each garment should in turn be worn. The same system was applied to the master's shoes.

In short, in the house on Savile Row – which must have been a temple of disorder in the time of the illustrious but dissipated Sheridan – everything was laid out for ease and comfort. There was no library, nor any books. These would have been of little use to Mr. Fogg, since he had two libraries at his disposal at the Reform Club: one devoted to literature, the other to law and politics. In the bedroom stood a safe of medium size, whose construction could resist fire as well as theft. There were no weapons in the house – no implements of war or of the hunt – and every detail indicated a life of tranquillity and of peaceable habits.

As he completed his detailed examination of the house, Passepartout broke into a broad smile. He rubbed his hands together and exclaimed, "This is just what I'd hoped for! We shall get on perfectly, Mr. Fogg and I! What a domestic and regular gentleman. A veritable machine! Well, I don't mind serving a machine."

CHAPTER III

IN WHICH A CONVERSATION TAKES PLACE THAT COULD COST PHILEAS FOGG DEARLY

Phileas Fogg, having left his house on Savile Row at half past eleven, and having placed five hundred and seventy-five times his right foot before his left and five hundred and seventy-six times his left foot before his right, arrived in due course at the Reform Club, an imposing edifice in Pall Mall that could not have cost less than three million pounds to build.

Phileas Fogg proceeded directly to the dining room, where nine windows gave onto a handsome garden, its trees already gilded by autumn. He took a seat at his usual table, where his place had already been laid. His lunch consisted of an

hors-d'oeuvre, a boiled fish dressed with a 'Reading Sauce' of the first quality, rare roast beef accompanied by mushrooms, a rhubarb and gooseberry cake, and a wedge of Cheshire cheese – all of which was washed down with several cups of an excellent tea selected specially for the Reform Club.

At twelve forty-seven, the gentleman rose and directed himself to the grand salon, a sumptuous room hung with lavishly framed paintings. There, a servant presented him with a copy of *The Times*, uncut, and Phileas Fogg proceeded to cut the pages with a sureness of hand that betrayed an easy familiarity with this delicate operation. He was occupied in reading this newspaper until three forty-five, and with the reading of *The Standard* – which succeeded it – until dinner. This meal was a nearly perfect repetition of his lunch, varying only in the addition of 'Royal British Sauce'.

At twenty to six, the gentleman reappeared in the grand salon, and was soon absorbed in reading *The Morning Chronicle*.

Half an hour later, several members of the Reform Club came in and gathered around the fireplace, where a coal fire was burning. These were Mr. Phileas Fogg's usual companions and, like him, avid players of whist: the engineer Andrew Stuart, the bankers John Sullivan and Samuel Fallentin, the brewer Thomas Flanagan, and Gauthier Ralph, one of the administrators of

the Bank of England. These were rich and highly respected personages, even in a club that counted among its members the captains of English finance and industry.

"So, Ralph," said Thomas Flanagan, "what's the latest in this robbery business?"

"Well," replied Andrew Stuart, "the Bank will surely lose the money."

"On the contrary," said Gauthier Ralph, "I hope that we may still lay hands on the thief. Some of our most skillful police detectives have been sent abroad to watch the principal ports of America and Europe, and this fellow will have a hard time slipping past them."

"But have you got a description of the thief?" asked Andrew Stuart.

"First of all, he isn't a thief," Gauthier Ralph replied.

"What! A person who makes off with fifty-five thousand pounds isn't a thief?" exclaimed Andrew Stuart.

"No," said Gauthier Ralph firmly.

"What would you call him then – a manufacturer?" asked John Sullivan.

"*The Morning Chronicle* asserts that he is a gentleman."

This response came from none other than Phileas Fogg, whose head now emerged from behind his newspapers. He

greeted his friends and joined in their conversation.

The matter they were discussing, which was headline news in all the papers of the United Kingdom, had taken place at the Bank of England just three days before, on the 29th of September. A bundle of banknotes, amounting to the enormous sum of fifty-five thousand pounds, had been lifted from the counter of the principal cashier.

For some, it was a surprise to learn that so great a theft could seemingly be carried off with so little effort. But, as the Bank's Vice-Governor Gauthier Ralph explained, the cashier had at that very moment been busy registering the receipt of three shillings and sixpence, and he could not be expected to keep track of everything at once.

It should be observed (and this goes some way to clearing up the matter) that this admirable institution of the Bank of England appears to have a touching confidence in the honesty of the general public. It relies neither on guards, nor on bars, nor on gratings. The gold, silver and banknotes are freely exposed and are at the mercy, so to speak, of all comers. After all, one would never wish to doubt the honor of an innocent passerby. One keen observer of English customs has this story to tell: one day, when passing through one of the rooms of the Bank, he was moved to examine more closely an ingot of gold, weighing seven

or eight pounds, which lay exposed on the table of a cashier. He took up the ingot, examined it, and passed it to his neighbor – who passed it to another, and so on, until the ingot, going from hand to hand, had traveled to the end of a dark corridor, only returning to its place a half hour later. Meanwhile, the cashier hadn't so much as raised his head.

However, on the 29th of September, events took a rather different course. The bundle of banknotes did not return, and when the magnificent clock presiding over the 'drawing office' sounded five o'clock and the closing of the offices, the Bank of England was obliged to move the fifty thousand pounds onto the account of profits and losses.

The theft duly acknowledged, several of the most able officers or 'detectives' were selected and dispatched to the principal ports – to Liverpool, to Glasgow, to the Havre, to Suez, to Brindisi, to New York, etc. – with the promise, should they meet with success, of a prize of two thousand pounds and five percent of the amount recovered. A judicial investigation had immediately been set in motion, and while they waited for more information to come to light, the detectives were tasked with scrupulously observing all arriving and departing travelers.

Indeed, as *The Morning Chronicle* had stated, there was cause to believe that the perpetrator did not actually belong to any of

England's criminal gangs. On that day of the 29th of September, a well-dressed gentleman, with polished manners and a distinguished air, had been seen coming and going in the paying room where the crime was committed. The investigation had produced a fairly detailed description of this gentleman, which was promptly dispatched to all the detectives in the United Kingdom and the continent. As a result, some people – and Gauthier Ralph was one of them – found reason to hope that the thief would not escape.

As might be expected, this affair was widely discussed in London and throughout England. People everywhere speculated on the probability that the Metropolitan Police Service would capture the thief. It is hardly surprising, therefore, that members of the Reform Club were also considering the matter – especially since their number included one of the Bank's Vice-Governors.

The honorable Gauthier Ralph was confident that the investigation would produce results, since he believed that the promised reward would significantly sharpen the zeal and the intelligence of the officers. But his colleague, Andrew Stuart, was far from convinced. The gentlemen continued to argue the matter as they sat down to the whist-table – Stuart opposite Flanagan, and Fallentin opposite Phileas Fogg. During the game, the players were still, but between rubbers, they picked up their

conversation where they had left off.

"I maintain," said Andrew Stuart, "that the chances are in favor of the thief, who must certainly be a capable fellow!"

"Come now!" replied Ralph, "there isn't a country in the world that will be safe for him."

"Pshaw."

"Where do you expect him to go?"

"I have no idea," rejoined Andrew Stuart, "but, after all, the Earth is more than big enough."

"It was once," said Phileas Fogg, in a low tone. Then, handing the cards to Thomas Flanagan: "It is your turn to cut, sir."

The conversation was suspended for the duration of the rubber. But soon Andrew Stuart picked it up again, saying:

"What do you mean, 'it was once'? Has the world shrunk in size, somehow?"

"Without a doubt," returned Gauthier Ralph. "I agree with Mr. Fogg. The world has shrunk, because one can go round it ten times more quickly than a hundred years ago. And that, in the affair at hand, will make our pursuit of the thief all the more swift."

"And his escape all the more certain!"

"Be so good as to play, Mr. Stuart," said Phileas Fogg.

But the incredulous Stuart was not convinced, and when the

hand was finished, said eagerly: "I must say, Mr. Ralph, you have a funny way of proving that the world has grown smaller. So, because one can go around it in three months—"

"In just eighty days," said Phileas Fogg.

"That's exactly right, gentlemen," added John Sullivan, "in eighty days, now that the Great Indian Peninsula Railway has opened the connection between Rothal and Allahabad. And here is the calculation made by *The Morning Chronicle*:

From London to Suez via Mont-Cenis and Brindisi,
by rail and steamboat . . . . 7 days
From Suez to Bombay, by steamboat . . . . 13 days
From Bombay to Calcutta, by rail . . . . 3 days
From Calcutta to Hong Kong by steamboat . . . . 13 days
From Hong Kong to Yokohama by steamboat . . . . 6 days
From Yokohama to San Francisco, by steamboat . . . . . . 22 days
From San Francisco to New York, by rail . . . . 7 days
From New York to London, by steamboat and rail . . . . 9 days

Total . . . . 80 days

"Yes, eighty days exactly!" exclaimed Andrew Stuart, who in his excitement overlooked a trump card, "but that doesn't

include bad weather, contrary winds, shipwrecks, derailments, etc."

"All included," returned Phileas Fogg, who continued playing as, for once, the conversation intruded on the whist.

"But what if the Hindus or the American Indians pull up the rails?" asked Andrew Stuart. "What if they stop the trains, pillage the carriages, scalp the passengers!"

"All included," repeated Phileas Fogg calmly. And, laying down his cards, he added, "Two trumps."

Andrew Stuart, whose turn it was to deal, gathered the cards.

"You're right in theory, Mr. Fogg," he said. "But in practice…"

"In practice as well, Mr. Stuart."

"I'd like to see you try it in eighty days."

"It's entirely up to you. Let's leave together."

"God forbid!" cried Stuart. "But I would wager four thousand pounds that such a voyage, made under those conditions, would be impossible."

"Perfectly possible, on the contrary," returned Mr. Fogg.

"Well, make it, then!"

"A journey around the world in eighty days?"

"Yes."

"I should be glad to."

"I'd like to see you try it in eighty days."

"When?"

"At once."

"This is madness!" exclaimed Andrew Stuart, increasingly frustrated by his partner's insistence. "Come. Let's play instead."

"In that case, deal the cards again," replied Phileas Fogg, "as there has been a misdeal."

Andrew Stuart took up the deck with a feverish hand; then, suddenly, he put it down again.

"Very well then – yes, Mr. Fogg," he said, "yes, I wager the four thousand pounds!"

"My dear Stuart," said Fallentin, "calm yourself. Nobody's taking this seriously."

"When I make a wager," returned Andrew Stuart, "it's always serious."

"So be it!" said Mr. Fogg. Then, turning to his colleagues:

"I have a sum of twenty thousand pounds deposited at Baring Brothers. I will gladly wager it…"

"Twenty thousand pounds!" exclaimed John Sullivan. "Twenty thousand pounds that may be lost with a single unforeseen delay!"

"The unforeseen does not exist," Phileas Fogg replied calmly.

"But, Mr. Fogg, that span of eighty days represents the bare minimum required to complete the journey!"

"A minimum properly deployed is always enough."

"But to stay within the eighty days, one must jump with mathematical precision from trains to steamships, and from steamships back to trains!"

"I will jump – mathematically."

"You are joking!"

"A proper Englishman never jokes where it concerns something so serious as a wager," replied Phileas Fogg. "I wager twenty thousand pounds against anyone who wishes that I will travel around the world in eighty days or less – that is, in nineteen hundred and twenty hours, or one hundred and fifteen thousand and two hundred minutes. Do you accept?"

"We accept," replied Messrs. Stuart, Fallentin, Sullivan, Flanagan, and Ralph, after a brief consultation.

"Good," said Mr. Fogg. "The train for Dover departs at forty-five minutes past eight o'clock. I will be on board."

"This very evening?" asked Stuart.

"This very evening," replied Phileas Fogg. "Therefore," he added, consulting a pocket calendar, "since it is today Wednesday the 2nd of October, I should be back in London, in this very salon of the Reform Club, on Saturday the 21st of December, at forty-five minutes past eight o'clock in the evening – failing which, gentlemen, the twenty thousand

pounds currently deposited on my account at Baring Brothers will be yours in fact and by right. Here is a check for the same amount."

The terms of the wager were at once drawn up and signed by the six interested parties. Phileas Fogg maintained his cold demeanor. He had certainly not wagered for the sake of profit, and had only staked those twenty thousand pounds – half of his entire fortune – because he foresaw that he might need to spend the other half in order to achieve his difficult (not to say impracticable) project. As for his adversaries, they appeared rather discomposed – not because of the sums at stake, but because they had some scruples about competing under these terms.

The clock struck seven o'clock, and Mr. Fogg's companions offered to suspend the game of whist so that he could begin the preparations for his departure.

"I am always ready," replied that impassive gentleman, dealing the cards. "Diamonds are trumps. It is your turn to play, Mr. Stuart."

CHAPTER IV

IN WHICH PHILEAS FOGG ASTOUNDS HIS SERVANT, PASSEPARTOUT

At twenty-five past seven, having won some twenty guineas at whist, Phileas Fogg bade farewell to his honorable colleagues and left the Reform Club. At ten to eight, he opened the door to his house and walked in.

Passepartout, who had conscientiously studied his new program, was quite surprised to find Mr. Fogg, guilty of inexactitude, appearing at this unusual hour. According to the schedule, the inhabitant of Savile Row was not meant to return until precisely midnight.

Phileas Fogg went straight up to his bedroom, and then he

called out, "Passepartout."

Passepartout did not reply. The call couldn't be for him. It wasn't the right time.

"Passepartout," repeated Mr. Fogg, without raising his voice in the slightest.

Passepartout appeared.

"This is the second time I've summoned you," said Mr. Fogg.

"But it's not yet midnight," replied Passepartout, consulting his watch.

"I'm aware," continued Phileas Fogg, "and I make no reproach. We are departing in ten minutes for Dover and Calais."

A kind of grimace spread across the Frenchman's round face. Clearly, he had misheard his master.

"Monsieur is going out?" he asked.

"Yes," replied Phileas Fogg. "We are going on a journey around the world."

Passepartout's eyes widened. His eyelids peeled back, his eyebrows arched, his arms hung limp, and his body sagged. He showed all the symptoms of an astonishment approaching stupefaction.

"Around the world…!" he murmured.

"In eighty days," affirmed Mr. Fogg. "We have, therefore, not a moment to lose."

"But what about the luggage?" asked Passepartout, who stood dazedly shaking his head from side to side.

"No luggage. Just an overnight bag. And in it, two woollen shirts, and three pairs of stockings for me. Pack the same for yourself. The rest we can purchase as we go. You'll bring down my mackintosh and my traveling rug. Be sure to wear sturdy shoes – although, in fact, we will do little or no walking. Go."

Passepartout wanted to reply, but he could not. He left Mr. Fogg's room and went up to his own, where he fell into a chair, uttering a rather vulgar phrase in his own language:

"Well! I'll be a monkey's uncle! And here I was hoping to lead a quiet life!"

Then, he mechanically set about making the preparations for departure. A journey around the world in eighty days! Could this be the whim of a madman? No… So was it a prank of some kind? They were bound for Dover – very well. To Calais, even – so be it. After all, that would hardly trouble Passepartout, who hadn't set foot in his native country for five years. Maybe they would even go so far as Paris – and indeed, he would be happy to see the great capital again. But certainly a gentleman so sparing of his movements would go no further…? No, absolutely not – but all the same, it was no less certain that this gentleman, until now so domestically inclined, was departing!

By eight o'clock, Passepartout had prepared the modest overnight bag containing his wardrobe and that of his master; then, still unsettled by this turn of events, he left his room — carefully closing the door — and rejoined Mr. Fogg.

Mr. Fogg was ready. Under his arm he carried a copy of the *Bradshaw's Continental Railway, Steam Transit, and General Guide*, which would provide all the information necessary to his journey. He took the bag from Passepartout, opened it, and slipped in a thick roll of those handsome English banknotes that are accepted as currency in every country.

"You haven't forgotten anything?" he asked.

"Nothing, Monsieur."

"My mackintosh and travel rug?"

"Here they are."

"Good. Take this."

Mr. Fogg returned the overnight bag to Passepartout.

"And do be careful with it," he added. "There are twenty thousand pounds inside."

The bag nearly slipped from Passepartout's hands — as if the twenty thousand pounds were all in gold, and weighed a ton.

Master and servant then stepped out, and the front door was double-locked behind them. A carriage stand was located at the end of Savile Row. Phileas Fogg and his servant climbed into

a cab, which carried them rapidly in the direction of Charing Cross, a station where one of the branches of the South Eastern Railway terminated. At twenty past eight, the cab stopped in front of the station. Passepartout jumped down. His master followed, and paid the coachman.

At that moment, a poor beggar-woman, leading a child by the hand, approached Mr. Fogg and asked for alms. She stood barefoot in the mud, wearing a tattered shawl to cover her rags, and a threadbare hat from which a single lamentable feather hung.

Mr. Fogg drew from his pocket the twenty guineas that he had just won at whist. Presenting them to the woman, he said, "Here you are, my good woman. I am pleased to have met you!" Then he passed on.

Passepartout had what might have been a moist sensation around his eyes. His master had taken a step up in his heart.

He and Mr. Fogg continued into the station. There, Phileas Fogg ordered Passepartout to purchase two first-class tickets for Paris. Then, turning around, he spotted his five colleagues from the Reform Club.

"Gentlemen, I am off," he said, "and on my return, all the visas stamped in the passport I have brought with me for that purpose will enable you to confirm my itinerary."

"Oh! Mr. Fogg," Gauthier Ralph replied politely, "that's not

necessary. We put our trust in your word as a gentleman!"

"Nevertheless, I will see that the passport is stamped," said Mr. Fogg.

"Don't forget that you will need to return..." observed Andrew Stuart.

"I will return in eighty days," finished Mr. Fogg, "on Saturday the 21st of December, 1872, at eight forty-five in the evening. Good-bye, gentlemen."

At eight forty, Phileas Fogg and his servant took their seats in the same compartment. At eight forty-five, a whistle sounded, and the train began to move.

The night was dark, and a fine rain was falling. Phileas Fogg, settled snugly in his corner, didn't say a word. Passepartout, still reeling from the day's events, clung mechanically to the overnight bag with its cargo of banknotes. Then, just as the train was passing through Sydenham, Passepartout suddenly gave a cry of deep despair!

"What is it?" asked Mr. Fogg.

"I... In my hurry... my confusion... I forgot..."

"What?"

"I forgot to put out the gas light in my bedroom!"

"Well, my boy," Mr. Fogg replied coldly, "it burns at your expense!"

"I will return in eighty days, on Saturday the 21st of December, 1872,
at eight forty-five in the evening."

CHAPTER V

IN WHICH A NEW STOCK APPEARS
ON THE LONDON EXCHANGE

When he left London, Phileas Fogg could hardly have imagined the great commotion that his departure would provoke. First, the news of his wager spread rapidly through the Reform Club, sparking passionate debate among the members of that distinguished circle. Then, from the club, that passion was transmitted by journalists to the newspapers, and by the newspapers to the public of London and the entire United Kingdom.

This question of a 'journey around the world' was discussed, debated, and dissected with as much passion and ardor as if it

had been a new national controversy like the 'Alabama Affair'.
Some people took the side of Phileas Fogg, but the rest – and
they soon formed a considerable majority – declared themselves
against him. To actually complete this journey around the world
– not just in theory and on paper – and to do it within eighty
days, with the means of transportation actually available, was not
merely impossible. It was absurd!

The Times, The Standard, The Evening Star, The Morning
Chronicle, and twenty other highly respectable newspapers,
declared themselves against Mr. Fogg. Only The Daily Telegraph
dared to support him to any extent. Phileas Fogg was generally
held to be a maniac and an eccentric, and his colleagues of the
Reform Club were condemned for having accepted the wager,
which so clearly demonstrated an enfeeblement of the mental
faculties of its author.

Articles appeared on the question, written in language no less
passionate than it was logical. The English are notorious for
their interest in all matters touching on geography, and readers
of every class devoured the columns dedicated to the case of
Phileas Fogg.

Initially, a few audacious spirits – chiefly women – supported
him, particularly when The Illustrated London News published
his portrait, based on a photograph registered in the archives

of the Reform Club. Certain gentlemen were heard to murmur, "Heh, heh, heh! And why not, after all? More extraordinary things have happened!" These were mostly readers of *The Daily Telegraph* – but soon, one felt that even *The Daily Telegraph* began to falter in its support.

At last, on the 7th of October, a long article appeared in the Bulletin of the Royal Geographical Society. It considered the question from every point of view, and demonstrated conclusively the utter folly of the enterprise. According to this article, everything stood in the way of the traveler: obstacles both natural and human. In order to achieve his goal, Phileas Fogg would need to benefit from a miraculous concordance of scheduled arrivals and departures – a concordance that did not exist, and which could not exist. At best, in Europe, which represented only a moderate part of the total distance around the world, one could depend on the prompt arrival of scheduled trains. But where trains would take three days to cross India, or seven days to cross the United States, could one rely on their punctuality to the degree required by the terms of the wager? What about mechanical failures, derailments, collisions, bad weather, the accumulation of snow – were all these not awaiting Phileas Fogg? Aboard steamships, in the approaching winter, would he not find himself at the mercy of unpredictable storms

and fogs? Is it not common for even the best and fastest vessels of the transoceanic shipping lines to experience delays of two or three days? And in fact, one delay – one single delay – would be enough to break the entire chain of correspondences. If Phileas Fogg missed, even by a few hours, the departure of a steamship, he would be forced to wait for the next sailing – and his whole endeavor would be irrevocably compromised.

This article caused quite a stir. Nearly all the newspapers reprinted it, and shares of Phileas Fogg fell sharply in value.

In the first few days following the gentleman's departure, large amounts of money were ventured on the success of his enterprise. Betting is ingrained in the English character, and the betting community in England is more enlightened and refined than any other. As a result, not only did various members of the Reform Club wager considerable sums on the outcome of Phileas Fogg's journey, but the public also began to take part. Phileas Fogg was set down in the betting books as if he were a prized racing horse. 'Phileas Fogg' bonds were issued, and were immediately launched on the London Stock Exchange. Phileas Fogg was asked for, and offered, at par or at a premium, and traded in vast quantities. But five days after his departure, with the appearance of the article in the Bulletin of the Geographic Society, demand began to falter. Phileas Fogg fell in value. It was

sold in bulk – at first in quantities of five, then of ten, until at last it sold only by the twenties, the fifties, the hundreds!

One sole supporter remained: the aged paralytic, Lord Albemarle. This honorable gentleman, restricted to his armchair, would have given his entire fortune to be able to journey around the world – even if it took him ten years! And he wagered five thousand pounds on Phileas Fogg's success. When the folly, as well as the uselessness, of this adventure was pointed out to him, he contented himself with replying, "If the thing can be done, the first to do it ought to be an Englishman."

So the partisans of Phileas Fogg became more and more rare. It seemed that everyone – and not without reason – turned against him. The bookmakers' odds on his adventure were already spiraling to one hundred and fifty or two hundred to one when, seven days after his departure, an unexpected incident occurred which deprived him of backers at any odds whatever.

On that day, at nine o'clock in the evening, the Commissioner of the Metropolitan Police Service, received the following telegraphic dispatch:

Suez to London.

Rowan, Commissioner of Police, central administration, Scotland Yard.

Am tailing Bank of England robber, Phileas Fogg. Send arrest

warrant without delay to Bombay.

FIX, detective.

The effect of this dispatch was instantaneous. The honorable gentleman vanished, giving way to the snatcher of banknotes. His photograph, on file at the Reform Club along with those of all his colleagues, was carefully re-examined. It corresponded in every feature with the man whose description had been put forward by the police investigation. Then, in turn, the mysteries of Phileas Fogg's existence were recalled: his solitude, his sudden departure… and it seemed evident that this personage, in making a journey around the world, on the pretext of a senseless wager, could have no other aim than to elude the officers of the police.

CHAPTER VI

IN WHICH DETECTIVE FIX DEMONSTRATES
A VERY NATURAL IMPATIENCE

The circumstances which led to the sending of the telegraphic dispatch concerning Mr. Phileas Fogg are as follows:

On Wednesday, the 9th of October, the population of Suez was awaiting the eleven o'clock arrival of the steamship *Mongolia*, of the Peninsular and Oriental Steam Navigation Company – an iron-hulled vessel with a screw propeller and spar deck, displacing 2,800 tons and boasting a nominal output of five hundred horsepower. The *Mongolia* regularly covered the route from Brindisi to Bombay via the Suez Canal. It was one of the fastest steamers belonging to the Company, and it had

always surpassed the official running speeds of 10 knots between Brindisi and Suez, and 9.53 knots between Suez and Bombay.

As they waited for the *Mongolia* to appear, two men strolled along the quay, through the crowd of natives and foreigners who flock to the city – a city that had, until recently, been little more than a hamlet, and which, thanks to the great engineering project of Mr. De Lesseps, is now assured a considerable future.

One of these two men was the British consul at Suez, who – despite the prognostications of the British government and the sinister predictions of the engineer Stephenson – saw English vessels passing through the canal on a daily basis, thereby reducing by half the length of their voyage from England to India, which would formerly have passed by the route around the Cape of Good Hope.

The other was a small, slightly built personage, with nervous yet intelligent features, who with remarkable persistence held his facial muscles tensed in a perpetual squint. Bright, piercing eyes flashed from beneath his long eyelashes – eyes whose expressiveness he had learned to mask when necessary. At that moment, however, he was showing certain signs of impatience, pacing up and down, and utterly unable to keep still.

This man was named Fix, and he was one of those English police 'detectives', who had been sent to various ports following

the theft at the Bank of England. It was his task to watch, with the greatest care and attention, every traveler on the Suez route, and if one of them seemed suspicious, to 'tail' him until he could obtain a warrant for his arrest. And in fact, just two days previously, Fix had received from the Commissioner of the Metropolitan Police Service the complete description of the presumed criminal — that well-dressed and distinguished person who had been observed at the cashier's counter in the Bank. The detective, evidently inspired by the splendid reward offered for the successful capture of the thief, therefore awaited the arrival of the *Mongolia* with an understandable impatience.

"So you say, Mr. Consul," he repeated for the tenth time, "that this ship cannot fail to arrive on time?"

"No, Mr. Fix," replied the Consul, "she was spotted yesterday in the offing at Port Saïd, and the canal's one hundred and sixty kilometers count as nothing for such a speedy craft. I tell you again, the *Mongolia* has always won the prize of twenty-five pounds that the government awards for an advance of twenty-four hours on the official timetable."

"And the steamer comes directly from Brindisi?" asked Fix.

"Yes, from Brindisi, where she took onboard the mail for India, and from where she departed on Saturday at five o'clock in the evening. So be patient — she can't be much longer in arriving.

But really, I don't see how, from the description you received, you'll be able to recognize your culprit, even if he is on board the *Mongolia*."

"Mr. Consul," responded Fix, "that sort of fellow must be felt rather than recognized. You must have a scent for them – a special scent like a sixth sense along with hearing, sight and smell. I've arrested more than one of these gentlemen in my career, and should my thief be on board the ship today, I can assure you that he won't slip out of my hands."

"I hope not, Mr. Fix, for it was a very costly robbery."

"A magnificent robbery," the detective replied enthusiastically. "Fifty-five thousand pounds! We don't often have such windfalls. These days our criminals are unambitious and petty. The descendants of the great Jack Sheppard are nothing like him. Thieves now go to the gallows for the sake of a few shillings."

"Mr. Fix," said the Consul, "you speak so passionately that I heartily wish you may succeed – but I repeat, with the conditions you face, I fear it will be most difficult. Do you realize that, according to the description you've received, this burglar resembles in every respect an honest man?"

"Mr. Consul, the great robbers always resemble honest men," the detective remarked dogmatically. "You understand, of course, that those with the features of scoundrels have no choice but to remain law-abiding citizens – otherwise they would all too quickly be arrested. The honest physiognomies – those are the ones we should most suspect. Mine is a difficult job, I admit, and one that's less a craft than an art."

It is evident that this Mr. Fix was not lacking in self-respect.

Little by little, the quay was getting busier. Sailors of various nationalities, merchants, ship-brokers, porters, and fellahs bustled to and fro. The arrival of the steamship was clearly imminent. The weather was fine, but the air was chilled by the east wind. Several minarets, rising above the city, were glazed by the pale rays of the sun. To the south, a jetty two thousand meters long extended like an arm into the roadstead of Suez. On the Red Sea, a few fishing boats and small coasting vessels rolled among the swells, some of them recalling in their rigging the elegant aspect of the ancient galleys.

As he passed through the busy crowd, Fix, according to the habit of his profession, scrutinized the passers-by with a quick, keen glance. It was then half past ten.

"Will this steamer never come!" he cried, as the harbor clock rang out.

"She can't be far off now," replied the Consul.

"How long will she stop at Suez?" asked Fix.

"Four hours. Just time enough to take on more coal. The distance from Suez to Aden, at the other end of the Red Sea, is thirteen hundred and ten miles, and the steamer will need an ample provision of fuel."

"And will she go from Suez directly to Bombay?" asked Fix.

"Yes, without putting in anywhere."

"Well then," said Fix with satisfaction, "if the thief has chosen this route and this ship, he must be planning to disembark in Suez, in order to reach by some other means the Dutch or French territories in Asia. He ought to know that he cannot be safe in India, which is English territory."

"Unless, that is, your thief is a particularly bold fellow," rejoined the Consul. "You know that an English criminal is always better concealed in London than he would be abroad."

This observation gave the detective much food for thought, and the Consul presently returned to his offices, located a short distance away. Fix, left alone, was again seized with impatience, and suddenly overcome with a strange presentiment that his thief would indeed be found aboard the *Mongolia* – and in truth, if that rascal had left England with the intention of reaching the New World, he would naturally have chosen the route passing east by way of India, as it was less well guarded and more difficult to monitor.

Fix was again seized with impatience, and suddenly overcome with a strange presentiment that his thief would indeed be found aboard the *Mongolia*.

These reflections, however, were soon interrupted by a succession of sharp whistles announcing the arrival of the steamship. Abruptly, all the porters and fellahs rushed toward the quay in a tumult that was rather dangerous to the clothing and, indeed, the limbs of the waiting passengers. A dozen boats pushed off from the shore and sailed off to meet the *Mongolia*.

Soon, the gigantic hull of the *Mongolia* came into view, passing between the banks of the canal and, as the clocks sounded eleven o'clock, the steamship anchored in the roadstead, the steam from its boilers rushing noisily up through its two high funnels.

There were many passengers on board. Some remained on the spar deck, contemplating the picturesque panorama afforded by the city, but the majority disembarked in the small shore boats that had come out to the steamer.

Fix scrupulously examined each passenger as they came ashore. One of these passengers, having vigorously shrugged off the fellahs who were assailing him with offers of their services, suddenly approached the detective. With the utmost politeness, the passenger asked if Fix might point out the office of the British consul — at the same time displaying a passport, which he undoubtedly wished to have stamped with a British visa.

Instinctively, Fix took the passport in his hands, and with a

rapid glance he read the description of its owner. He was just able to restrain himself from making an involuntary movement. The document trembled slightly in his hand. The description laid down in the passport was identical in every respect to the one he had received from the Commissioner of the Metropolitan Police Service!

"This passport isn't yours?" he said to the passenger.

"No," the passenger replied. "It belongs to my master."

"And your master is...?"

"He stayed on board."

"But," the detective continued, "he must present himself in person at the Consul's office, in order to establish his identity."

"What! Is that absolutely necessary?"

"It's indispensable."

"And where is this office?"

"There, in the corner of the square," the detective replied, indicating a house at a distance of two hundred paces.

"Well then, I'll go and fetch my master — although he won't like being disturbed!"

And with that, the passenger bowed to Fix, and returned to the steamer.

CHAPTER VII

WHICH ONCE AGAIN DEMONSTRATES THE USELESSNESS OF PASSPORTS IN POLICE MATTERS

The detective descended the quay and directed himself rapidly towards the Consul's office. At his urgent insistence, he was at once admitted to that official's presence.

"Mr. Consul," he said without any preamble, "I have good reason to believe that our man has taken passage on board the *Mongolia*."

And Fix related what had passed between himself and the servant regarding the passport.

"Very well, Mr. Fix," the Consul replied, "I wouldn't mind seeing the rascal's face. But perhaps he won't present himself

in my office, if he is indeed what you suspect him to be. A thief doesn't like to leave behind any trace of his passage – and besides, the formality of stamping passports is no longer obligatory."

"Mr. Consul," replied the detective, "if this man is as shrewd as I think he is, he will come!"

"To obtain a visa for his passport?"

"Yes. Passports serve no other purpose than to inconvenience honest people, and to cover the escape of scoundrels. I can assure you that this passport will be perfectly in order, but nevertheless I hope you will refuse to stamp it."

"And why not?" asked the Consul. "If the passport is in order, I have no right to refuse the visa."

"And yet, Mr. Consul, it is essential that I keep this man here in Suez until I've received the warrant for his arrest from London."

"Ah! Mr. Fix, that is your business," replied the Consul, "but I'm afraid that I cannot…"

The Consul was unable to finish his sentence. At that moment, there came a knock at his door, and the office boy showed in two strangers – one of whom was the servant whom Fix had encountered earlier.

These were, in fact, both the master and the servant. The master

presented his passport, requesting laconically that the Consul kindly stamp it with a visa. The official took up the passport and examined it closely, while Fix, in a corner of the office, observed the stranger – or, rather, devoured him with his eyes.

The Consul finished reading the document.

"You are Phileas Fogg, Esquire?" he asked.

"Yes, sir," replied the gentleman.

"And this man is your servant?"

"Yes. A Frenchman named Passepartout."

"You've come from London?"

"Yes."

"And you are going to…?"

"To Bombay."

"Very good, sir. You are aware that the visa is a mere formality, and that we no longer require the presentation of the passport?"

"I know it, sir," replied Phileas Fogg, "but I wish to prove, by your visa, that I have passed through Suez."

"Very well, sir."

The Consul, having signed and dated the passport, applied his stamp. Mr. Fogg paid the visa tariff and, with a curt nod, departed, followed by his servant.

"Well?" asked the detective.

"Well," replied the Consul, "he seems a perfectly honest man!"

"Perhaps," said Fix, "but that is beside the point. Do you not find, Mr. Consul, that this phlegmatic gentleman resembles in every feature the description I have received of the thief?"

"I confess that he does – but, you know, all descriptions of that sort…"

"I must get to the bottom of this," interrupted Fix. "The servant seems to me less inscrutable than the master. And besides, if he's a Frenchman, he won't be able to stop himself from talking. Good day, Mr. Consul."

With this, the detective left the Consul's offices and set out in search of Passepartout.

Meanwhile, Mr. Fogg, on leaving the consular offices, had directed himself towards the quay. There, he gave a few orders to his servant, then he embarked in a small boat, boarded the *Mongolia*, and returned to his cabin. He took out his notebook, which contained the following entries:

Left London, Wednesday 2 October, 8:45 p.m.
Arrived in Paris, Thursday 3 October, 7:20 a.m.
Left Paris, Thursday, 8:40 a.m.
Arrived in Turin via Mont Cenis, Friday 4 October, 6:35 a.m.
Left Turin, Friday, 7:20 a.m.

Arrived in Brindisi, Saturday 5 October, 4:00 p.m.
Embarked on the Mongolia, Saturday, 5:00 p.m.
Arrived in Suez, Wednesday 9 October, 11:00 a.m.
Total number of hours used: 158 ½, or 6 ½ days.

Mr. Fogg inscribed these dates in an itinerary divided into columns which set out, from the 2nd of October to the 21st of December, the month, the day, and the date, the scheduled arrivals at each principal waypoint – Paris, Brindisi, Suez, Bombay, Calcutta, Singapore, Hong Kong, Yokohama, San Francisco, New York, Liverpool, London – and the actual time of arrival, thereby enabling him to calculate the amount of time gained or lost at each stage of the journey.

This itinerary, therefore, provided a complete account of their progress, and Mr. Fogg always knew whether he was running ahead or behind schedule. So, on that day, Wednesday the 9th of October, he recorded his arrival in Suez – which, coinciding with the scheduled arrival, constituted neither a gain nor a loss of time.

After this, Mr. Fogg ordered lunch to be served to him in his cabin. The idea of touring the town never crossed his mind, since he was of that race of Englishmen who leave it to their servants to visit the countries in which they travel.

CHAPTER VIII

IN WHICH PASSEPARTOUT TALKS A BIT MORE,
PERHAPS, THAN IS PRUDENT

It took just a few moments for Fix to catch up with
Passepartout on the quay, where the Frenchman was ambling
along and enjoying the scenery – not feeling, himself, obliged to
ignore the sights.

"Well, friend," Fix said, greeting him, "did you get the visa
for your passport?"

"Ah, it's you again, Monsieur?" replied Passepartout. "Much
obliged. Yes, the papers are all perfectly in order."

"And you are admiring the country?"

"Yes, but we are traveling so quickly that it seems as if I'm

moving in a dream. So this is Suez?"

"Yes."

"In Egypt?"

"Certainly, in Egypt."

"And in Africa?"

"In Africa."

"In Africa!" repeated Passepartout. "I can't believe it. Do you know, Monsieur, I never thought we'd go any further than Paris – but that famous capital, I barely caught a glimpse of it between the hours of twenty past seven and twenty to nine in the morning, in a driving rain, through the windows of a carriage that took us from the Gare du Nord to the Gare de Lyon. How I regret it! I would have loved to see the Père Lachaise cemetery again, and the Champs-Élysées Circus!"

"Are you in much of a hurry, then?" asked the police detective.

"I am not, but my master is. And speaking of which, I must buy some socks and shirts! We left without luggage, with no more than an overnight bag."

"I'll take you to a bazaar where you can find everything you'll need."

"Monsieur," said Passepartout, "this is really too kind of you!"

The two men set off together, Passepartout chatting as they went.

"Above all," he said, "I must be sure not to miss the boat!"

"You have plenty of time," replied Fix. "It's only just twelve o'clock."

Passepartout pulled out his enormous watch.

"Twelve o'clock!" he said. "Come now – it's nine fifty-two in the morning!"

"Your watch is running slow," observed Fix.

"My watch! A family heirloom, passed down from my great grandfather! It's never been off by more than five minutes per year. It's a true chronometer!"

"I believe you," replied Fix. "But you've kept it on London time, which is roughly two hours behind Suez. You'll need to reset your watch at noon in every country you visit."

"Me? Reset my watch?" cried Passepartout, "never!

"Well then, it won't correspond with the sun."

"That's just too bad for the sun, Monsieur. It's the sun that'll be in the wrong!"

And with a defiant flourish, the worthy fellow returned the watch to his waistcoat pocket.

Presently, Fix resumed the conversation.

"So you say that you left London in a hurry?"

"I should think so! Wednesday last, at eight o'clock in the evening, in a violation of all his routines, Mr. Fogg returned from his club – and three quarters of an hour later we were off."

"But where is he going, then, your master?"

"Straight ahead! He's making a journey around the world!"

"Around the world?" cried Fix.

"Yes, in eighty days! It's all to do with a wager, he says – but between you and me, I don't believe a word of it. It just doesn't sound sensible. There must be something more to it."

"Ah! So he's a bit of a character, this Mr. Fogg?"

"I would say so."

"It sounds as though he must be rich."

"Evidently so, and he's brought a pretty sum of money along with him, all in brand-new banknotes! He certainly isn't skimping as we go! For example, he's promised a magnificent prize to the *Mongolia*'s mechanic, if we arrive in Bombay well ahead of schedule."

"Have you known him for long, this master of yours?"

"Me, know him!" Passepartout replied. "I entered into his service on the very day of our departure!"

One can easily imagine the effect that these responses had upon the already over-excited imagination of the police detective.

"But where is he going, then, your master?"

This sudden departure from London, immediately following the theft, this vast sum being carried abroad, this eagerness to reach distant countries, this pretext of an eccentric wager... all seemed to confirm, inevitably, Fix's suspicions. He led on the prattling Frenchman, learning that the fellow knew nothing of his master, and that this mysterious gentleman lived in isolation in London – that he was thought to be rich, although the origins of his fortune were unknown – and that the details of his life were impenetrably obscure. At the same time, Fix felt sure that Phileas Fogg would not disembark in Suez, and that he would indeed continue to Bombay.

"Is Bombay far from here?" asked Passepartout.

"Quite far," replied the detective. "It will take another ten days of sailing to get there."

"And in what country is Bombay?"

"India."

"In Asia?"

"Naturally."

"Oh, dear me! Oh – you must understand... There's just one thing that's bothering me... It's my burner!"

"What burner?"

"The gas-burner in my room, which I forgot to extinguish, and which is burning at my expense. I've worked out that

it's costing me two shillings per twenty-four hours, which is precisely six pence more than I earn – and so you can understand that the longer this journey takes…"

Did Fix indeed understand this matter of the gas-burner? It is most unlikely. He had stopped listening, and was coming to a decision. He and the Frenchman had arrived in the bazaar. Fix left his companion to make his purchases, urging him not to miss the departure of the *Mongolia*, and then returned with all haste to the Consul's office.

Now that his mind was made up, Fix had recovered all of his equanimity.

"Sir," he said to the Consul, "I no longer have any doubt. I've identified my man. He's passing himself off as an eccentric who is going around the world in eighty days."

"Then he's a crafty fellow," replied the Consul, "and he's planning to return to London, once he's shaken off all the police detectives of the two continents!"

"We shall see," said Fix.

"Are you sure you're not mistaken?" asked the Consul once again.

"I am not mistaken."

"But then why did the thief request a visa to prove that he had passed via Suez?"

"Why?... I have no idea, Mr. Consul," replied the detective, "but consider this."

And in a few words, he laid out the salient points of his conversation with Phileas Fogg's servant.

"There's no doubt about it," said the Consul. "All the evidence points to this man. And what will you do?"

"I'll send a dispatch to London, immediately requesting that an arrest warrant be sent to Bombay. Then I'll embark on the *Mongolia* myself, to track my thief to India – and there, in English territory, I'll politely accost him with the warrant in one hand and the other placed firmly on his shoulder."

Having uttered these words with an air of cool determination, the detective took leave of the Consul and proceeded to the telegraph office. There, he sent to the Commissioner of the Metropolitan Police the dispatch, with which we are already familiar.

A quarter of an hour later, Fix, with a lightly packed bag in hand, and well-furnished with the necessary funds, embarked on the *Mongolia*, and soon after, the vessel was cruising at full steam upon the waters of the Red Sea.

CHAPTER IX

IN WHICH THE RED SEA AND THE INDIAN OCEAN PROVE BENEFICIAL TO THE DESIGNS OF PHILEAS FOGG

The distance between Suez and Aden is precisely thirteen hundred and ten miles, and the regulations of the Company allow its steamships a period of one hundred and thirty-eight hours in which to traverse it. The *Mongolia*, whose fires had been vigorously stoked, was running at a rate that would put the ship well ahead of the stipulated arrival time.

Most of the passengers who had embarked at Brindisi were bound for India. Some were going to Bombay, others were going to Calcutta – but they, too, were traveling via Bombay, since the construction of a railroad crossing the width of the Indian

subcontinent meant it was no longer necessary to round the point of Ceylon.

Among the *Mongolia*'s passengers were functionaries and military officers of every rank. Of these last, some belonged to the regular British Army, while others commanded companies of native sepoys, and all were highly paid, since the government had assumed the rights and the charges of the former East India Company: for the sub-lieutenants earned £280, the brigadiers £2,400, and the generals £4,000 per year.

They led an easy life on board the *Mongolia*, therefore, this community of functionaries, and among them there could even be found a few young Englishmen who, with a million pounds in their pocket, had set off to establish new businesses in distant capitals. The ship's 'purser', a trusted official of the Company, and the equal of the Captain, ensured that the service on board was of the highest standard. At breakfast, at the two o'clock lunch, at the five-thirty dinner, and at the eight o'clock supper, the tables groaned beneath plates of fresh meat and side-dishes furnished by the kitchens and store-rooms of the steamship. The female passengers – of whom there were several – changed their clothes twice every day. There was music, and even dancing, when the sea would permit it.

But the Red Sea is capricious, and all too often rough, like

all long and narrow gulfs. When the wind blew from either the Asian or the African coast, the *Mongolia* – merely a long hull with a propeller – was taken abeam, and rolled dreadfully. Then, the ladies would disappear, the pianos fell silent, singing and dancing stopped at once. And yet, despite the wind, despite the swell, the steamship, propelled by its powerful engine, ran steadily towards the Strait of Bab-el-Mandeb.

What was Phileas Fogg doing all this time? One might expect that, ceaselessly worrying, gripped with anxiety, he attended to every contrary shift in the wind, every disordered movement of the swell which might cause damage to the engine – indeed, every possible source of damage that, by obliging the *Mongolia* to call at some port for repairs, might compromise his voyage.

Not a bit of it. Or at least, if that gentleman did consider such eventualities, he betrayed no sign of it. He was, as always, the impassive, imperturbable member of the Reform Club, whom no incident or accident could unsettle. He appeared no more emotional than the ship's chronometers. He was rarely seen on deck. He had little interest in observing the Red Sea, however rich it might be in memories of the earliest scenes of human history. He did not care to admire the curious little towns scattered along its shores, which sometimes raised their picturesque outlines against the sky. He was unperturbed by

the dangers of this Arabian gulf, of which the ancient historians – Strabo, Arrian, Artemidorus, al Idrisi – have always spoken with horror, and where, in times past, sailors never ventured unless they had first consecrated their voyages with prayers and sacrifices to the gods.

What was this personage doing then, while imprisoned in the *Mongolia*? First, he partook of four hearty meals every day, and neither the pitching nor the rolling of the vessel could unsettle a machine of such marvelous regularity. And second, he played whist.

Yes! He had found partners as devoted to the game as he was himself: a tax collector who was assuming his post in Goa, a minister, the Reverend Decimus Smith, who was returning to Bombay, and a brigadier general of the British Army, who was rejoining his regiment in Benares. All three passengers had the same passion for whist as Mr. Fogg, and together they played for hours on end in an absorbing silence.

As for Passepartout, he was entirely untroubled by seasickness. He occupied a forward cabin and dined, like his master, conscientiously. It should be said that he found such a journey, taking place under such conditions, by no means unpleasant. In fact, he quite enjoyed it. Well fed and comfortably lodged, he took in the scenery and contented himself with the

He partook of four hearty meals every day, and neither the pitching nor the rolling of the vessel could unsettle a machine of such marvelous regularity.

thought that this wild caper would surely come to an end in Bombay.

Furthermore, on the 10th of October, the day after their departure from Suez, he was rather pleased to encounter on deck the obliging personage with whom he had walked and chatted in Egypt.

"If I am not mistaken," he said, greeting Fix with his most amiable smile, "you are the person who so kindly served as my guide in Suez."

"Indeed," replied the detective, "I recognize you! You are the servant of that peculiar Englishman..."

"Just so, Monsieur...?"

"Fix."

"Monsieur Fix," replied Passepartout. "I am delighted to see you on board. And where are you bound?"

"Why, the same as you – to Bombay."

"Excellent! Have you already made this journey?"

"Several times," replied Fix. "I am an agent of the Peninsular Company."

"Then you know India well?"

"Well... Yes..." replied Fix cautiously.

"And is it quite a curious place, this 'India'?"

"Oh, very curious! There are mosques, minarets, temples,

fakirs, pagodas, tigers, serpents, and temple dancers. But I hope that you will have time to visit the country?"

"I hope so too, Monsieur Fix. You see, a man of sound mind can't very well spend his life leaping out of steamships and into trains, under the guise of going around the world in eighty days! No. You may be sure – all these gymnastics will end when we arrive in Bombay."

"And is Mr. Fogg getting on well?" asked Fix in the most natural tone in the world.

"Very well, Monsieur Fix. As, indeed, am I! I'm eating like a famished ogre. It must be all this fresh sea air."

"But I never see your master on deck."

"Never. He is not the least bit curious."

"Do you know, Mr. Passepartout, this supposed voyage in eighty days could easily be a cover for some secret errand… A diplomatic mission, for example!"

"Oh, Monsieur Fix, I have absolutely no idea – and in truth I wouldn't give up half a crown to know the truth of it."

Following this encounter, Passepartout and Fix got into the habit of chatting together. Little by little, Fix sought to gain the trust of Mr. Fogg's servant – which he felt might one day be useful to him. The police detective would often, in the bar-room of the *Mongolia*, offer the worthy fellow a few glasses of whisky

or pale ale, which Passepartout gladly accepted – thinking this Monsieur Fix to be a very honest gentleman.

Meanwhile, the steamship was making rapid progress. On the 13th, they came within sight of the city of Moka, sheltering within a ring of ruined battlements, above which floated a few green date palms. In the distance, on the flanks of the mountains, were vast plantations of coffee. Passepartout was delighted to contemplate this famous city, and it seemed to him that, with its high, circular walls, and a dilapidated fort shaped somewhat like a handle, the whole structure resembled an enormous coffee cup.

During the following night, the *Mongolia* passed through the Strait of Bab-el-Mandeb, whose Arabic name is translated as the Gate of Tears, and the next day, the 14th, the ship put in at Steamer Point, to the northwest of the port of Aden. It was there that they would take on coal.

The supplying of steamships with combustibles – at such great distances from their centers of production – is a serious matter. To this end the Peninsular Company alone is forced to spend a sum, every year, of eight hundred thousand pounds. It has been necessary, in fact, to establish coal depots in a string of ports, and in these distant seas, coal is valued at more than three pounds sterling per ton.

The *Mongolia* still had to cover a distance of sixteen hundred

and fifty miles before reaching Bombay, and so she was obliged to wait four hours at Steamer Point while her holds were filled. But this delay could have no adverse effect on the schedule of Phileas Fogg. It was foreseen. And in fact, instead of arriving at Aden in the morning of the 15th of October, the *Mongolia* arrived in the evening of the 14th. She had made a gain of fifteen hours.

Mr. Fogg and his servant went ashore. The gentleman wished to obtain a visa for his passport. Fix followed him, unseen. Once the formality of the visa had been completed, Phileas Fogg returned to the ship to continue his game of whist.

Passepartout, on the other hand, as was his habit, wandered among the local population of Somalis, Baniyas, Parsees, Jews, Arabs, and Europeans who made up the twenty-five thousand inhabitants of Aden. He admired the fortifications that made this city the Gibraltar of the Indian Ocean, and the vast cisterns where the English engineers were still hard at work, two thousand years after the engineers of King Solomon.

"Very curious, very curious," Passepartout said to himself as he returned to the steamer. "It seems that travel is quite the thing, if one wishes to see new sights."

At six o'clock in the evening, the *Mongolia*'s propeller began churning the waters of the Aden roadstead, and soon afterwards

she was cruising on the Indian Ocean. The steamer had one hundred and sixty-eight hours to complete the crossing between Aden and Bombay.

As it happened, the conditions were ideal: the wind held in the northwest, and the sails were set to assist the engine. The vessel rolled far less. The ladies, in new dresses, reappeared on the deck. Singing and dancing resumed. In this way the journey proceeded smoothly, and Passepartout was delighted by the charming companion that his good fortune had found for him in the person of Fix.

On Sunday, the 20th of October, at about noon, the coast of India was sighted. Two hours later, the pilot came on board to guide the steamer into port. On the horizon, a distant line of hills was delicately traced against the sky. Soon, the rows of palm trees that cover the city came distinctly into view. The steamship entered the roadstead formed by the islands of Salcette, Colaba, Elephanta, and Butcher, and at four thirty she hauled up at the quays of Bombay.

Phileas Fogg was just then finishing the thirty-third rubber of the day, and thanks to an audacious maneuver, he and his partner, having won all thirteen tricks, completed the crossing with an admirable grand slam.

The *Mongolia* was not due in Bombay before the 22nd

of October, but she arrived on the 20th. This constituted, therefore, a gain of two days since Phileas Fogg's departure from London, and he calmly inscribed it in the appropriate column of his itinerary.

CHAPTER X

IN WHICH PASSEPARTOUT IS ONLY TOO GLAD
TO ESCAPE WITH THE LOSS OF HIS SHOES

Everyone knows that India – that great, inverted triangle with its base in the north and its apex in the south – covers an area of fourteen hundred thousand square miles, across which is spread unevenly a population of one hundred and eighty million inhabitants. The British government exercises direct control over a portion of this immense territory. It has established a Governor-General in Calcutta, governors in Madras, in Bombay and in Bengal, and a lieutenant-governor in Agra.

But British India, properly defined, consists of just seven

hundred thousand square miles and a population of one hundred to one hundred and ten million inhabitants. Which is to say that a significant part of the entire territory still falls outside the authority of the Queen. In fact, among certain rajahs of the interior (fierce and terrible rulers), the Hindus still hold absolute independence.

From 1756 – when the first English outpost was established where the city of Madras stands today – to 1857, the year that saw the eruption of the great Sepoy Mutiny, the famous East India Company was all-powerful. It annexed, bit by bit, the various provinces, purchasing territory from the Rajahs in exchange for rents which it seldom paid, if at all. It appointed its own Governor-General and all of its own civil and military officials. But the East India Company no longer exists, and England's possessions in India are directly controlled by the Crown.

The appearance, the customs, and the ethnographic divisions of the peninsula are changing day by day. In the past, one might commonly travel here by all the ancient modes of transport: on foot, on horseback, in a wagon, in a wheelbarrow, in a palanquin, on the back of a man, in a coach, etc. Today, steamboats travel at great speed along the Indus and the Ganges, and a railroad, spanning the entire breadth of India, with numerous branch lines

spreading along its way, puts Bombay at just three days' travel from Calcutta.

The route described by this railroad is not a straight line across the continent. The distance, as the crow flies, is only eleven hundred miles, and a train running at no more than average speed could cover that distance in less than three days — but the route is extended by at least a third by the detour the railway makes in order to reach Allahabad in the north of the peninsula.

Here is a summary of the itinerary followed by the Great Indian Peninsular Railway. On departing from the island of Bombay, it traverses Salsette, crosses to the continent opposite Thana, runs through the chain of the Western Ghats, continues to the northeast as far as Burhanpur, traces through the more-or-less independent territory of Bundelkhand, rises to Allahabad, turns towards the east, encounters the Ganges at Benares, angles slightly away from it, and, descending to the southeast via Burdwan and the French city of Chandernagore, reaches its terminus in Calcutta.

It was half past four in the evening when the passengers of the *Mongolia* disembarked in Bombay. The train for Calcutta was scheduled to depart at precisely eight o'clock.

Mr. Fogg took leave of his partners, left the steamship, gave

his servant a few errands to do, ordered him expressly to present himself at the station before eight o'clock, and, with a step as regular as the second hand of an astronomical clock, made his way to the passport office.

Of all the marvels of Bombay, there was none that he intended to see: neither the city hall, nor the magnificent library, nor the forts, nor the docks, nor the cotton market, nor the bazaars, nor the mosques, nor the synagogues, nor the Armenian churches, nor the splendid temple of Malabar Hill, ornamented with two polygonal towers. He would contemplate neither the masterpieces of Elephanta, nor its mysterious subterranean hypogea, hidden to the southeast of the docks, nor the Kanheri Caves on the island of Salcette, those admirable remnants of Buddhist architecture!

No! Nothing. On exiting the passport office, Phileas Fogg proceeded tranquilly to the station, and there he ordered dinner. Among several dishes on offer, the head waiter especially recommended to him a certain giblet of 'native rabbit', which he praised lavishly.

Phileas Fogg accordingly ordered the dish and tasted it conscientiously – but, despite its heavily spiced sauce, he found it wholly unpalatable. He rang for the head waiter.

"Sir," he said, fixing the man with his gaze, "is this rabbit?"

"Yes, milord," replied the offended waiter, "it is jungle rabbit."

"And tell me, did this rabbit meow when it was killed?"

"Meow? Oh! Milord! A rabbit! I swear to you..."

"Sir, be so good not to swear," interrupted Mr. Fogg coldly, "and remember this: there was a time, in India, when cats were considered sacred animals. It was a good time."

"For the cats, Milord?"

"And perhaps for the travelers as well!"

Having made this observation, Mr. Fogg calmly continued with his meal.

Following shortly after Mr. Fogg, Detective Fix also disembarked from the *Mongolia*, and he hurried to the offices of the police commissioner of Bombay. He made himself known as a London detective, explained his mission, and laid out his situation with regard to the suspected thief. Had they received an arrest warrant from London...? No such warrant had arrived. And indeed, the warrant, departing after Fogg himself, could not possibly have arrived before him.

Fix was sorely disappointed. He requested that the commissioner issue an order for Mr. Fogg's arrest, but the commissioner refused. This was a matter concerning the metropolitan police administration, and only that body could

legally issue a warrant. Such strict principles, and such rigorous observance of legal practice is perfectly in line with English customs, which, in matters of individual liberty, admit no arbitrary interference.

Fix, realizing that he would have to await his warrant, did not insist. But he resolved that he would not let this inscrutable rogue out of his sight, so long as the man stayed in Bombay. He had no doubt that Phileas Fogg would remain in Bombay – this had also been, as we know, the belief of Passepartout – and he felt certain that there would be time for the warrant to arrive.

However, since receiving his master's orders on disembarking from the *Mongolia*, Passepartout had understood that their visit to Bombay would resemble those to Suez and Paris – that the journey would not end here; that it would continue, at the very least, to Calcutta, and perhaps even further. And he began to wonder whether this wager of Mr. Fogg's was not in fact perfectly real, and whether fate would not compel him – he, who wished only to live in peace – to complete a journey around the world in eighty days.

In the meantime, having purchased some new shirts and socks, he strolled through the crowded streets of Bombay. There, he rubbed shoulders with Europeans of all nationalities, with Persians in pointed bonnets, Baniyas in round turbans,

Sindhis in square bonnets, long-robed Armenians and Parsees
in black miters. It was, in fact, a day of celebration for these
Parsees or Guebres, the direct descendants of the sect of
Zoroaster, who are the most industrious, civilized, intelligent
and austere of the Hindus – and among whom are counted
the wealthy native merchants of Bombay. That day, they were
celebrating a sort of religious carnival, with processions and
performances, featuring temple dancers dressed in fabrics of pink
gauze fastened with gold and silver pins, and who, to the sound
of fiddles and the beat of the tambourine, danced marvelously,
and in perfect decency.

It goes without saying that Passepartout took in these curious
ceremonies with his eyes and ears wide open, eager to grasp every
last detail, and his expression and demeanor marked him out as
the greenest 'booby' imaginable.

Unfortunately for him and for his master, whose journey
he risked compromising, his curiosity led him on further than
was prudent. Indeed, having seen the Parsee celebrations,
Passepartout was making his way toward the station when,
passing before the admirable Malabar Hill Temple, he was struck
with the unfortunate idea of stepping inside for a visit.

He was ignorant of two things: first, that Christians are
officially forbidden entry to certain Hindu temples, and

secondly, that even members of the Hindu faith may not enter without removing their shoes and leaving them at the door. It should be noted that, as a matter of sound policy, the English government (wishing to respect and to promote respect of local religious beliefs, even to the slightest detail) severely punishes whoever violates their practices.

Passepartout, entering as a simple tourist, without any ill intent, was admiring the interior of Malabar Hill – a shimmering eruption of Brahmanical ornamentation – when he suddenly found himself upended on the sacred flagstones. Three angry priests threw themselves on Passepartout, tearing the shoes and socks from his feet, and with savage cries they began to rain down blows upon him.

The Frenchman, vigorous and agile as he was, quickly found his feet again. With a blow of his fist and a sharp kick, he knocked down two of his adversaries, who were hampered by their long robes. Then, scampering out of the temple with all the speed of his young legs, he soon outran the third Hindu, who was raising a furious crowd in his pursuit.

At five to eight, just minutes before the train's departure, hatless, shoeless, and having lost, in his flight, the packet containing his purchases, Passepartout arrived at the railway station. Fix was there too, waiting on the platform. He had

followed Mr. Fogg to the station, and when he realized that his quarry was planning to leave Bombay, he had resolved immediately to follow him to Calcutta — or even further, should the need arise. Passepartout didn't notice Fix, who was lurking in the shadows, but Fix heard clearly the recital of all Passepartout's adventures, which he conveyed in a few sentences to his master.

"I hope this will not happen again," responded Phileas Fogg simply, as he took his place in one of the train carriages. The unfortunate servant, barefoot and distressed, followed his master without another word.

Fix was about to climb into another of the carriages, when something occurred to him that held him back, and abruptly altered his plans.

"No, I'll stay here," he said to himself. "An offense committed on Indian territory… I've got him now."

At that moment, the locomotive whistled sharply, and the train rumbled out into the night.

CHAPTER XI

IN WHICH PHILEAS FOGG ACQUIRES A CURIOUS
MOUNT FOR A FABULOUS PRICE

The train departed at the scheduled hour. It carried a number of travelers, several military officers, government officials, and opium and indigo merchants, whose business called them to the eastern part of the peninsula.

Passepartout occupied the same compartment as his master. A third traveler took his place in the corner opposite. It was the brigadier general, Sir Francis Cromarty, one of Mr. Fogg's partners at whist during the crossing from Suez to Bombay, who was rejoining his troops stationed near Benares.

Sir Francis Cromarty was tall, blond, about fifty years old,

and had distinguished himself during the most recent Sepoy revolt. He could with some justification be termed a native: he had lived in India since his earliest years, and had made only a few, rare appearances in the country of his birth. He was a deeply knowledgeable man, who would gladly have provided information on the customs, history and administration of India, had Phileas Fogg been the type of man to request it. But that gentleman requested nothing. He was not traveling – he was tracing a circumference. He was nothing more than a satellite, pursuing its orbit around the terrestrial globe, according to the laws of rational mechanics. At that moment, he was reviewing in his mind the number of hours that had passed since his departure from London, and he would have rubbed his hands together in satisfaction, had it been in his nature to make so useless a gesture.

Sir Francis Cromarty had not failed to notice the oddity of his traveling companion, despite having observed him only with cards in his hands, and between rubbers of whist. He had seen enough to wonder if a human heart could beat beneath that cold exterior, and if Phileas Fogg had a soul that was susceptible to the beauties of nature, and moral aspirations. It was a perplexing question. Of all the eccentric persons that the brigadier general had encountered, not one compared with this product of the

science of exactitude.

Phileas Fogg had not concealed from Sir Francis Cromarty his project of traveling around the world, nor the conditions under which he made his journey. The brigadier general saw in this wager no more than pointless eccentricity, and felt it lacked any hint of the principle of greater good — which ought to guide every reasonable man. If this bizarre gentleman continued along his path, he would end up achieving nothing, either for himself, or for other people.

One hour after its departure from Bombay, the train, passing along the viaducts, had crossed the island of Salcette and was running on the continent. At the Kalyan Station it passed the junction for the railway branch descending via Kandallah and Poona to the southeast of India, and the train continued on to the station of Pawule. At that point, it entered the foothills of the Eastern Ghats, a chain of mountains rising from a foundation of basalt and other trapp rock, and whose highest summits are covered with thick forests. From time to time, Sir Francis Cromarty and Phileas Fogg had exchanged a few words — and at this moment, the brigadier general revived their conversation.

"Only a few years ago, Mr. Fogg, you would have met with a delay, here, which would probably have compromised your itinerary."

"Why is that, Sir Francis?"

"Because the railway stopped at the base of these mountains, which travelers could only cross in palanquins or on ponies, to reach the station of Kandallah on the other side."

"Such a delay would not have upset my plans in the least," replied Mr. Fogg. "I have naturally anticipated the eventuality of certain obstacles."

"And yet, Mr. Fogg," the brigadier general continued, "you could certainly have faced a spot of serious trouble with this young fellow's adventure at the temple."

Passepartout, his bare feet wrapped in his traveling rug, was sleeping deeply, blithely unaware that he formed the subject of their discussion.

"The English government treats these offences with extreme severity," continued Sir Francis Cromarty, "and with good reason. It wishes above all to see that the religious customs of the Indians are respected – and if your servant had been apprehended ..."

"Well, if he had been apprehended, Sir Francis," replied Mr. Fogg, "he would have been convicted, he would have served his sentence, and then he would have returned peacefully to Europe. I fail to see in what manner this affair might have delayed his master!"

And with this comment, the conversation lapsed again. During the night, the train crossed the Ghats and passed through Nashik. The following day, the 21st of October, it proceeded through fairly flat country, belonging to the territory of Khandeish. The landscape was well-cultivated, and dotted with villages, above which the spires of temples appeared in place of the steeples of European churches. Numerous little waterways, most of them tributaries of the Godavari, irrigated this fertile country.

Passepartout, awake once again, stared out of the windows, unable to believe that he was crossing the country of the Indians in a train belonging to the Great Peninsular Railway. It seemed fantastical to him – and yet it was so! The locomotive, tended by the hands of an English engineer and stoked with English coal, sent its smoke billowing across plantations of cotton, of coffee, of nutmeg, of cloves, of red peppers. Steam swirled into spirals around clusters of palm trees, among which there appeared picturesque bungalows, and the occasional *vihara* – a kind of abandoned monastery – and marvelous temples, enriched by the inexhaustible ornamentation so typical of Indian architecture. Then, immense tracts of land stretched out as far as one could see: jungles lacking neither serpents nor wild tigers which fled at the screams of the engine's steam whistle, and then forests,

divided by the railway line, still populated by elephants which, with a pensive eye, watched the passing of the passenger cars.

In the course of the morning, beyond the station of Malegaon, the travelers crossed that somber region so often stained with blood by the followers of the goddess Kali. Not far off rose Ellora, with its admirable temples. Not far off lay the famous Aurungabad, the capital of the ferocious Aureng-Zeb, today simply the chief town of one of the detached provinces of the kingdom of the Nizam. It was over this country that Feringhea, the leader of the Thugs, king of the Stranglers, exercised his dominion. Those murderers, united in a secret society, strangled victims of all ages in the name of the goddess of Death – without spilling a drop of blood – and there was a time when one could not disturb the ground in any part of that country without uncovering a corpse. The English government has been able to put a stop to most of these murders, but the appalling assassin's guild persists, and still continues to function.

At half past twelve, the train stopped at the station of Burhanpur, and Passepartout was able to purchase, for a princely sum, a pair of slippers: exotic babouches stitched with false pearls, into which he stepped with evident vanity. The travelers ate hurriedly, and departed again for the station of Assergur, following for a brief moment the bank of the Tapti, a small river

that flows into the gulf of Cambay, near Surat.

One might well wonder what Passepartout's thoughts were at this point in the journey. In fact, before his arrival in Bombay, he could and did believe that the whole matter would end there. But now, racing at full steam across India, a profound reversal was taking place in his mind. His true nature returned to him. He rediscovered the fantastical ideas of his youth, and he began to take his master's project seriously. He believed now in the truth of the wager, in the journey around the world, and in the time limit which they must not exceed. Already, he was worrying about possible delays, and the accidents which might befall them on their route. He felt a personal interest in the outcome of this endeavor, and trembled at the thought that he might have compromised its success with his unpardonable folly of the day before. And, with a nature much less phlegmatic than that of Mr. Fogg, he was much more restless. He counted and recounted the days that had passed, uttered curses every time the train stopped, accusing it of sluggishness, and secretly blaming Mr. Fogg for having omitted to bribe the engineer. The worthy fellow didn't realize that, while this might yield results aboard a steamship, it was useless aboard a train, whose speed is strictly regulated.

Towards evening, the train entered the defiles of the Sutpoor

Mountains, which separate the territories of Khandeish and Bundelkhand.

The next day, on the 22nd of October, in response to a question from Sir Francis Cromarty, Passepartout, having consulted his watch, stated that it was three o'clock in the morning. Indeed, that famous timepiece, still carefully set to the Greenwich meridian, which could now be found approximately seventy-seven degrees to the west, should be – and was – running four hours late.

Sir Francis corrected the hour given by Passepartout, and made the same observation that the Frenchman had already heard from Fix. He tried to make Passepartout understand that he should reset the watch to each new meridian, and that, since he was going constantly eastwards – that is to say, against the movement of the sun – each day was shortened by four minutes for every degree by which they advanced. It was no use. Whether or not the stubborn fellow understood the brigadier general's explanations, he refused to touch his watch, maintaining it invariably on London time. It was, at least, an innocent obsession, which could harm no one.

At eight o'clock in the morning, at a distance of fifteen miles past the station of Rothal, the train stopped in the middle of a vast clearing, bordered by a few bungalows and the workmen's

cabins. The train conductor passed along the line of passenger carriages, crying: "All passengers will get out here!"

Phileas Fogg looked at Sir Francis Cromarty, who himself seemed baffled by this stop in the middle of a forest of tamarinds and date palms.

Passepartout, no less surprised, jumped out onto the tracks – but he returned almost immediately. "Monsieur," he cried, "No more railroad!"

"What do you mean?" asked Sir Francis Cromarty.

"I mean that the train can't go any further!"

The brigadier general climbed down from the carriage. Phileas Fogg followed him, without haste, and the two men went to address the train conductor.

"Where are we?" asked Sir Francis Cromarty.

"In the village of Kholby," replied the conductor.

"We're stopping here?"

"Certainly. The railway hasn't been finished…"

"What? Hasn't been finished?"

"No. There is still a section of about fifty miles to be built between this point and Allahabad, where the line begins again."

"And yet the newspapers have announced the completion of the railway in its entirety!"

"What can I say, General? The newspapers were wrong."

"And yet you've sold tickets from Bombay to Calcutta!"
continued Sir Francis Cromarty, who was beginning to get
angry.

"Indeed," replied the conductor, "but the passengers know
that they must find their own transportation between Kholby
and Allahabad."

Sir Francis Cromarty was furious. Passepartout would
willingly have knocked the conductor down, and he didn't dare
to look his master in the face.

"Sir Francis, if you please," said Mr. Fogg calmly, "let us find
another way of reaching Allahabad."

"Mr. Fogg, this is a delay which must absolutely jeopardize
your project!"

"No, Sir Francis, it was foreseen."

"What! Did you know that the railway…"

"By no means — but I knew that, sooner or later, some
obstacle would appear along the way. And therefore nothing
has been compromised. I have an advance of two days which I
can sacrifice. There is a steamer which departs from Calcutta for
Hong Kong on the 25th at noon. Today is only the 22nd, and we
will reach Calcutta in time."

To a statement made with such complete assurance, there was
no possible response.

"Mr. Fogg, this is a delay which must absolutely jeopardize your project!"

It was all too true that construction of the railway terminated at this point. The newspapers resembled certain watches with a tendency to run fast, and they had announced prematurely the completion of the line. Most of the passengers were aware of this interruption in their journey and, descending from the train, they had availed themselves of every kind of vehicle which the village had to offer: four-wheeled palki-gharries, carts drawn by zebus (a species of humped cow), traveling coaches resembling movable pagodas, palanquins, ponies, etc. So, although Mr. Fogg and Sir Francis Cromarty searched through the entire village, they found nothing left at all.

"I'll go on foot," said Phileas Fogg.

Passepartout, overhearing this as he rejoined his master, looked worriedly down at his magnificent – but impractical – babouches. Luckily, he had made a discovery of his own, which now he somewhat hesitatingly shared.

"Monsieur," he said, "I think I've found a – a means of transport."

"What is it?"

"An elephant! An elephant belonging to an Indian who lives just a hundred paces from here."

"Let us go to see this elephant," replied Mr. Fogg.

Five minutes later, Phileas Fogg, Sir Francis Cromarty and

Passepartout arrived at a hut beside an enclosure formed by a high palisade. In the hut, there was an Indian; and in the enclosure, an elephant. At their request, the Indian admitted Mr. Fogg and his two companions into the enclosure.

There, they found themselves in the presence of a half-tamed animal, which was being raised by its proprietor not as a beast of burden, but for warlike purposes. With this in mind, he had begun to alter the naturally gentle disposition of the animal, feeding it exclusively on sugar and butter for a period of three months, so as to lead it gradually toward that paroxysm of rage referred to in the Hindu language as 'mutsh'. This may seem an unlikely method of achieving such a result, but it is employed with no less success by elephant trainers. Luckily for Mr. Fogg, the elephant in question had only recently begun this regimen, and the 'mutsh' had not yet declared itself.

Kiouni – this was the name of the animal – could, like all of its kind, maintain a swift pace over long periods of time, and so, lacking any other mount, Phileas Fogg resolved to hire it. But elephants are expensive in India, where they are becoming rare. Male elephants, which alone are suitable for combat in the circuses, are much sought-after. Once brought into a state of domesticity, these animals only rarely reproduce, so that new specimens can only be procured in the wild. They are the subject

of extreme cares, and when Mr. Fogg asked the Indian if he might hire his elephant, the Indian refused him outright.

Fogg persisted, offering for the animal an excessive price of ten pounds per hour. The man refused. Twenty pounds? Refusal once again. Forty pounds? Refusal still. Passepartout jumped at every doubling of Mr. Fogg's offer, but the Indian would not be tempted. And yet the sum was magnificent. Assuming that it would take the elephant fifteen hours to reach Allahabad, the beast would earn for its proprietor a sum of six hundred pounds.

Phileas Fogg, without betraying the least animation, then proposed to buy the animal from the Indian, and immediately offered to pay one thousand pounds. The Indian didn't want to sell! Perhaps the fellow could sense an opportunity to strike a magnificent deal.

Sir Francis Cromarty took Mr. Fogg aside and urged him to consider before going any further. Phileas Fogg replied to his companion that he was not in the habit of acting rashly, that this was ultimately a matter of a wager of twenty thousand pounds, that this elephant was necessary to him, and that, even if he had to pay twenty times its true value, the elephant would be his.

Mr. Fogg returned to the Indian, whose small eyes, blazing with covetousness, showed clearly that this was for him only a question of price. Phileas Fogg made successive offers of twelve

hundred pounds, fifteen hundred pounds, and finally two thousand. Passepartout's usually ruddy complexion turned white with suspense.

At two thousand pounds, the Indian gave in.

"By my babouches," exclaimed Passepartout to himself, "what a fabulous price per pound of elephant!"

Once the deal was struck, it only remained to find a guide. This was much easier. A young Parsee with intelligent features offered his services. Mr. Fogg accepted and promised him a hefty remuneration which could not help but redouble his intelligence.

The elephant was led out and equipped without delay. The Parsee was perfectly well acquainted with the trade of 'mahout' or elephant driver. He covered the back of the elephant with a type of saddle-cloth and arranged, on either side against the animal's flanks, two cacolets: rather uncomfortable hanging seats.

Phileas Fogg paid the Indian in banknotes which he drew from the famous overnight bag – but it seemed almost as if he were pulling them from the vitals of poor Passepartout. Then, Mr. Fogg offered to convey Sir Francis Cromarty to the station of Allahabad. The brigadier general accepted. An additional passenger, after all, was unlikely to tire the enormous animal.

Provisions were purchased in Kholby. Sir Francis Cromarty

took his place in one of the cacolets, and Phileas Fogg in the other. Passepartout sat astride the elephant's back, on the saddle-cloth between his master and the brigadier general. The Parsee straddled the elephant's neck, and at nine o'clock the animal, leaving the village, took the shortest route into a dense forest of palms.

CHAPTER XII

IN WHICH PHILEAS FOGG AND HIS COMPANIONS MAKE THEIR WAY THROUGH THE FORESTS OF INDIA, AND WHAT ENSUES

In order to shorten the distance they should have to cover, the guide left on his right hand the path being traced by the railway still under construction. That route, which had to contend with the capricious windings of the Vindhya Mountains, did not follow the shortest possible path, which it was in Phileas Fogg's interest to take. The Parsee, who knew every road and track in the country, proposed to gain some twenty miles by cutting through the forest, and the three travelers agreed.

The mahout urged the elephant on to a swift pace. Phileas Fogg and Sir Francis Cromarty, buried to the neck in their

cacolets, were rudely shaken by the animal's jerky trot. However, they suffered this discomfort with true British phlegm, speaking little, and scarcely able to catch a glimpse of one another.

As for Passepartout, posted on the back of the animal, and directly subjected to the concussions caused by every step, he was careful to keep his tongue behind his teeth (as his master had recommended) because it could easily have been cut in two. The brave fellow was thrown now onto the elephant's hindquarters, now onto its neck, and seemed to perform acrobatics like a clown on a trampoline. But he was laughing and joking as he tumbled back and forth, and from time to time he drew from his pocket a piece of sugar, which the intelligent Kiouni seized with the tip of his trunk, without interrupting for one moment his swift and steady progress.

After two hours' journey, the guide stopped the elephant and gave him an hour of rest. The animal, having drunk his fill from a nearby lake, devoured branches torn from trees and bushes. Sir Francis Cromarty, too, was glad of the halt. He was shattered. Mr. Fogg, however, appeared as perfectly refreshed as if he had just stepped out of bed.

"Why, he must be made of iron!" said the brigadier general, regarding him with admiration.

"Of forged iron," agreed Passepartout, who was busy

preparing a hasty luncheon.

At noon, the guide gave the signal of departure. The countryside soon took on a savage aspect. The high forests were succeeded by copses of tamarinds and dwarf palms, and then by vast, arid plains, studded with scraggly bushes and strewn with great blocks of syenite. Travelers seldom visit this portion of the upper Bundelkhand, which is inhabited by a fanatical people, hardened by the most terrible practices of the Hindu religion. The English have not been able to extend their complete dominion over this territory, as it is still subject to the influence of the rajahs – Indian princes who, in turn, would have been difficult to assail in their inaccessible retreats among the peaks of the Vindhyas.

Several times, the party caught sight of bands of ferocious Indians, who made angry and threatening gestures on seeing the rapid quadruped pass by. And, in fact, the Parsee avoided them as much as possible, judging them dangerous to encounter. They saw few animals in the course of the day, apart from a handful of monkeys that fled before them, performing a thousand grimaces and contortions, which made Passepartout roar with laughter.

And yet there was one thought, among many, which worried the poor fellow. What would Mr. Fogg do with the elephant, when he arrived at the station of Allahabad? Would he bring him

along on their journey? Impossible! The cost of transporting the animal, added to the cost of its acquisition, would be ruinous. Would they sell it, or set it free? This worthy animal certainly deserved every consideration… But if, for example, Mr. Fogg made a gift of it to Passepartout himself, he would find the elephant rather a burden. This question kept him preoccupied for quite some time.

By eight o'clock, they had traversed the principal chain of the Vindhyas, and the travelers made a halt in a ruined bungalow at the foot of the northern slopes. They had come, in the course of the day, a distance of some twenty-five miles, and would need to cover as much again to reach the station of Allahabad.

The night was cold. Inside the bungalow, the Parsee built a fire of dry branches, whose warmth was much appreciated. Dinner consisted of provisions purchased in Kholby. The travelers were harassed and weary. Their conversation, which began with a few, disconnected phrases, soon gave way to noisy snoring. The guide kept watch beside Kiouni, who slept standing up, leaning against the trunk of a large tree.

The night passed without incident. The silence was broken from time to time by the scattered roars of leopards and panthers, mingled with the sharp chattering of monkeys. But the great carnivores were heard, not seen, and they made no

hostile approach to the occupants of the bungalow. Sir Francis Cromarty slept heavily, like an honest soldier overcome with fatigue. Passepartout, in an agitated state, rehearsed in his sleep the acrobatics of the day before. As for Mr. Fogg, he rested as peacefully as if he had lain in his tranquil house on Savile Row.

At six o'clock in the morning, the travelers set out once again. The guide hoped to reach the station of Allahabad that very evening. That way, Mr. Fogg would use up only part of the advance of forty-eight hours gained in the early stages of his journey.

They descended the lower slopes of the Vindhyas. Kiouni had resumed his rapid pace. Towards noon, the guide made a detour around the hamlet of Kallinger, situated on the banks of the Cani – one of the smaller tributaries of the Ganges. He was always careful to avoid places of habitation, feeling it safer to keep to the deserted landscapes of those first depressions of the great river basin. The station of Allahabad was now no more than twelve miles away to the northeast, and the party stopped among a cluster of banana trees, whose fruits – as nutritious as bread and, according to many travelers, 'as succulent as cream' – they much enjoyed.

At two o'clock, the guide led them into the cover of a dense forest, through which they would need to march for several

miles. He preferred to travel in the shelter of the trees. They had not, so far, had any unpleasant encounters, and the journey seemed destined to pass without incident, when the elephant, betraying clear signs of alarm, suddenly came to a stop.

It was then four o'clock.

"What is it?" asked Sir Francis Cromarty, craning forward from the depths of his cacolet.

"I don't know, officer," replied the Parsee. He listened attentively to a confused murmur that came through the dense foliage.

A few moments later, the murmur became more distinct. One might have said it resembled a concert – still far off – of human voices mingling with brass instruments. Passepartout was all ears – all eyes. Mr. Fogg waited patiently, without saying a word.

The Parsee jumped to the ground, tied the elephant to a tree, and disappeared into the thickest part of the undergrowth. A few minutes passed, and he returned, announcing, "A procession of Brahmins – and it's heading this way. If possible, let us avoid being seen."

The guide untied the elephant and led him into a thicket, advising the travelers not to dismount. He held himself ready to leap astride the animal at a moment's notice, should flight become necessary. But he thought it likely that the troop of worshippers

would pass by without noticing them, for they were almost entirely hidden by the overlapping leaves and branches.

The discordant racket of voices and instruments drew nearer. Monotone chanting mingled with the sound of drums and cymbals. Soon, the head of the procession appeared beneath the trees, some fifty paces from the hiding place of Mr. Fogg and his companions. Through the branches, they were able easily to observe the curious participants of this religious ceremony.

At the head of the procession were priests wearing miters and dressed in long, brocaded robes. They were surrounded by men, women, and children who gave voice to a strange, funereal song, interrupted at regular intervals by the striking of tom-toms and cymbals. Following behind them, drawn by two pairs of richly caparisoned zebus, there appeared a hideous statue, riding on a heavy car with massive wheels, whose spokes and rims depicted interlacing serpents. The statue had four arms, and its body was painted a somber shade of red. It had haggard eyes and tangled hair, a lolling tongue, and lips tinted with henna and betel juice. Upon its breast hung a necklace of skulls. Around its waist was drawn a girdle of dismembered human hands. It stood upright, triumphant, on the headless carcass of a giant.

Sir Francis Cromarty recognized the statue.

"The goddess Kali," he murmured, "goddess of love and

Through the branches, they were able easily to observe
the curious participants of this religious ceremony.

of death."

"Of death, perhaps, but of love? Never!" said Passepartout. "That ugly old woman!"

The Parsee signaled to him to be quiet.

Around the statue there thronged and cavorted and convulsed a group of ancient fakirs, striped with bands of ocher, and covered in cuts from which their blood oozed drop by drop – mindless fanatics who, in the great Hindu ceremonies, still throw themselves beneath the wheels of the Car of Juggernaut.

Next there came a few Brahmins, in all the sumptuousness of their oriental dress, dragging along a woman who was barely able to keep her feet. The woman was young, and as pale as a European. Her head, her neck, her shoulders, her ears, her arms, her hands, her toes, were laden with jewels, necklaces, bracelets, bangles and rings. A tunic woven through with golden threads, and covered with a robe of light muslin, disclosed the outlines of her form.

Behind this young woman – a shocking contrast – there came a troop of guards, armed with naked sabers thrust into their belts and with long, damascened pistols, and carrying a corpse upon a litter. It was the body of an old man, dressed in the opulent clothing of a rajah, wearing, as in life, a turban embroidered with pearls, robes of woven silk and gold, a belt of diamond-studded cashmere and, at his side, the magnificent weapons of an Indian prince.

Finally, to close the procession, there came musicians, and a rear-guard of fanatics, whose shouts from time to time drowned out the deafening racket of the instruments.

Sir Francis Cromarty observed all this pageantry with an air of singular sadness, and he turned to the guide.

"A *suttee*!" he said.

The Parsee nodded, but raised a warning finger to his lips. The long procession wound slowly among the trees, and soon the stragglers disappeared into the depths of the forest. Little by little, the chanting died away. There were a few last, distant shouts, and then at last the tumult gave way to a deep silence.

Phileas Fogg had overheard the word uttered by Sir Francis Cromarty, and he spoke up as soon as the procession had passed.

"What is a *suttee*?" he asked.

"A *suttee*, Mr. Fogg," replied the brigadier general, "is a human sacrifice – but a willing one. The woman that you have just seen will be burned tomorrow in the early hours of the morning."

"What? The scoundrels!" cried Passepartout, unable to hold back his cry of indignation.

"And what of the corpse?" inquired Mr. Fogg.

"It is the body of the prince, her husband," replied the guide, "an independent rajah of the Bundelkhand."

"Can it be," continued Phileas Fogg, his voice betraying not the slightest hint of emotion, "that these barbaric customs still persist in India, and that the English have not succeeded in stamping them out?"

"Throughout the greater part of India," replied Sir Francis Cromarty, "these sacrifices no longer take place; but over these savage regions we exert little influence, and still less over this territory of the Bundelkhand. All of the northern slopes of the Vindhyas are the scene of incessant murders and pillaging."

"The poor woman!" murmured Passepartout. "Burned alive!"

"Yes," said the brigadier general. "Burned. And if she were not, you could scarcely imagine to what a miserable condition she would be reduced by her closest friends and family. They would shave off her hair, and feed her no more than a few, scanty handfuls of rice. Regarded by all as an unclean creature, she would be shunned, and would perish in some corner like a mangy dog. The prospect of such an awful existence often drives these poor women to their sacrifice — much more than love or religious fanaticism. There are cases, nevertheless, when the sacrifice is truly voluntary, and then the government must intervene most energetically to prevent it. A few years ago, I was living in Bombay when a young widow came to ask the governor for authorization to burn herself with the body of her husband.

As you can imagine, the governor refused. So the widow left the city, took refuge in the court of an independent rajah, and there she carried out her sacrifice."

The guide was shaking his head as the brigadier general related these events – and when the tale was over, he spoke.

"The sacrifice that will take place tomorrow at dawn is not voluntary," he said.

"How do you know?"

"This affair is known to everyone in the Bundelkhand," replied the guide.

"And yet that unfortunate woman seemed to offer no resistance," observed Sir Francis Cromarty.

"That is because she has been drugged with hemp smoke and the fumes of opium."

"But where are they taking her?"

"To the Pillaji Temple, two miles away from here. She will spend the night there and await the hour of her sacrifice."

"And this sacrifice will take place...?"

"Tomorrow, at the first light of dawn."

With this, the guide led the elephant out of the dense undergrowth and climbed back into place on the animal's neck. But just as he was about to spur the animal on with a peculiar whistle, Mr. Fogg stopped him and addressed Sir Francis

Cromarty.

"What if we were to save that woman?" he said.

"Save her, Mr. Fogg...?" cried the brigadier general.

"I am still twelve hours ahead of schedule. I can use those twelve hours for this purpose."

"Well! So you are a man of heart!" said Sir Francis Cromarty.

"Sometimes," replied Phileas Fogg simply. "When I have the time."

CHAPTER XIII

IN WHICH PASSEPARTOUT PROVES ONCE MORE
THAT FORTUNE FAVORS THE BRAVE

This was a hazardous undertaking, bristling with difficulties, perhaps impracticable. Mr. Fogg would be risking his life – or at the very least his liberty – and would risk at the same time the success of all his projects. But he did not hesitate. And he found, in fact, a resolute ally in Sir Francis Cromarty.

As for Passepartout, he stood ready. They could count on him. His master's idea exhilarated him. He could sense a heart – a soul within that icy exterior. He was starting to like Phileas Fogg.

There remained the guide. What part would he play in this

affair? Would he not take the side of the Hindus? If he refused to aid Phileas Fogg and his companions, they would need to assure themselves, at least, of his neutrality.

Sir Francis Cromarty put the question to him frankly.

"Officer," replied the guide, "I am a Parsee, and that woman is a Parsee. I am at your command."

"Very well, guide," said Mr. Fogg.

"But know this," continued the Parsee. "Not only do we risk our lives, but horrible tortures await us should we be captured. So consider well."

"It is considered," replied Mr. Fogg. "I think we should wait for nightfall before we take any action?"

"I think so too," replied the guide.

The worthy Indian then gave a further account of the victim. She was an Indian woman of the Parsee race, celebrated for her beauty, the daughter of wealthy merchants in Bombay. She had received, in that city, a thoroughly English education, and from her manners and learning one would have thought her to be a European. Her name was Aouda.

After the death of her parents, she was married, against her wishes, to the old rajah of the Bundelkhand. Three months later, she became a widow. Knowing what fate awaited her, she escaped, but was immediately recaptured – and the rajah's

relatives, who stood to profit from her death, sentenced her to that sacrifice which now it seemed impossible to avert.

The details of this narrative could only serve to strengthen Mr. Fogg and his companions in their generous resolve. It was decided that the guide would direct the elephant towards the Pillaji Temple, which they would approach as nearly as possible.

Half an hour later, they stopped in a dense copse some five paces from the temple wall. They could not see the nearby structure, but the wild cries of the fanatics were clearly audible.

Then they discussed how they might reach the victim. The guide knew the Pillaji Temple, in which he affirmed that the young woman was imprisoned. Would it be possible to enter by one of the doors, while the entire party was plunged in an intoxicated slumber – or would they need to make some breach in the wall? These were questions which could only be decided in the very place and time of their undertaking. But it was absolutely certain that the rescue would need to be attempted that same night – before sunrise, at which time the victim would be led out to the funeral pyre. For then, no human intervention could possibly save her.

Mr. Fogg and his companions waited for night. As soon as darkness fell, at about six o'clock in the evening, they resolved to carry out a reconnaissance of the temple. The last cries of

the fakirs were dying out. It is probable that those Indians, as was their custom, were now sinking into the deep intoxication brought on by 'hang' – liquid opium, mixed with an infusion of hemp – and it might just be possible to slip past them and reach the temple itself.

The Parsee, followed by Mr. Fogg, Sir Francis Cromarty and Passepartout, moved silently through the forest. For ten minutes they crept along beneath the leaves and branches, and then they reached the edge of a little stream – and there, in the glow of iron torches tipped with burning resins, they perceived a mass of stacked wood. It was the pyre, composed of precious sandalwood, and already impregnated with a scented oil. On a platform at the top reposed the embalmed corpse of the rajah, ready to be burned at the same time as his widow. At another hundred paces beyond this funeral pyre, there stood the temple, whose spires rose through the shadows, piercing the canopy of the forest.

"Come!" said the guide in a whisper. And, with redoubled caution, followed by his companions, he slipped noiselessly through the tall brush.

The silence around them was broken only by the murmur of the wind among the branches.

Soon, the guide stopped at the edge of a clearing. A few

torches lit up the space. The ground was littered with small groups of sleepers, overcome in their intoxication. It resembled a battleground, strewn with the bodies of the dead. Men, women and children lay mingled together. Here and there, a few drunkards were still groaning to themselves.

In the background, flanked on either side by the dark mass of trees, the temple of Pillaji rose through the gloom. But to the great disappointment of the guide, the rajah's guards stood watch at the doors in the light of smoking torches, and patrolled with naked sabers. It was to be supposed that, within the temple, the priests were standing watch as well.

The Parsee advanced no further. He recognized that it would be impossible to force an entry to the doors of the temple, and he led his companions back into the forest.

Phileas Fogg and Sir Francis Cromarty, too, had understood that they could attempt nothing in that direction. They stopped, and conferred in whispers.

"Let's wait," said the brigadier general. "It's only eight o'clock now, and it's possible that the guards will eventually fall asleep."

"It's possible, yes," replied the Parsee.

So Phileas Fogg and his companions stretched out on the ground at the foot of a tree and waited.

The rajah's guards stood watch at the doors in the light of
smoking torches, and patrolled with naked sabers.

The hours were long in passing! From time to time, the guide left them to observe the temple from the edge of the woods. The rajah's guards were still watching in the torchlight, and a faint glow filtered out through the windows of the temple.

They waited until midnight, but there was no change in the surveillance of the temple door. It became clear that they could not expect the guards to give in to sleep. They had probably been spared the intoxicating fumes of 'hang'. It would be necessary, then, to try another tack, and to get in by making some breach in the walls of the temple. The question remained whether the priests within would be guarding their victim with as much diligence as the soldiers at the temple door.

After one last consultation, the guide announced that he was ready to go. Mr. Fogg, Sir Francis and Passepartout followed. They made a rather long detour, and approached the temple from the rear.

At about half past midnight, they arrived at the foot of the walls. They had not encountered anyone, and there was no watch set on this side of the building – but there was a total absence here of windows or doors.

The night was dark. The moon, then in its last quarter, was just lifting over a horizon encumbered with heavy clouds. The height of the forest trees helped deepen the shadows around them.

But it was not enough merely to reach the foot of the walls; they would still need to make some opening in them. To accomplish this, Phileas Fogg and his companions had no other tools than their pocket knives. Happily, the temple walls were built from a mixture of wood and bricks which ought not to be difficult to pierce. Once they had removed the first brick, the others would come out easily.

They set to work, making as little noise as possible. The Parsee, on one side, and Passepartout, on the other, labored to release the bricks, in order to make an opening two feet wide. They were making progress, when a sudden cry was heard within the temple – and almost immediately it was answered by more cries from without.

Passepartout and the guide suspended their labor. Had they been discovered? Had the alarm been given? Simple prudence dictated that they retreat to a safe distance – and so, with Phileas Fogg and Sir Francis Cromarty, they plunged back into the cover of the woods. They planned to wait, if possible, until the disturbance died down, and then immediately to resume their operation.

But, in an unlucky development, a troop of guards now appeared at the rear of the temple, and took up a position rendering any approach impossible.

It would be difficult to describe the disappointment of the four men whose attempt had been so decisively thwarted. Now that they could no longer reach the victim, how could they possibly save her? Sir Francis Cromarty was biting his knuckles. Passepartout was beyond himself, and it was with difficulty that the guide was able to restrain him. The impassive Fogg waited, without betraying any emotion.

"I suppose there's nothing for us to do but go?" asked the brigadier general in a whisper.

"There's nothing to do but go," replied the guide.

"Wait," said Fogg. "I only need to reach Allahabad tomorrow before noon."

"But what can you hope to accomplish?" replied Sir Francis Cromarty. "In a few hours, the sun will rise, and then…"

"The chance that has escaped us may still present itself at the last moment."

The brigadier general would have given much to know what was going on behind Phileas Fogg's tranquil gaze. What was that Englishman, with his icy demeanor, planning to do? Did he intend, at the moment of the sacrifice, to rush forward and tear the young woman from the grasp of her executioners? It would be pure folly – and could one really believe that this man was mad enough to try it? At any rate, Sir Francis Cromarty agreed

to wait for the conclusion of this terrible scene. The guide did not let his companions linger on in the spot where they had taken refuge, leading them instead to the back of the clearing. There, hidden by a dense cluster of trees, they could observe the groups of sleepers.

Meanwhile, Passepartout, resting among the lower branches of a tree, was turning over an idea which had, at first, flashed through his mind like lightning, and which now fixed itself firmly in his brain.

At first he had told himself, "This is madness!" – but now he murmured quietly, "Why not, after all? It's an opportunity, and perhaps it's the only one we'll get. And we are dealing with such cretins…!"

With that, Passepartout sprang into action, slipping with the grace of a serpent along the low branches, whose tips arched down toward the ground.

The hours passed, and soon, although the darkness still lay heavily around them, some brighter nuances began to hint at the approaching day.

The moment had arrived. In that unconscious crowd, a kind of resurrection seemed to take place. The little groups began to stir. The sound of the tom-tom rang through the clearing. Songs and cries broke out again. The hour had come in which the

unlucky woman was doomed to die.

Indeed, the doors of the temple now swung open. A harsher light poured out from within. In the bright glare Mr. Fogg and Sir Francis Cromarty could see the victim, as two priests were dragging her out between them. For a moment it seemed to them that, shaking off the numbness of intoxication through some supreme instinct of self-preservation, the poor woman tried to escape from her executioners. Sir Francis Cromarty's heart leapt inside his breast. Convulsively grasping Phileas Fogg's hand, he found that it held an open pocket knife.

At that moment, the crowd surged forward. The young woman had fallen back into the torpor brought on by the hemp smoke. She passed among the ranks of the fakirs, who accompanied her with their fanatical cries. Phileas Fogg and his companions followed, mingling with the stragglers on the edge of the crowd.

After two minutes, they reached the bank of the river, and stopped at less than fifty paces from the funeral pyre, on which lay the body of the rajah. In the dim half-light, they could make out the young victim, absolutely motionless, stretched out beside her husband's corpse.

Then a burning torch dipped toward the pyre – and the wood, impregnated with oil, immediately burst into flame.

At once, Sir Francis Cromarty and the guide took hold of Phileas Fogg who, in a moment of generous folly, had thrown himself toward the burning pyre... But just as Phileas Fogg managed to wrestle free of his companions, the scene suddenly changed. A cry of terror lifted from the crowd, and around them the people fell to the ground in horror.

Could it be that the old rajah was not actually dead? For he was suddenly seen to rise, like a ghost, from his resting place – and, lifting the young woman in his arms, he stepped down from the flaming pyre amid the swirling smoke that so enhanced his spectral appearance.

The fakirs, guards and priests, gripped by terror, lay with their faces turned to the ground, not one of them daring to lift his eyes to behold this awful phenomenon.

The unconscious victim lay, seemingly weightless, in the strong arms that held her. Mr. Fogg and Sir Francis Cromarty had remained standing. The Parsee had bowed his head, and Passepartout was, one imagines, scarcely less surprised...

The resuscitated rajah approached the place where Mr. Fogg and Sir Francis Cromarty stood and, coming abreast of them, he spoke.

"Let's get out of here!" he said abruptly.

It was Passepartout – Passepartout himself, who had slipped

toward the funeral pyre through the billowing smoke! It was Passepartout who, taking advantage of the last gloom of night, had snatched the young woman back from death! It was Passepartout who, playing his role with audacious delight, had strolled through the crowd amid the general terror!

A moment later, all four men had disappeared into the forest, and the elephant was carrying them away at a rapid trot. But renewed cries and clamor, and even a whistling musket ball which pierced Phileas Fogg's hat, alerted them that their ruse had been discovered.

Indeed, the body of the old rajah could now be clearly seen among the fierce flames of the pyre. The priests, recovering from their fright, realized that an abduction had taken place.

Immediately they rushed into the forest. The guards followed, firing their weapons at the fugitives, but the young woman's captors were fleeing swiftly and, in just a few seconds, had passed beyond the range of bows and muskets.

CHAPTER XIV

IN WHICH PHILEAS FOGG TRAVELS THE LENGTH OF THE VALLEY OF THE GANGES RIVER WITHOUT ONCE THINKING TO LOOK AT IT

The daring abduction was a success. One hour later, Passepartout was still laughing gleefully at his victory. Sir Francis Cromarty had shaken the intrepid fellow's hand. His master had told him, "Good," which, coming from that gentleman, was a mark of high praise. To which Passepartout had replied that all the honor of the affair belonged to his master. As for himself, he had only struck upon a 'funny idea' – and he laughed to think that, for a few fleeting moments, he, Passepartout, the former gymnast and ex-sergeant of the fire brigade, had been a venerable, embalmed rajah, the widower

of a charming woman!

As for the young Indian woman, she was unaware of all that had occurred. Wrapped in the travel rugs, she was resting in one of the cacolets.

All this time, the elephant, guided with extreme care by the Parsee, was racing through the twilit forest. One hour after leaving the Pillaji Temple, it strode out onto an immense plain. At seven o'clock, the party made a halt. The young woman was still in a state of complete unconsciousness. The guide helped her to drink a few sips of water and brandy, but it appeared that the stupefying effects of the drug would last for some time yet.

Sir Francis Cromarty, who was familiar with the effects of intoxication produced by the inhalation of hemp fumes, had no worries at all on her account.

But although the young Indian woman's recovery seemed beyond question to the brigadier general, he was much less certain about her future. He did not hesitate to point out to Phileas Fogg that, if Mrs. Aouda remained in India, she would inevitably fall back into the hands of her would-be executioners. These fanatics were scattered throughout the entire peninsula, and despite the efforts of the English police, they would certainly succeed in retaking their victim – whether it be in Madras, in Bombay, or in Calcutta. And Sir Francis Cromarty

cited, in support of this view, a similar case that had taken place only recently. In his opinion, the young woman would be truly safe only when she had left India.

Phileas Fogg replied that he would take these observations into account, and that he would consider the matter.

Towards ten o'clock, the guide announced that they were arriving at the station of Allahabad. Here, the interrupted railway line resumed operation, and its trains crossed, in less than a day and a night, all the remaining distance to Calcutta. Phileas Fogg should therefore arrive in time to board the steamship that would depart at noon the next day, the 25th of October, for Hong Kong.

The young woman was deposited in a room at the station. Passepartout was instructed to go and buy for her all manner of items: toiletries, a dress, a shawl, furs, and so forth – whatever he could find. His master gave him an unlimited budget.

Passepartout set out directly, hunting through all the streets of the city. Allahabad is a holy city, and one of the most venerated sites in India, because it is built at the confluence of two sacred rivers, the Ganges and the Jumna, whose waters attract pilgrims from all parts of the peninsula. In fact, according to the sacred Hindu legends of the *Ramayana*, the Ganges has its source in the sky – from where, by the grace of Brahma, it

descends to the earth.

In making his various purchases, Passepartout had soon visited much of the city. It had once been defended by a magnificent fort, but this has now become a state prison. There is no more commerce, no more industry in this city, which once was both industrial and mercantile. Passepartout searched in vain for a department store, as if he had stood in Regent Street just a few steps from Farmer & Co., but at last, in a second-hand shop run by a difficult, elderly Jewish man, he succeeded in finding the objects he needed: a dress of Scottish wool, a large coat, and a magnificent pelisse — a soft cloak of otter skin for which he did not hesitate to pay seventy-five pounds. Then, he returned triumphantly to the train station.

Mrs. Aouda was beginning to come to. Little by little, the intoxication to which the priests of Pillaji had subjected her was beginning to dissipate, and her lovely eyes were resuming their expression of Indian softness.

When the poet-king, Uçaf Uddaul, celebrates the charms of the queen of Ahmehnagara, he says this:

"Her shining tresses, divided in two equal parts, frame the harmonious contours of her white and delicate cheeks, brilliantly smooth and fresh. Her ebony eyebrows possess the shape and power of the bow of Kama, god of love, and beneath long, silky

lashes, in the dark pupils of her large, clear eyes, there swim – as in the sacred lakes of the Himalayas – the purest reflections of the celestial light. White, even, and finely shaped, her splendid teeth appear between her smiling lips, like droplets of dew caught in the half-closed center of a pomegranate flower. Her ears, sweetly and symmetrically curved, her vermillion hands, her tiny feet, rounded and tender as lotus buds, glitter with the finest pearls of Ceylon, and the rarest diamonds of Golconda. Her slender and supple waist, which one hand alone might encircle, enhances the elegant camber of her curving back and bust, where the flowering of youth displays its most perfect treasures, and, beneath the silken folds of her tunic, she seems to have been modeled in pure silver by the divine hand of Vishwakarma, the eternal sculptor."

But without resorting to such extravagance, it will suffice to say that Mrs. Aouda, the widow of the rajah of the Bundelkhand, was a charming woman in every European sense of the word. She spoke English with great refinement, and the guide had not exaggerated in affirming that this young Parsee had been transformed by her education.

Meanwhile, the train was preparing to leave the station of Allahabad. The Parsee stood waiting. Mr. Fogg paid him his salary, handing over exactly the agreed-upon fee, with not

a penny more or less. This was something of a surprise to Passepartout, who knew what his master owed to the devotion of the guide. Indeed, the Parsee had willingly risked his life in the affair of Pillaji and if, later on, the Hindus learned of his complicity, he would find it difficult to escape their vengeance.

There remained as well the question of Kiouni. What would they do with the elephant, purchased at such a high cost?

But Phileas Fogg had already made a decision in this regard.

"Parsee," he said to the guide, "you have proved yourself both serviceable and devoted. I have paid for your service, but not for your devotion. Do you want this elephant? It is yours."

The guide's eyes shone.

"Your Honor is offering me a fortune!" he cried.

"Accept it, guide," replied Mr. Fogg, "and I will still be in your debt."

"Oh, happy day!" shouted Passepartout. "Take him, friend! Kiouni is a worthy and courageous beast!"

And rushing to the elephant, he gave it several lumps of sugar, saying, "Here, Kiouni; here, here!"

The elephant made some grunts of satisfaction. Then, grasping Passepartout around the waist and rolling him up in his trunk, he lifted him as high as his head. Passepartout, not at all frightened, warmly caressed the animal, who then placed

The elephant made some grunts of satisfaction. Then, grasping Passepartout around the waist and rolling him up in his trunk, he lifted him as high as his head.

him gently back on the ground. The honest Kiouni offered him the tip of his trunk, which the young man grasped warmly in a vigorous handshake.

A few moments later, settled into a comfortable carriage where Mrs. Aouda occupied the very best seat, Phileas Fogg, Sir Francis Cromarty and Passepartout were racing at full steam towards Benares.

Eighty miles at most separate this city from Allahabad, and they covered this distance in two hours.

During the trip, the young woman recovered herself completely. The stupefying hemp fumes had dissipated. How great was her astonishment when she found herself on that train, in that compartment, clad in European clothes, amid a group of travelers who were utter strangers to her!

From the first, her companions offered her every assistance, reviving her with a few drops of brandy. Then, the brigadier general related all that had occurred. He placed special emphasis on the devotion of Phileas Fogg, who had without hesitation put his life in play to save her; and on the climax of their adventure, in which the audacious imagination of Passepartout held sway.

Mr. Fogg let Sir Francis speak, saying nothing himself. Passepartout, blushing, kept repeating that, "It was really nothing!"

Mrs. Aouda thanked her rescuers effusively — more with tears than with words. Her lovely eyes were better interpreters of her gratitude than her lips. But then, her thoughts transporting her back to the scene of the *suttee*, and recalling that vast Indian territory where so many dangers might still lay in wait for her, she gave a shiver of fear.

Phileas Fogg could guess what was passing through Mrs. Aouda's mind and, to reassure her, he offered — rather coldly, in fact — to conduct her to Hong Kong, where she could live until this affair had safely died down.

Mrs. Aouda accepted the offer gratefully. It so happened that one of her relatives — like her, a Parsee — resided in Hong Kong. He was one of the prominent merchants in that city, which is wholly English, despite being located on the coast of China.

At half past noon, the train stopped in the station of Benares. Brahmanic legends hold that this city was built on the ancient site of Kashi — which at one time was suspended in space, between the zenith and the nadir, like the tomb of Mohammed. But, in this more rational epoch, Benares — which orientalists regard as the Athens of India — rests prosaically on the ground, and for a few moments Passepartout caught glimpses of brick houses and wattle-and-daub huts, which gave the city an aspect of desolation, without any hint of local color.

This was Sir Francis Cromarty's destination. The troops that he would rejoin were encamped just a few miles north of the city. The brigadier general bade farewell to Phileas Fogg, wishing him all possible success, and expressing the hope that he would someday repeat the journey – in a manner less original, but more profitable. Mr. Fogg lightly pressed the hand of his companion. Mrs. Aouda's words of parting were more affectionate. She would never forget what she owed to Sir Francis Cromarty. As for Passepartout, he was honored with a hearty handshake from the brigadier general. Deeply moved, he wondered where and when he might once again be at the officer's service. And then they separated.

On departing from Benares, the railway followed part of the valley of the Ganges. Through the windows of the carriage, under clear skies, appeared the varied landscapes of Bihar, followed by mountains covered in greenery, fields of barley, maize and wheat, gullies and lakes swarming with green crocodiles, well-kept villages, and yet more green forests. A few elephants, and zebus with their great humps, came to bathe in the waters of the sacred river – as did, despite the advanced season and falling temperature, some groups of Hindus of either sex, who piously performed their holy ablutions. These votaries, the sworn enemies of Buddhism, are the fervent devotees of

the Brahmanic religion, which is dedicated to the worship of
these three figures: Vishnu, the solar deity, Shiva, the divine
personification of natural forces, and Brahma, the supreme
master of priests and legislators. But how might Brahma, Shiva
and Vishnu look upon this 'Britannic' India now, when some
whistling steam-boat comes past, troubling the consecrated
waters of the Ganges, and scattering the gulls that fly along its
surface, the turtles that crowd its edges, and the faithful gathered
along the length of its banks?

The whole of this panorama passed before them like a flash,
and from time to time a cloud of white steam obscured the
details. The travelers were just able to glimpse, twenty miles
to the south-east of Benares, the fort of Chunar – former
stronghold of the rajahs of Bihar – then, Ghazipur and its great
rose-water factories, the tomb of Lord Cornwallis rising over
the left bank of the Ganges, the walled city of Buxar, Patna, the
great manufacturing and trading city, which boasts the biggest
opium market in India, and Monghir, a city not just European
in style but as English, in fact, as Manchester or Birmingham. It
was a city famous for its iron foundries and factories, whose high
chimneys poured their thick black smoke into the sky of Brahma
– punching up into the realm of dreams!

Then came the night, and the train passed at high speed

through the midst of howling tigers, bears and wolves which fled before the locomotive, and they saw no more of the wonders of Bengal, nor of Golgonda, nor of the ruined Gour, nor of Murshidabad, once a capital city, nor of Burdwan, nor of Hooghly, nor of Chandernagore, that French speck within the Indian territory, over which Passepartout would have been proud to see his nation's flag flying.

At last, at seven o'clock in the morning, they reached Calcutta. The steamship, bound for Hong Kong, would only weigh anchor at noon. So, Phileas Fogg still had five hours ahead of him.

According to his itinerary, the gentleman was meant to arrive in the capital of India on the 25th of October, twenty-three days after his departure from London, and he was arriving on the day in question. He was therefore neither ahead nor behind schedule. Sadly, the two days' advance which he had won between London and Bombay had been used up, as we have seen, in their traversing of the Indian peninsula – but it is to be supposed that Phileas Fogg did not regret their loss.

CHAPTER XV

IN WHICH THE BAG OF BANKNOTES IS LIGHTENED BY ANOTHER FEW THOUSAND POUNDS

The train had stopped at the station. Passepartout was the first to descend from the carriage, followed by Mr. Fogg, who helped his young companion to find her footing on the platform. Phileas Fogg intended to present himself immediately aboard the steamship for Hong Kong, in order to see Mrs. Aouda comfortably settled in. He did not want to leave her side, as long as she remained in a country which held such dangers for her.

Just as Mr. Fogg was leaving the station, a policeman approached and spoke to him.

"Mr. Phileas Fogg?"

"I am he."

"And this man is your servant?" added the policeman, pointing to Passepartout.

"Yes."

"Please follow me, both of you."

Mr. Fogg made no movement which might have betrayed in him any surprise whatever. This agent was a representative of the law – and, for every Englishman, the law is sacred. Passepartout, more accustomed to the French manner, made some protest, but the policeman touched him with his stick, and Phileas Fogg signaled to him that he should obey.

"May this young woman accompany us?" asked Mr. Fogg.

"She may," replied the policeman.

The policeman conducted Mr. Fogg, Mrs. Aouda and Passepartout toward a palki-gharry – a type of four-wheeled, four-seater carriage, drawn by two horses. They departed. No one spoke for the duration of the journey, which lasted roughly twenty minutes.

The carriage first passed through the 'black town', with its narrow streets lined by shacks in which swarmed a filthy, squalid, cosmopolitan populace. Then, it passed through the European quarter, made cheerful by handsome brick houses,

shaded by coconut palms, and bristling with masts, where already, despite the early hour, elegant horsemen and well-kept carriages were passing back and forth.

The palki-gharry stopped before a house of modest appearance, which did not seem destined for domestic purposes. The policeman made his prisoners step down — one could in all truth call them that — and he brought them into a room with barred windows.

"At half past eight," he informed them, "you will appear before Judge Obadiah."

Then he withdrew, and shut the door.

"Well! We've been caught!" cried Passepartout, collapsing into a chair.

Mrs. Aouda turned to Mr. Fogg, trying in vain to disguise the emotion in her voice.

"Sir, you must abandon me," she said. "It is because of me that you are being charged! It is because you saved me!"

Phileas Fogg replied simply that this was impossible. Prosecuted for an affair of *suttee*? Unthinkable! How could the plaintiffs dare to stand before the court? There must be some mistake. Mr. Fogg added that, at any rate, he would not abandon the young woman, and that he would escort her to Hong Kong.

"But the boat sails at noon!" observed Passepartout.

"And we shall be on board before noon," replied the unflappable gentleman.

This was so succinctly asserted, that Passepartout could not help saying to himself, "*Parbleu!* That much is certain! Before noon, we'll all be on board!" But he was somehow not much reassured.

At half past eight, the door opened. The policeman reappeared, and he conducted the prisoners into the neighboring room. It was a public courtroom, and a fairly large crowd of Indians and Europeans already filled the stalls at the back of the chamber.

Mr. Fogg, Mrs. Aouda and Passepartout were seated on a bench facing the seats reserved for the magistrate and the clerk.

This magistrate, Judge Obadiah, promptly entered the courtroom, followed by the clerk. The judge was a big man, and perfectly round. He took down a wig hanging from a nail, and hurriedly arranged it on his head.

"The first case, please," he said.

But then he raised his hand to his head.

"Why – this is not my wig!"

"Indeed not, Mr. Obadiah. It is mine," replied the clerk.

"My dear Mr. Oysterpuf, can you reasonably expect a judge to pass a proper sentence from beneath the wig of a clerk?"

The exchange of wigs was made. During these preliminary exchanges, Passepartout was boiling over with impatience. Across from him, the hands of the big courtroom clock appeared to be racing around the dial at a terrible speed.

"The first case," resumed the judge at last.

"Phileas Fogg?" called Mr. Oysterpuf.

"I am here," replied Mr. Fogg.

"Passepartout?"

"Present!" replied Passepartout.

"Good," said Judge Obadiah. "For two days now, our agents have been watching for the arrival of the accused by every train from Bombay."

"But of what are we accused?" cried Passepartout impatiently.

"You'll soon find out," replied the judge.

"Sir," said Mr. Fogg, "I am an English citizen, and I have the right..."

"Have you been subjected to any ill treatment?" demanded Mr. Obadiah.

"None at all."

"Good! Bring in the plaintiffs."

Upon the judge's command, a door opened, and a bailiff ushered in three Hindu priests.

"So that's it," murmured Passepartout. "It's those rascals who

wanted to burn our young lady!"

The priests took their places before the judge, and the bailiff read out, in a booming voice, a charge of sacrilege, made against the gentleman Phileas Fogg and his servant, who were accused of violating a place consecrated by the Brahmanic religion.

"You have heard the charge?" the judge inquired of Phileas Fogg.

"Yes, sir," replied Mr. Fogg, glancing at his watch, "and I confess."

"Ah! You confess...?"

"I confess – and I call upon these three priests to confess in turn what they were planning to do at the Pillaji Temple."

The priests looked at one another. They appeared not to have the slightest idea what Phileas Fogg meant.

"That's right!" Passepartout cried impetuously. "At the Pillaji Temple, where they were planning to burn their victim alive!"

Again, the priests looked utterly baffled, and Judge Obadiah was thrown into profound confusion.

"What victim?" he asked. "Burn who alive? In the middle of Bombay?"

"What do you mean, Bombay?" asked Passepartout.

"I mean Bombay, of course. This has nothing to do with the Pillaji Temple. This matter concerns the Malabar Hill Temple,

in Bombay."

"And here, as proof, are the desecrator's very shoes," added the clerk, placing on the desk before him a pair of shoes.

"My shoes!" cried Passepartout who, in his surprise, was unable to restrain himself from this ill-advised exclamation.

It will be easy to understand the confusion which had arisen in the mind of both master and servant. They had completely forgotten the incident in the temple in Bombay — and it was that incident which had brought them now before the magistrate of Calcutta.

Indeed, detective Fix had quickly realized just what advantage could be gained from that unfortunate affair. Delaying his departure by twelve hours, he had gained the confidence of the priests of Malabar Hill. He had promised to win for them substantial damages and punitive fines, knowing well that the English government would severely punish this type of infraction. Then, boarding the very next train, he had thrown himself back on the trail of the desecrator. Because of the added time it took to rescue the young widow, Fix and the Hindu priests arrived in Calcutta before Phileas Fogg and his servant, whom the magistrates, alerted by special dispatch, intended to arrest when they stepped from the train.

Fix had been gravely disappointed when he learned that

"My shoes!" cried Passepartout who, in his surprise, was unable
to restrain himself from this ill-advised exclamation.

Phileas Fogg had not yet been spotted in the capital of India. He was forced to conclude that his thief, stopping at one of the stations of the Peninsular Railway, had taken refuge somewhere in the northern provinces. For twenty-four hours, racked with anguish and doubt, Fix lay in wait at the station. At last, that very morning, with the utmost joy, he had spotted his quarry stepping down from a railway carriage – accompanied, it was true, by a young woman whose presence he could not explain. Immediately, he directed a policeman to detain them – and that was how Mr. Fogg, Passepartout, and the widow of the rajah of the Bundelkhand were brought before Judge Obadiah.

If Passepartout had been somewhat less preoccupied, he would have spotted the detective in a corner of the courtroom, where he was following the proceedings with understandable interest – for here in Calcutta, as in Bombay, as in Suez, he lacked the warrant for Mr. Fogg's arrest!

Meanwhile, Judge Obadiah had taken notice of the admission that had escaped Passepartout, who would have given everything he owned to take back his imprudent words.

"The charge is admitted?" asked the judge.

"It is," Mr. Fogg replied coldly.

"Given the fact," the judge continued, "given the fact that the English law seeks to provide equal and rigorous protection

for all the religions of the peoples of India, and it being admitted by Mr. Passepartout that he violated, with his sacrilegious steps, the floors of the Malabar Hill Temple, in Bombay, on the day of the 20th of October, we do hereby sentence the aforementioned Passepartout to fifteen days in prison and a fine of three hundred pounds."

"Three hundred pounds?" cried Passepartout, who was indifferent to the prison sentence but deeply dismayed by this hefty fine.

"Silence!" commanded the bailiff shrilly.

"Furthermore," Judge Obadiah added, "since it has not been materially proven that no connivance took place between the servant and the master, and since the master ought at any rate be held responsible for the actions and transgressions of a servant in his employment, we will also detain the aforementioned Phileas Fogg and sentence him to eight days in prison and a fine of one hundred and fifty pounds. Clerk, bring up the next case!"

In his corner, Fix was overcome by an indescribable sense of satisfaction. Phileas Fogg would be held in Calcutta for eight days, and this was more than enough time for the arrest warrant to catch up with them.

Passepartout was stunned. This conviction would ruin his master. A wager of twenty thousand pounds lost – and

all because, like a gawping tourist, he had stepped into that ridiculous temple!

Phileas Fogg had not so much as wrinkled his brow. He appeared perfectly unruffled, as though the sentence passed had nothing at all to do with him. But just as the clerk prepared to call the next case, he rose from his seat.

"I offer bail," he said.

"You have that right," replied the judge.

At this, Fix felt a chill run down his spine – but he took courage again when he heard the judge's pronouncement. Because of their status as foreigners, bail for Phileas Fogg and his servant would be set at the enormous sum of one thousand pounds each.

If he failed to serve out the judge's sentence, it would cost Mr. Fogg two thousand pounds.

"I'll pay," said the gentleman. From the overnight bag that Passepartout still carried, Phileas Fogg drew a bundle of banknotes and placed it upon the clerk's desk.

"This sum will be returned to you on your release from prison," said the judge. "Until your sentence is due to begin, you are free on bail."

"Come," said Phileas Fogg to his servant.

"Well then, at the very least, let them give me back my

shoes!" cried Passepartout angrily.

His shoes were returned to him.

"*Parbleu*! This is an expensive pair," he muttered. "Each one cost us more than a thousand pounds – and on top of it all they pinch my feet!"

The dejected Passepartout followed Mr. Fogg, who had offered his arm to the young woman. Detective Fix still clung to the hope that his quarry would be unwilling to abandon the sum of two thousand pounds, and that he would serve the eight days in prison. So he threw himself once more on Fogg's trail.

Mr. Fogg immediately flagged down a carriage, into which he stepped with Mrs. Aouda and Passepartout. Fix ran after the vehicle, which soon stopped at one of the quays of the city.

Half a mile away, the *Rangoon* lay at anchor in the roadstead, with its signal of departure fluttering from the masthead. The clocks were striking eleven. Mr. Fogg was one hour ahead of schedule. Fix saw him step down from the carriage with Mrs. Aouda and his servant. The party pushed off in a boat for the steamer, and the detective stamped his feet with rage.

"The scoundrel!" he cried. "He's leaving! Two thousand pounds sacrificed – he's as spendthrift as any thief. Ah! I'll follow him to the edge of the Earth if need be, but at this rate he'll have spent every penny he's stolen!"

The police detective had good reason to make this observation. Indeed, since leaving London, Phileas Fogg's total expenditure on train and steamer tickets, on rewards and inducements, on the purchase of elephants, on bonds and fines, amounted to more than five thousand pounds – and the percentage of the total recovered sum, which had been promised to the detective who would apprehend the bank robber, was therefore constantly diminishing.

CHAPTER XVI

IN WHICH FIX SEEMS NOT TO UNDERSTAND
IN THE SLIGHTEST WHAT IS SAID TO HIM

The *Rangoon*, one of the ships employed by the Peninsular and Oriental Company on the seas surrounding China and Japan, was an iron-built steamer, with a screw propeller, displacing some seventeen-hundred and seventy tons, and driven by engines of four hundred horsepower. It was the *Mongolia*'s equal in speed, but not in comfort. As a result, the quality of Mrs. Aouda's accommodation was not all that Phileas Fogg would have wished. However, this was to be a cruise of just three thousand and five hundred miles, or between eleven and twelve days, and the young woman proved not to be a difficult passenger.

During the first few days of the crossing, Mrs. Aouda gradually became better acquainted with Phileas Fogg. She frequently expressed to him the keen gratitude she felt. The phlegmatic gentleman listened to her, by all appearances, with the utmost coldness – and not the slightest gesture or intonation ever betrayed in him a hint of emotion. He made sure that the young woman wanted for nothing. He visited regularly, at certain hours – if not to converse with her, then at least to listen. He paid her every kind attention which the requirements of the strictest etiquette could demand, but with no more grace or verve than an automaton whose movements had been coordinated for that purpose. Mrs. Aouda wasn't sure what to make of this, but Passepartout had explained to her some of the eccentric characteristics of his master. He had told her about the wager that had prompted the gentleman's journey around the world. Mrs. Aouda had smiled at this, but, after all, she owed him her life, and viewed through the prism of her gratitude, her savior could in no way be diminished.

Mrs. Aouda confirmed the account that the Hindu guide had made of her own touching history. She belonged, indeed, to that race which occupies the first rank among the native populations. Several Parsee merchants have made vast fortunes in India, in the cotton industry. One of them, Sir James Jejeebhoy, has even

been ennobled by the English government, and Mrs. Aouda was a relative of this wealthy inhabitant of Bombay. It was, in fact, a cousin of Sir Jejeebhoy's – the Honorable Jejeeh – whom she planned to seek out in Hong Kong. Would he be able to offer her refuge and assistance? Of this she could not be certain. But Mr. Fogg assured her that she should worry about nothing, and that everything would be mathematically arranged. That was the term he used: mathematically.

Did the young woman understand the significance of that horrible adverb? Impossible to say. At any rate, she fixed her large eyes upon those of Mr. Fogg – her large eyes 'clear as the sacred lakes of the Himalayas'. But the intractable Fogg, as straitlaced as ever, did not seem to be the kind of man who throws himself into such lakes.

This first part of the *Rangoon*'s crossing took them across part of the immense Bay of Bengal. The weather was favorable, the conditions perfectly suited to assist the swift progress of the steamer. The *Rangoon* soon came in sight of the Great Andaman, the principal islands in a notable group, whose picturesque Saddle Peak, at a height of two thousand and four hundred feet, is a landmark well known among mariners.

The steamer passed quite close to shore, but the island's Papuan savages did not reveal themselves. They are creatures

belonging to the lowest rung of the human ladder — but they are wrongly described as cannibals.

The panorama offered by these islands was superb. In the foreground lay immense forests of palms, bamboos, nutmeg and teak, of giant mimosas and tree ferns. Beyond them rose the elegant silhouette of the mountains. Along the coast, the air was filled with thousands of flocking birds: the precious swiftlets, whose edible nests are a delicacy much sought after by the Chinese of the Celestial Empire. However, the varied spectacle of the Andaman island group soon passed, and the *Rangoon* proceeded quickly toward the strait of Malacca, which gave onto the China Seas.

But what had become, during this crossing, of Detective Fix, the officer of law so haplessly caught up in a voyage of circumnavigation? In Calcutta, having left instructions that the arrest warrant be forwarded to him in Hong Kong, he was able to embark on the *Rangoon* without being seen by Passepartout, and he hoped to remain hidden on board until the steamer's arrival. Indeed, it would have been difficult for him to explain his presence on the ship without awaking the suspicions of Passepartout, who still believed him to be in Bombay. But despite all his designs, circumstances soon forced him to renew his acquaintance with the honest fellow. How? We shall find out.

All the hopes, all the desires of the police detective, were now focused on a single point in all the world: Hong Kong. For the steamer would stop far too briefly in Singapore for him to carry out any operation in that city. The arrest, therefore, would need to take place in Hong Kong, or else the thief would slip from his grasp, so to speak, for good.

Indeed, Hong Kong was still English soil – but it was the last that would be found on their route. Beyond it, China, Japan, and America offered more or less certain refuge to Mr. Fogg. In Hong Kong, if he could get hold of the arrest warrant that had evidently been following in his footsteps all this time, Fix would arrest Fogg and deliver him into the hands of the local police. Nothing could be simpler. But, beyond Hong Kong, a straightforward arrest warrant would no longer suffice. He would need an act of extradition. And as a result, there would be delays, impediments, obstacles of all kinds, which the rogue would use to make his final escape. If the operation failed in Hong Kong, it would be difficult – if not impossible – to continue with any chance of success.

"So," Fix told himself for the hundredth time as he paced through the long hours in his cabin, "so either the warrant will be waiting in Hong Kong and I'll arrest my suspect, or it won't, and I'll need to delay his departure – this time at any cost! I

failed in Bombay, and I failed in Calcutta. If I miss my chance in Hong Kong, my reputation is as good as ruined. No matter what it takes, I must succeed. But how can I be sure to delay, if necessary, the departure of that dastardly Fogg?"

Fix made up his mind that, as a measure of last resort, he would reveal everything to Passepartout. He was evidently not an accomplice in the theft, and Fix would reveal to the innocent fellow just what kind of master he served. Feeling the force of that revelation, and facing the risk of being implicated in the affair, Passepartout would in all probability come over to Fix's side. But, of course, this was a hazardous plan, to be attempted only if every other failed. A single word from Passepartout to his master would be enough to compromise Fix's stratagems once and for all. However, having come to these conclusions, the police detective was once again thrown into disarray by the appearance of Mrs. Aouda on board the *Rangoon*, in Phileas Fogg's company.

Who was this woman? What circumstances had conspired to bring her together with Fogg? It was clear that they had met somewhere between Bombay and Calcutta. But in what part of the peninsula? Was it chance alone that had united Phileas Fogg and the young traveler? Or, on the contrary, had the gentleman planned his journey across India with the express aim of joining

this charming person? For she was charming indeed! Fix had
observed her carefully in the courtroom in Calcutta.

The detective was naturally intrigued by this new appearance.
He began to wonder if the case might not involve some element
of criminal abduction. Indeed, it must be so! The idea took hold
of Fix's brain, and he began to consider just what advantages he
could gain from the circumstance. Whether the young woman
was married or not, there was likely a case to be made for
abduction – and it would be possible, in Hong Kong, to raise
such obstacles for the kidnapper that this time he could not
escape for any sum of money.

But Fix could not afford to wait for the arrival of the *Rangoon*
in Hong Kong. He knew Phileas Fogg had a frustrating habit of
jumping from one ship to another, and the gentleman might be
well under way again before Fix had a chance to set his trap.

It was therefore essential that Fix notify the English
authorities and alert them to the approach of the *Rangoon* –
before Fogg could disembark. And nothing could be easier: the
ship was scheduled to stop in Singapore, and Singapore is linked
to the Chinese coast by a telegraph wire.

Still, before taking action, in order to be sure of his next steps,
Fix resolved to interrogate Passepartout. He knew that it wasn't
very difficult to draw the young fellow into conversation, and he

decided at last to come out of hiding. Indeed, there was no time to lose. It was the 30th of October, and the very next day the *Rangoon* would reach Singapore.

That afternoon, Fix left his cabin and stepped out on deck, intending to 'bump into' Passepartout with all the outward appearances of the most extreme surprise. The Frenchman was strolling on the foredeck, when the detective sprang towards him.

"You, of all people," cried Fix, "on board the *Rangoon*!"

"Monsieur Fix!" replied Passepartout in amazement, recognizing his companion from the crossing on the *Mongolia*. "What! I leave you in Bombay, and I find you again en route to Hong Kong! Can it be that you, too, are making a journey around the world?"

"No, no," replied Fix, "and I plan to end my journey in Hong Kong – for a few days, at least."

"Ah!" said Passepartout, who seemed, for a moment, taken aback. "But how is it that I haven't seen you on board since our departure from Calcutta?"

"What can I say – I was under the weather… a bout of sea-sickness… I've stayed in my cabin, in bed… The Bay of Bengal hasn't been as kind to me as the Indian Ocean. And how is your master, Mr. Phileas Fogg?"

"In perfect health, and quite as punctual as his itinerary! Not a

day behind schedule. Ah! Monsieur Fix, you won't know this yet, but we've also got a young woman with us."

"A young woman?" replied the detective, who seemed for all the world not to understand a word of what his interlocutor was saying to him. But Passepartout had soon brought him completely up to date. He described the incident in the temple in Bombay, the acquisition of the elephant at a cost of two thousand pounds, the affair of the *suttee*, the rescue of Aouda, their conviction in the courthouse of Calcutta, and their freedom on bail. Fix, already perfectly familiar with the last of these incidents, seemed ignorant of them all, and Passepartout let himself go in the pleasure of relating his adventures to such an interested and attentive listener.

"But tell me," said Fix, "does your master ultimately intend to bring this young woman back to Europe?"

"Certainly not, Monsieur Fix, certainly not! We will merely restore her to the care of one of her relatives, a wealthy merchant in Hong Kong."

"There's nothing in it," said the detective to himself, hiding his disappointment. And he said aloud, "A glass of gin, Mr. Passepartout?"

"With pleasure, Monsieur Fix. It's the least we can do to celebrate our meeting on board the *Rangoon*!"

CHAPTER XVII

WHICH DEALS WITH VARIOUS MATTERS TAKING PLACE DURING THE CROSSING FROM SINGAPORE TO HONG KONG

From that day forward, Passepartout and the detective met frequently – but the detective trod carefully around his companion, and did not press him for further information. Only once or twice did he spot Mr. Fogg, who preferred to remain in the grand salon of the *Rangoon*, either in Mrs. Aouda's company or, according to his unvarying custom, playing whist.

As for Passepartout, he had been considering very seriously the unexpected stroke of luck that had placed Mr. Fix, yet again, on the same route as his master. Indeed, the circumstances were surprising, to say the least. This was a gentleman (amiable and

obliging, to be sure) whom they had met first in Suez, who had then embarked on the *Mongolia*, who had disembarked in Bombay, which was supposedly his destination, who then turned up again on the *Rangoon*, bound for Hong Kong – who, in a word, was following step by step the same itinerary as Mr. Fogg. This was a bizarre concordance, and it certainly merited some attention. What was this Fix fellow up to? Passepartout was prepared to bet his babouches – which he had carefully preserved – that Fix would leave Hong Kong at the same time as Mr. Fogg's party, and probably aboard the same ship.

Passepartout might have pondered the matter for a hundred years without ever guessing the true nature of the detective's mission. He could never have imagined that Phileas Fogg would be 'tailed' like a burglar around the entire globe. However, it is human nature to advance an explanation for all things. In a flash of inspiration, Passepartout settled on a theory explaining Fix's presence on board – and really, this theory was perfectly plausible. According to Passepartout, Fix could be nothing other than an agent dispatched in pursuit of Mr. Fogg by his colleagues in the Reform Club, in order to ensure that the journey around the world was undertaken properly, according to the agreed-on itinerary.

"It's obvious! It's obvious!" repeated the honest fellow, filled

with pride at his own perspicacity. "He's a spy, set on our trail by those gentlemen! That is unworthy of them. To have Mr. Fogg – so upright, so honorable – spied on by an undercover agent! Ah! You gentlemen of the Reform Club, you'll pay for this!"

Passepartout, elated by his discovery, resolved nonetheless to say nothing to his master, fearing that he would be understandably offended by the mistrust shown him by his adversaries. But he promised himself that he would mock and chaff Fix whenever the occasion arose, in guarded terms and without revealing his new insights.

On Wednesday the 30th of October, in the afternoon, the *Rangoon* entered the Straits of Malacca, which separate the peninsula of the same name from the large island of Sumatra. The passengers' view of this island was framed by numerous mountainous islets, steep and picturesque, rising from the waters of the strait.

The following day, at four in the morning, the *Rangoon*, having gained an advance of half a day on its official schedule, put in at Singapore in order to replenish its supply of coal.

Phileas Fogg noted this advance in the column of gains and then, for once, he came ashore – to accompany Mrs. Aouda, who had expressed a wish to take the air for a few hours. Fix,

to whom any act on Fogg's part appeared suspect, followed him, making every effort not to be seen. As for Passepartout, he merely chortled at Fix's maneuvers, and went off to run his usual errands about town.

The island of Singapore is neither large nor imposing of aspect. It lacks mountains – that is to say, it lacks contour. And yet, it is charming in its narrowness. It is a park, cut through with lovely avenues. A neat carriage, drawn by those elegant horses imported from New Holland, conveyed Mrs. Aouda and Phileas Fogg among dense stands of palms with their lurid foliage, and of clove trees, whose famous cloves are formed from the very bud of the tree's open flower. There, pepper bushes could be found instead of the thorny hedges of the European countryside. Sago palms and giant ferns, with their magnificent fronds, varied the aspect of that tropical region. Nutmegs with their glossy foliage filled the air with a penetrating aroma. There was no shortage of monkeys, in lively, grimacing gangs among the trees; nor perhaps of tigers in the jungles. To those surprised to learn that, even on this relatively small island, such terrible carnivores have not been hunted down to the last specimen, suffice it to say that they come from Malacca, and are able to swim across the Straits.

Having driven through the countryside for two hours,

Mrs. Aouda and her companion – who seemed unmoved by the scenes around him – returned to the city, a vast agglomeration of heavily built houses, surrounded by charming gardens in which mangos and pineapples grew, along with all the best fruits in the world.

At ten o'clock they returned to the steamer, never suspecting that they had been followed every step of the way by the police detective – who also had resorted to hiring a carriage.

Passepartout was waiting for them on the deck of the *Rangoon*. The good fellow had purchased some dozens of mangoes. These are roughly the size of an apple, dark brown on the outside, and a striking red on the inside, and their white flesh, as it melts between the lips, affords to keen gourmets a pleasure without equal. Passepartout was only too happy to offer them to Mrs. Aouda, who thanked him gracefully.

At eleven o'clock, the *Rangoon*, having replenished its stocks of coal, cast off its moorings – and, a few hours later, the high mountains of Malacca, whose forests shelter the finest tigers in all the world, were lost to sight.

Roughly thirteen hundred miles separate Singapore from the island of Hong Kong, that tiny English territory which lies detached from the Chinese coast. Phileas Fogg needed to complete the crossing in six days at most, in order to catch the

At ten o'clock they returned to the steamer, never suspecting that they
had been followed every step of the way by the police detective.

ship that would sail from Hong Kong on the 6th of November, bound for Yokohama, one of the principal ports of Japan.

The *Rangoon* was rather crowded. Many passengers had embarked at Singapore: Hindus, Ceylonese, Chinese, Malays, and Portuguese who, for the most part, occupied the second class cabins.

The weather, which had been fair until now, changed with the last quarter of the moon. There was a heavy swell. The wind was at times severe, but happily it blew from the southeast, which rather favored the progress of the steamer. Whenever possible, the captain passed the order to make sail. The *Rangoon*, rigged as a brig, often deployed courses and topsails together, and its speed duly increased under the double action of wind and steam. In this fashion they labored on through short and often very tiring seas, along the shores of Annam and Cochinchina.

But these conditions were the fault of the *Rangoon*, rather than the sea, and the passengers – most of whom had fallen ill – should have held the steamer accountable for their discomfort.

Indeed, the vessels of the Peninsular and Oriental Company which ply the routes on the China Seas suffer from a serious defect in their construction. There had been a miscalculation in the ratio of their molded depth to their draft when fully laden and, as a result, they are particularly vulnerable to the action of

the swells. Their volume – that part of the ship enclosed and impenetrable to the water – is insufficient. They have therefore a tendency to 'wallow', to use the maritime expression. It only takes a few swells, breaking over the side, to check their progress. These vessels are much inferior – if not in their engines, at least in their construction – to those employed by the French Messageries Maritimes Company, such as the *Impératrice* and the *Cambodge*. Whereas those ships, according to the calculations made by engineers, can take on a weight of water equal to their own before sinking, the ships of the Peninsular Company – the *Golgonda*, the *Corea*, and finally the *Rangoon* – could not bear a sixth of their own weight without promptly going under.

That is why it was necessary, in foul weather, to take extensive precautions. The captain sometimes had to modify the vessel's heading and proceed at reduced speed. The resulting delay appeared not to affect Phileas Fogg in the slightest – but Passepartout was obviously extremely irritated. He railed against the captain, the engineer, and the Company, and roundly cursed all those involved in the business of transporting passengers. Perhaps the thought of the gas burner – still burning brightly at his own expense in the house on Savile Row – contributed in no small part to his impatience.

"Are you really so anxious to reach Hong Kong?" the detective asked him one day.

"Incredibly anxious!" replied Passepartout.

"Do you think that Mr. Fogg is in a hurry to catch the steamer bound for Yokohama?"

"In a dreadful hurry."

"And so you've come to believe in this strange tale of a journey around the world?"

"Absolutely. And what about you, Monsieur Fix?"

"Me? I don't believe a word of it!"

"You joker!" replied Passepartout with a wink.

This remark left the detective unsettled. It worried him, although he wasn't quite sure why. Had the Frenchman guessed at his true intentions? He didn't know what to think. How could Passepartout possibly have discovered his identity as a detective – a fact he alone knew? And yet, if his manner of speaking was any indication, Passepartout certainly meant more than he said.

The young fellow went even further on another occasion. He was simply unable to resist – he could not hold his tongue.

"I say, Monsieur Fix," he remarked to his companion with a hint of malice, "when we arrive in Hong Kong, will we have the misfortune of parting ways with you?"

"Well…" replied Fix, somewhat embarrassed, "I don't know!

It's possible that…"

"Ah!" said Passepartout, "I would be so happy if you were to accompany us! Come – an agent of the Peninsular Company shouldn't stop at the halfway point! You were going no further than Bombay, and yet here you are nearly in China! America isn't far off now, and then it's just a skip and a jump from America to Europe!"

Fix observed his interlocutor closely, but saw nothing more in Passepartout's features than an infectious amiability, and he decided that the best course was to laugh along with him. But then the Frenchman, growing confident, asked him "if the pay was very good, in that line of work?"

"Yes and no," replied Fix evenly. "One may have good luck and bad. But of course you understand that I don't travel at my own expense!"

"Oh! As for that, I'm quite sure of it!" crowed Passepartout, laughing even harder.

The conversation over, Fix returned to his cabin and set to thinking. It was evident that his identity had been discovered. One way or another, the Frenchman had recognized in him the police detective. But had he warned his master? What role did he play in all of this? Was he an accomplice, yes or no? Had Fix's mission been exposed, and thereby been doomed to failure?

The detective spent several difficult hours in this manner – now thinking all was lost, now clinging to the hope that Fogg was still none the wiser, and uncertain at last what to believe.

Eventually, he was able to calm himself, and he resolved to take a frank and open course with regard to Passepartout. If the necessary conditions were not in place for him to arrest Fogg in Hong Kong, and if Fogg was preparing once and for all to depart from English territory, he, Fix, would reveal all to Passepartout. Either the servant was his master's accomplice, and the master knew all – in which case all was lost – or the servant had nothing to do with the robbery, and it would be in his own self interest to give up the thief.

So it was that matters lay between those two travelers – and meanwhile, far above them, Phileas Fogg soared on in his majestic indifference. He was completing, in the most rational manner, his orbit around the world, and was in no way concerned with the lesser asteroids that might gravitate around him.

Of course there was, nearby, a wayward star – to use the astronomers' expression – which ought to have produced certain perturbations in that gentleman's heart. But no! The charm of Mrs. Aouda had no effect, to the great surprise of Passepartout, and the perturbations, if they existed, would have been more

difficult to calculate than those, in the orbit of Uranus, which led to Neptune's discovery.

Yes! It was a source of perpetual surprise to Passepartout, who read in the young woman's eyes so much gratitude to his master! Clearly, Phileas Fogg had heart enough to conduct himself heroically – but not amorously. As for any preoccupations which might have stirred in him concerning the success of their journey, of these there was not the slightest trace. Passepartout, however, lived in a state of perpetual crisis. One day, leaning against the handrail of the engine room, he watched the powerful machine straining as some violent pitching of the vessel lifted the furious propeller from the water. Whenever this happened, jets of steam blasted out from the safety valves, provoking the honest fellow's rage.

"These valves aren't full enough!" he cried. "They're emptying out! We're hardly moving! Ah, this is typically English! If the ship were American, the boiler might explode, but we'd be going much faster!"

CHAPTER XVIII

IN WHICH PHILEAS FOGG, PASSEPARTOUT, AND FIX
GO SEPARATELY ABOUT THEIR BUSINESS

In the last days of the crossing, the weather got gradually worse. The wind was blowing very hard. It held steady in the northwest, thereby impeding the steamer's progress. The *Rangoon*, too unstable, rolled considerably, and the passengers regarded with justifiable rancour the long, foaming waves that the wind lifted from the sea.

During the third and fourth days of November, there rose a kind of storm. The wind beat the sea with relentless fury. For half a day, the *Rangoon* was forced to adjust her heading and speed – keeping barely enough headway, with the propeller

turning just ten times per minute, to steer among the waves. Every sail was tightly reefed, and the bare rigging shrieked and whistled in the gale.

The steamer's rate of travel, as one may imagine, was significantly reduced, and it was estimated that the ship would arrive in Hong Kong some twenty hours behind schedule – and even more, if the storm did not abate.

Phileas Fogg regarded the spectacle of the furious sea, which seemed bent on fighting him at every turn, with characteristic detachment. His expression never altered for a moment, even though a delay of twenty hours might force him to miss the departure of the Yokohama steamer, and thereby compromise his entire journey. But that nerveless creature felt neither impatience nor anxiety. It seemed actually as though this storm were part of his itinerary – as if it had been expected. Mrs. Aouda, who discussed this new setback with her companion, found him as calm as ever.

Detective Fix, of course, saw the matter from a different perspective. The storm delighted him, and he would have been happy beyond measure if the *Rangoon* had been obliged to fly before its fury. Every hour's delay strengthened his hand, as it could force Mr. Fogg to remain in Hong Kong for several days. At long last, the sky, with its squalls and gales, was on his

side. He might be slightly seasick – but what of it! He thought nothing of a bit of nausea, and while his body was twisting in discomfort, his spirit was unbending in immense satisfaction.

As for Passepartout, one can easily imagine the ill-disguised rage which carried him through this ordeal. Up till now, all had gone well: land and water both had seemed at his master's service. Ships and railways obeyed his command. Wind and steam united to further his aims. Had the hour of disappointments come at last? It was as if the wager's twenty thousand pounds were to come from his own purse: Passepartout was at the end of his tether. The storm exasperated him, the fury of the wind only fed his own, and like the wind he would happily have thrashed that disobedient sea! Poor fellow. Fix was careful to hide from Passepartout his own satisfaction – a wise decision, for if Passepartout had guessed at Fix's secret delight, the detective would have had a difficult time of it.

Passepartout spent the duration of the storm on the deck of the *Rangoon*. He could not have stayed below. He clambered in the rigging; he astonished the crew, and assisted them in every task with the eager dexterity of a monkey. A hundred times, he interrogated the captain, the officers, and the sailors – who couldn't help chuckling at the sight of a fellow so excessively distressed – asking how long the storm would last. They sent

him to examine the barometer, whose indicator, however, refused to rise. Passepartout shook the barometer, but nothing seemed to help: neither the shaking, nor the imprecations that he heaped upon the unresponsive instrument.

At last, however, the gale subsided. Throughout the 4th of November, the state of the sea gradually improved. The wind veered into the south by two quarters, returning to a favorable direction.

Passepartout's mood cleared with the weather. The topsails and courses were unfurled, and the *Rangoon* continued its journey with a remarkable turn of speed. But they could not regain the time they had lost. There was no getting around it, and they sighted land only on the 6th, at five o'clock in the morning. Phileas Fogg's itinerary listed the steamer's arrival for the 5th. Instead, it would arrive on the 6th – so they were twenty-four hours behind schedule, and would certainly have missed the departure for Yokohama.

At six o'clock, the pilot came on board the *Rangoon* and took up his position by the helm, in order to guide the vessel through the channels to the harbor of Hong Kong.

Passepartout was dying to question the man, and to ask him if the steamer for Yokohama had left Hong Kong. But he didn't dare do it, wanting instead to preserve to the very last some

shred of hope. He had confided his fears to Fix who – the sly fox – tried to console him, telling him that Mr. Fogg, after all, would be able to continue his journey on the very next steamer. This merely served to infuriate Passepartout.

Passepartout had avoided questioning the pilot – but Mr. Fogg, having consulted his Bradshaw's, inquired of the man in his quiet manner if he knew when a ship would next depart from Hong Kong for Yokohama.

"Tomorrow, on the morning tide," replied the pilot.

"Ah!" said Mr. Fogg, without showing any surprise.

Passepartout, who had overheard this exchange, would happily have kissed the pilot – and Fix would happily have wrung his neck.

"What is the name of the steamer?" asked Mr. Fogg.

"The *Carnatic*," replied the pilot.

"Was it not meant to depart yesterday?"

"Yes, sir, but one of its boilers needed repairing, and its departure has been pushed back until tomorrow."

"Thank you," replied Mr. Fogg, and he returned, with his mechanical tread, to the salon of the *Rangoon*.

As for Passepartout, he grasped the pilot's hand and shook it violently, saying, "Pilot, you're an excellent fellow!"

The pilot would probably never know why his

straightforward responses had won him such a demonstration of friendship. The blast of a whistle sounded, and he returned to the helm to guide the steamer through the flotilla of junks, of sampans, of fishing boats, of shore boats of all kinds, which crowd the waterways of Hong Kong.

At one o'clock, the *Rangoon* was moored at the quay, and the passengers disembarked.

In this case, it must be said that chance had distinctly favored Phileas Fogg. If it had not been necessary to repair the *Carnatic*'s boilers, the vessel would have departed on the 5th of November, and travelers bound for Japan would have had to wait another eight days for the departure of the next steamer. Mr. Fogg, it is true, was still twenty-four hours behind schedule, but this delay could not have any negative effect on the rest of the journey.

In fact, the steamer that makes the crossing from Yokohama to San Francisco was scheduled to make a direct connection with the steamer arriving from Hong Kong, and it could not depart until that vessel had arrived. Obviously they would still be twenty-four hours behind at Yokohama – but it would be easy to make up that time in the course of the twenty-two days that it takes to cross the Pacific. So, thirty-five days after leaving London, Phileas Fogg found himself within twenty-four hours of

The pilot guided the steamer through the flotilla of junks, of sampans, of fishing boats, of shore boats of all kinds, which crowd the waterways of Hong Kong.

his planned itinerary.

Since the *Carnatic* wasn't due to depart until five o'clock the next morning, Mr. Fogg still had sixteen hours ahead of him in which to look to his affairs – which is to say, those concerning Mrs. Aouda. On disembarking from the steamer, he offered the young woman his arm and led her to a palanquin. He asked the porters to recommend a hotel, and they suggested he go to the Club Hotel. The palanquin set off, followed by Passepartout, and twenty minutes later they arrived at their destination.

They engaged a room for the young woman, and Phileas Fogg made sure that she had everything she might require. Then he told Mrs. Aouda that he intended to begin immediately the search for the Hong Kong relative in whose care he intended to leave her. At the same time, he ordered Passepartout to remain at the hotel until his return, so that the young woman might have some company.

The gentleman made his way to the Exchange. It was certain that people there would be acquainted with a personnage such as the Honorable Jejeeh, who numbered among the wealthiest merchants of the city.

Mr. Fogg consulted a broker who, indeed, knew of the Parsee businessman – but Mrs. Aouda's relative had left China two years earlier. Having made his fortune, he had established

himself in Europe – in Holland, it was thought, because of the many connections he had developed with that country in the course of his business dealings.

Phileas Fogg returned to the Club Hotel. He immediately asked Mrs. Aouda if he might speak to her – and, without further preamble, informed her that the Honorable Jejeeh no longer lived in Hong Kong, and that he was probably residing in Holland.

To this, Mrs. Aouda at first had no reply. She raised one hand to her forehead, and for a few moments sat in thought. Then she said softly, "What should I do, Mr. Fogg?"

"It's very simple," replied the gentleman. "Return to Europe."

"But I cannot impose…"

"You are not imposing, and your presence in no way hinders my project. Passepartout?"

"Monsieur?" replied Passepartout.

"Go to the *Carnatic*, and reserve three cabins."

Passepartout was delighted to continue his journey in the company of the young woman, who had been exceedingly kind to him, and he immediately left the Club Hotel.

CHAPTER XIX

IN WHICH PASSEPARTOUT TAKES TOO KEEN
AN INTEREST IN HIS MASTER, AND WHAT ENSUES

Hong Kong is no more than an island, which the treaty of Nanking, following the war of 1842, made an English territory. In the space of a few years, the colonizing genius of Great Britain had built it up into a major city and a port: Victoria Harbor. The island is situated at the mouth of the Canton River, and a mere sixty miles separate it from the Portuguese city of Macao, on the opposite shore. It was inevitable that Hong Kong would defeat Macao in the competition for commerce, and today the majority of Chinese freight passes through the English city. With its docks, hospitals,

wharfs, warehouses, a gothic cathedral, a government house, and paved, modern roads, it looks as if it belonged in the counties of Kent or Surrey – as if, having traversed the terrestrial sphere, some English commercial center had emerged at its antipodes, in China.

Passepartout, his hands in his pockets, proceeded towards Victoria Harbor, admiring the palanquins and sailing wheelbarrows – which are still used in the 'Celestial Empire', as China is known – and the vast crowd of Chinese, Japanese, and European people who filled the streets. There were few differences to be found, here, with the cities of Bombay, Calcutta, and Singapore, which the Frenchman had already visited on his journey. It might be said that they belong to a string of English cities extending all around the world.

Passepartout arrived at Victoria Harbor. There, the mouth of the Canton River was thronged with ships belonging to all nations: English, French, American, Dutch – both warships and trading vessels – Japanese and Chinese boats: junks, sampans, houseboats, and even those flower-boats that gather to form as many ornamental gardens floating on the water. As he strolled along, Passepartout noticed a number of Hong Kong natives, all of them very old, and all of them dressed in yellow. He entered a Chinese barber shop to have himself shaved 'in the

Chinese style'. The local Figaro, who spoke rather good English, informed him between strokes of the razor that those ancient persons were all at least eighty years old, and that by attaining that age they earned the privilege of wearing yellow – the imperial color. Passepartout found this rather funny, although he wasn't sure why.

His face cleanly shaven, he continued to the quay where the *Carnatic* was moored, and there he was not at all surprised to see Fix, pacing to and fro. The police detective's face bore unmistakable signs of severe disappointment.

"Well!" said Passepartout to himself, "things are going badly for the gentlemen of the Reform Club!"

And he greeted Fix with his usual happy smile, without seeming to notice his companion's apparent distress.

As it happened, the detective had good reason to curse the bad luck that had pursued him so far. He still had no arrest warrant! Clearly, the warrant was still following behind him, and would only catch up if he remained in the city for a few more days. And, since Hong Kong was the last English territory along Phileas Fogg's route, unless Fix was able to retain him there, the gentleman would escape his grasp entirely.

"So, Monsieur Fix, have you made up your mind to accompany us all the way to America?" asked Passepartout.

"Yes," replied Fix through clenched teeth.

"I knew it!" cried Passepartout, with a resounding laugh. "I knew that you couldn't bear to part company with us! Come, come, let's book our places!"

The two entered the office of marine transport and reserved cabins for four people. But the company agent there informed them that, the repairs on the *Carnatic* having been completed, the steamer would depart that very evening at eight o'clock, and not the following morning as had been announced.

"Excellent!" replied Passepartout. "That will suit us perfectly. I'll go and tell my master."

In that moment, Fix decided to take a risk. He would reveal everything to Passepartout. It was perhaps the only means left by which to keep Phileas Fogg in Hong Kong for a few more days.

As they left the office, Fix suggested to his companion that they take some refreshment in a tavern. Passepartout still had plenty of time, and he accepted Fix's invitation. An agreeable-looking tavern stood nearby on the edge of the quay, and the two men entered. Inside, they found a large, well-decorated room and, at the back, a long, low bed, littered with cushions. On this bed, a number of people were lying fast asleep.

Some thirty customers sat at small tables made from braided rushes. Some were draining pints of English beer – ale or porter

— while others drank cups of gin or brandy. In addition, most of them were smoking long pipes made of red clay, stuffed with little balls of some substance mixed with essence of rose. From time to time, a smoker overcome by the fumes would slip beneath his table, and two waiters, taking him by the head and the feet, carried him to the bed to join his comrades. There were perhaps twenty of these drunkards lying side by side in the final stages of stupefaction.

Fix and Passepartout realized that they had entered a den haunted by those miserable, emaciated, befuddled idiots to whom the English merchants sell each year ten and a half million pounds' worth of that dismal drug called opium. Those are sorry millions indeed, raised by one of the deadliest vices known to human nature.

The Chinese government has tried to combat this scourge with strict laws, but in vain. Use of the drug spread from the wealthy elite, to whom the use of opium was at first formally restricted, to the lower classes, and its ravages could not be stopped. Opium is smoked in every place and at every time in the Middle Kingdom. Men and women both surrender to this deplorable passion, and once they are accustomed to those constant inhalations, they can no longer go without, lest they suffer debilitating stomach cramps. A heavy smoker can consume up to eight pipes per day, but he will die within five years.

So it was one of these many opium dens – which proliferate, even in Hong Kong – that Fix and Passepartout had entered in search of refreshment. Passepartout had no money, but he willingly accepted the generosity of his companion, with the understanding that it would be returned in due course.

They ordered port, to which the Frenchman applied himself energetically, while Fix – rather more reserved – observed his companion closely. They chatted of one thing and another, and agreed what a good idea it had been for Fix to book his passage on the *Carnatic*. And speaking of the steamer, whose departure had been brought forward by several hours, and with the bottles now empty, Passepartout finally rose to share the news with his master.

Fix held him back.

"Just a moment," he said.

"What is it, Monsieur Fix?"

"There's something important I need to say to you."

"Something important!" cried Passepartout, draining the few drops of wine left at bottom of his glass. "Well then, we can discuss it tomorrow. I don't have time today."

"Stay," said Fix. "It concerns your master!"

At this Passepartout paused, and looked attentively at his

interlocutor. Fix's expression seemed odd to him. He sat down again.

"What is it you have to tell me?" he asked.

Fix laid a hand on his companion's arm and said, lowering his voice, "Have you already guessed who I am?"

"*Parbleu!*" said Passepartout, smiling.

"Well then I'll confess everything..."

"You'll confess – what I already know? Ah, that's a bit rich, friend! Well, have it your way. But before you go any further, let me tell you that those gentlemen have laid out a lot of money for nothing!"

"For nothing!" said Fix. "That's easy for you to say! It's obvious that you don't know how much it is we're talking about!"

"Of course I know," replied Passepartout. "Twenty thousand pounds!"

"Fifty-five thousand!" retorted Fix, grasping Passepartout by the hand.

"What!" cried Passepartout. "Could Monsieur Fogg have dared...! Fifty-five thousand pounds! Well! All the more reason not to lose a moment." And the Frenchman again got up to leave.

"Fifty-five thousand pounds!" continued Fix, forcing Passepartout back into his seat and signaling to the waiter for

another bottle. "And if I succeed, I'll earn a bounty of two thousand pounds. Five hundred of it is yours – on the condition that you help me."

"Help you?" exclaimed Passepartout, his eyes widening in shock.

"Yes, help me to delay Mr. Fogg for a few days in Hong Kong!"

"Huh? What are you saying?" cried Passepartout. "So not only do they have my master followed, and cast doubts upon his honor, but those gentlemen also intend to raise more obstacles in his path! I'm ashamed for them."

"But – what? What do you mean?" asked Fix.

"I mean that it's deeply unsportsmanlike. They might as well just waylay him, and take the money straight from his pocket!"

"Eh! But that's exactly what we plan to do!"

"Why, it's a conspiracy!" cried Passepartout – who was growing more animated under the influence of the brandy Fix was serving him, and which he drank without noticing – "It's a plot! To think these are gentlemen! And colleagues!"

Fix began to wonder what this was all about.

"Colleagues!" continued Passepartout. "Members of the Reform Club! Know this, Monsieur Fix: my master is an honorable man, and when he makes a wager, he sets out to win it

honestly."

"But then... who is it you think I really am?" asked Fix, fixing his gaze on Passepartout.

"*Parbleu!* An agent of the members of the Reform Club, and your mission is to observe and verify my master's itinerary – a singularly humiliating precaution! And you should know that, although I guessed your true identity some time ago, I've made sure to let nothing slip to Monsieur Fogg."

"He knows nothing...?" asked Fix urgently.

"Not a thing," replied Passepartout, emptying another glass.

The police detective raised a hand to his forehead. He hesitated a moment before replying. What should he do? It appeared that Passepartout had been sincerely mistaken – but his error made Fix's project more difficult. It was evident that the fellow spoke in absolute good faith, and that he was not his master's accomplice – which Fix might have feared.

"Well then," he thought, "if he's not an accomplice, he'll have to help me."

Once again, the detective decided to take a risk. After all, he was running out of time. He had to keep Fogg in Hong Kong at any cost.

"Listen," said Fix shortly, "and listen carefully. I am not what you think I am – an agent of these Reform Club members."

"Bah!" said Passepartout, regarding him with an air of mockery.

"I am a police detective, entrusted with a mission by Scotland Yard!"

"You… a police detective!…"

"Yes, and I can prove it," continued Fix. "Here is my commission."

And the detective, drawing a paper from his pocketbook, showed his companion a commission signed by the head of the Metropolitan Police Service. Passepartout was astounded. He stared at Fix, unable to utter a single word.

"Mr. Fogg's wager," said Fix, "is nothing more than a pretext, meant to deceive you – you and his colleagues of the Reform Club – because he needed to gain your unwitting complicity."

"But why?…" cried Passepartout.

"Listen. On the 28th of September, a theft of fifty-five thousand pounds was committed at the Bank of England by an individual whose description was passed on to the police. I have the description here – and, down to the last detail, it is that of Mr. Fogg."

"Come now!" objected Passepartout, banging his heavy fist on the table. "My master is the most honest man in the world!"

"How would you know?" retorted Fix. "You don't even know

"I am a police detective, entrusted with a mission by Scotland Yard!"

him! You entered his service the very day of his departure — a departure made suddenly, under a ridiculous pretext, without a single trunk, but with a large sum in crisp new banknotes! And you dare to affirm that he's an honest man!"

"Yes! Yes!" the poor fellow repeated mechanically.

"And do you want to be arrested as his accomplice?"

Passepartout held his head in his hands. He was unrecognizable. He didn't dare look the police detective in the face. Phileas Fogg, a thief? He — Aouda's rescuer, the brave and generous man! And yet, what a weight of evidence had been brought against him! Passepartout tried to drive away the suspicions that slipped into his mind. He didn't want to believe in the guilt of his master. He made a supreme effort to hold himself together.

"Well, what is it you want from me?" he said to the police detective.

"This," replied Fix. "I've trailed Mr. Fogg this far, but I haven't yet received the arrest warrant that I've requested from London. So I need you to help me keep him in Hong Kong…"

"Me! You want me to…"

"And I will share with you the bounty of two thousand pounds promised by the Bank of England!"

"Never!" replied Passepartout, who wanted to stand, but fell back down, feeling his strength and his reason abandoning

him at the same time. "Monsieur Fix," he stammered, "even if everything you've told me were true... if my master were the thief whom you seek... which I deny... I've been... I am in his service... I know him to be good and generous... Betray him – never... no, not for all the gold on Earth... That's not how we do things, where I come from!..."

"You refuse?"

"I refuse."

"Then let's pretend I never mentioned it," said Fix, "and let's drink."

"Yes, let's drink!"

Passepartout felt himself more and more overcome by drunkenness. Fix, realizing that it was necessary at all cost to separate him from his master, wanted to push him over the edge. There were several pipes filled with opium lying on the table. Fix slipped one into the Frenchman's hand, and Passepartout grasped it, raised it to his lips, lit it, drew in a few narcotic breaths, and fell back, his head heavy with the effects of the drug.

"At last," said Fix, seeing that Passepartout was completely out of commission. "Mr. Fogg won't be warned in time about the departure of the *Carnatic*, and even if he does leave, it will be without this cursed Frenchman!"

Then, having paid the bill, he left the tavern.

CHAPTER XX

IN WHICH FIX ENTERS INTO DIRECT CONTACT WITH PHILEAS FOGG

While this scene was taking place, which might so seriously compromise Mr. Fogg's future, that gentleman was accompanying Mrs. Aouda on a stroll through the streets of the English city. Now that Mrs. Aouda had accepted his offer to convey her to Europe, he had turned his thoughts to the various details involved in such a long journey. That an Englishman such as he might embark on a journey around the world with no more than an overnight bag was just about acceptable, but a woman could not undertake such an expedition under those conditions. It was therefore necessary to purchase the clothing and other

items needed for her journey. Mr. Fogg carried out this task with his characteristic composure, and in response to all the young widow's excuses and objections – she was embarrassed by his generosity – he said invariably, "It serves the interests of my journey. It is all part of the itinerary."

These purchases made, Mr. Fogg and the young woman returned to the hotel and enjoyed a sumptuous dinner in the restaurant. Then Mrs. Aouda, feeling slightly fatigued, shook the hand of her imperturbable rescuer in the English fashion, and retired to her room.

The honorable gentleman spent the evening absorbed in his reading of *The Times* and *The Illustrated London News*.

Had he been the type of man who feels surprise, he would have been surprised that his servant did not return to the hotel when it came time to sleep. But, knowing that the steamer for Yokohama was not due to leave Hong Kong before the following morning, he thought no more of it. However, when day broke, and Mr. Fogg rang his bell, Passepartout did not appear.

What the honorable gentleman thought when he learned that his servant had not returned to the hotel, none can say. Mr. Fogg simply took his bag, asked that Mrs. Aouda be notified, and sent for a palanquin.

It was then eight o'clock, and the high tide, which the *Carnatic* would use to pass through the channels, was expected at half past nine.

When the palanquin arrived at the entrance to the hotel, Mr. Fogg and Mrs. Aouda climbed into that comfortable vehicle, and their luggage was sent after them in a handcart. Half an hour later, the travelers stepped out on the quay, and there Mr. Fogg learned that the *Carnatic* had sailed the previous evening.

Mr. Fogg, who had expected to find both the steamer and his servant, was forced to make do without either. However, he betrayed no sign of disappointment, and when Mrs. Aouda gave him a worried look, he merely replied, "It is an incident, madam, nothing more."

At that moment, Mr. Fogg was approached by a person who had been observing him closely for some time. It was Detective Fix, who greeted him and asked, "Are you not, sir, like me, one of the passengers who arrived yesterday on board the *Rangoon?*"

"Yes, sir," replied Mr. Fogg coldly, "but I don't think I've had the honor…"

"I beg your pardon – but I expected to find your servant here."

"Do you know where he is, sir?" asked the young woman eagerly.

"What!" replied Fix, feigning surprise, "is he not with you?"

"No," said Mrs. Aouda. "He never returned yesterday evening. Could he have embarked on the *Carnatic* without us?"

"Without you, madam?..." replied the detective. "But — forgive my asking — were you then intending to depart on this steamer?"

"Yes, sir."

"So was I, madam, and you find me very disappointed. It seems that the *Carnatic*, having finished its repairs, left Hong Kong twelve hours early, without warning anyone, and now we'll need to wait eight days for the next departure!"

As he spoke the words 'eight days', Fix felt his heart leap with joy. Eight days! Fogg delayed for eight days in Hong Kong! There would be plenty of time for the arrest warrant to arrive. Finally, the police detective's luck appeared to be changing.

So one can imagine what a stunning blow it was to him when he heard Phileas Fogg say, in his quiet voice, "But there are other vessels besides the *Carnatic*, I believe, in the port of Hong Kong."

Then Mr. Fogg, offering Mrs. Aouda his arm, directed his steps towards the docks, in search of another vessel that was ready to set sail.

In a daze, Fix followed them. It seemed as though an invisible thread tied him to that gentleman.

And yet, despite his calm confidence, it really appeared as though luck had abandoned the man it had served so well until now. For three hours, Phileas Fogg searched among the docks. He was ready to charter a vessel, if need be, to transport him to Yokohama – but all the ships he found were in the process of loading or unloading their cargo, and consequently could not be ready to sail. Fix, once again, began to hope.

Still, Mr. Fogg was not about to give up, and he was preparing to continue his search, even if it meant going to Macao, when he was accosted by a seaman on the quay.

"Are you in need of a boat, sir?" the seaman said to him, doffing his cap.

"Do you have a boat ready to depart?" asked Mr. Fogg.

"Yes, sir, a pilot boat, no. 43 – the best in the fleet."

"Is it fast?"

"Between eight and nine knots, sailing close to the wind. Would you like to see her?"

"Yes."

"You will not be disappointed, sir. Is it a sailing excursion you're after?"

"No. A voyage."

"A voyage?"

"Will you undertake to convey me to Yokohama?"

At these words, the seaman stood with his arms dangling and his eyes bulging.

"Are you joking?" he asked.

"No. I missed the departure of the *Carnatic*, and I need to be in Yokohama by the 14th, at the latest, to catch the steamer for San Francisco."

"I'm sorry," said the pilot, "but that's not possible."

"I will pay you one hundred pounds per day, and a bounty of two hundred pounds if you get me there in time."

"Are you in earnest?" asked the pilot.

"Very much in earnest," replied Mr. Fogg.

The pilot stood aside for a moment. He looked at the sea, evidently torn between the desire to win such an enormous sum and the fear of venturing so far. Fix was on tenterhooks.

Meanwhile, Mr. Fogg had turned to Mrs. Aouda.

"You won't be frightened, madam?" he asked.

"Not with you, no, Mr. Fogg," the young woman replied.

The pilot again approached the gentleman, turning his cap in his hands.

"Well then, Pilot?" said Mr. Fogg.

"Well then, sir," replied the pilot, "I can risk neither my crew, nor myself, nor yourselves, on such a long crossing in a

boat of twenty tons at most, at this time of year. What's more, we wouldn't get there in time, for it's sixteen hundred and fifty miles from Hong Kong to Yokohama."

"Only sixteen hundred," countered Mr. Fogg.

"It amounts to the same."

Fix breathed a deep sigh of relief.

"But," the pilot added, "there may be another way to manage it."

Fix stopped breathing entirely.

"How?" asked Phileas Fogg.

"By going to Nagasaki, at the southern extremity of Japan, which is eleven hundred miles, or by going only as far as Shanghai, which is eight hundred miles from Hong Kong. During a crossing to Shanghai, we wouldn't stray far from the Chinese coast, which would be a great advantage – particularly since the currents there flow to the north."

"Pilot," replied Phileas Fogg, "I need to catch the American steamer in Yokohama, not in Shanghai or Nagasaki."

"And why not?" replied the pilot. "The San Francisco steamer doesn't start its journey in Yokohama. It stops in Yokohama and in Nagasaki, but its port of departure is Shanghai."

"You're certain of what you say?"

"Quite certain."

"And when will the steamer leave Shanghai?"

"The 11th, at seven o'clock in the evening. That means we have four days ahead of us. Four days – that's ninety-six hours, and with an average speed of eight miles an hour, if we're lucky, and the wind holds fair in the southeast, and the sea is calm, we could run the eight hundred miles that separate us from Shanghai."

"And when can you cast off?"

"In an hour. Just enough time to purchase supplies and fit out the boat."

"Then it's agreed. Are you the master of the boat?"

"Yes. John Bunsby, master of the *Tankadère*."

"Would you like me to pay a deposit?"

"If that's no inconvenience to you."

"Here is an advance of two hundred pounds. Sir," added Phileas Fogg, turning to Fix, "if you would like to take advantage of this situation…"

"Sir," replied Fix resolutely, "I was about to ask the favor."

"Very well. We will be on board in half an hour."

"But that poor boy…" said Mrs. Aouda, who was deeply distressed by Passepartout's disappearance.

"I will do everything that I can for him," replied Phileas Fogg.

And, while Fix – nervous, feverish, enraged – went on board

the pilot boat, the two of them directed their steps to the Hong Kong police station. There, Phileas Fogg submitted a description of Passepartout, and left behind a sum of money sufficient to repatriate him. They went through the same formality with the French consular agent, and then the palanquin, having stopped briefly at the hotel for their luggage, returned the travelers to the quay.

It was three o'clock. The no. 43 pilot boat, with its crew aboard and its stores carefully stowed away, was ready to cast off.

The *Tankadère* was a charming little schooner of twenty tons, very narrow in the bow, easy in her movements, long and graceful in her lines. She might be mistaken for a racing yacht. Her shining brasswork, her galvanized iron fittings and her deck white as ivory showed that the master John Bunsby liked to keep her in the best condition. Her two masts leaned slightly towards the stern. She carried a foresail, staysail, jib, flying jib, spanker, and could be rigged to run before the wind. She looked as though she would be a flyer, and indeed, she had already won several prizes in the 'matches' between rival pilot boats.

The crew of the *Tankadère* consisted of the master John Bunsby and four other men. They belonged to that class of seasoned mariners who venture forth in all weathers in search of approaching vessels, and who have gained broad knowledge of

the China seas. John Bunsby was a man roughly forty-five years old, vigorous, deeply tanned, with an energetic figure and a lively eye, and a confident demeanor that would have put even the most fearful passenger at ease.

Phileas Fogg and Mrs. Aouda came aboard. Fix was already on deck. Via a hatchway on the schooner's quarterdeck, one might descend into a square cabin, whose walls curved gently inwards over low settees. In the center of the room, a table was lit by a gimbal lamp. It was small, but clean.

"I regret that I have nothing better to offer you," said Mr. Fogg to Fix, who bowed without replying.

The police detective felt in some way humiliated for having profited from the kindness and generosity of Mr. Fogg.

"To be sure," he thought, "he's a very polite scoundrel, but he's a scoundrel all the same!"

At ten past three, the sails were raised. The English flag snapped at the schooner's masthead. The passengers were seated on the deck. Mr. Fogg and Mrs. Aouda gazed along the quay one last time, to see if Passepartout might still appear.

Fix could not suppress a sense of apprehension, for chance might still have directed to that very spot the unhappy fellow whom he had treated so unjustly – and then an explanation would have ensued, in which the detective would not have

Mr. Fogg and Mrs. Aouda gazed along the quay one last time,
to see if Passepartout might still appear.

appeared to much advantage. But the Frenchman was nowhere to be seen and, without a doubt, the stupefying narcotic still held him in its grasp.

At last, the master John Bunsby took the helm and the *Tankadère*, catching the wind in her foresail, her spanker and her jibs, set forth, bounding over the swells.

CHAPTER XXI

IN WHICH THE MASTER OF THE TANKADÈRE
RISKS LOSING A BOUNTY OF TWO HUNDRED POUNDS

This eight hundred mile crossing, on a sailing vessel of twenty tonnes, was a very daring undertaking – particularly at this time of the year. They are generally tumultuous, those China Seas, and can be subject to terrible gales, especially during the spring and autumn equinoxes – and it was now early November.

It would have been, clearly, in the pilot's interest to convey his passengers all the way to the port of Yokohama, since he was being paid a fixed sum per day. But it would have been deeply imprudent to attempt such a crossing in such conditions – and

it was already an audacious act, if not a brash one, to sail up to Shanghai. Still, John Bunsby trusted in his *Tankadère*, which rose to meet the waves like a seagull, and perhaps his trust was not misplaced.

In the waning hours of the day, the *Tankadère* sailed through the capricious channels of Hong Kong, and she handled most admirably in every point of sail, whether close to the wind or running before it.

"I'm sure there's no need, Pilot," said Phileas Fogg as the schooner emerged onto the open sea, "for me to recommend that you make all possible haste."

"You can depend on me, Your Honor," replied John Bunsby. "Every sail is aloft that the wind will permit us to carry. Our topsails would add nothing to our speed, and would only press her down in the water, and hamper her movement."

"It is your profession, Pilot, not mine, and I put my trust in you."

Phileas Fogg, his carriage erect, his legs apart, straight-backed as any sailor, gazed unflinchingly at the rough sea. The young woman, seated in the stern, was moved by the sight of that ocean, already shadowed by twilight, on which she had ventured in this frail craft. Above her head stretched the white sails, which bore her through space like vast wings. The schooner, lifted by

the wind, seemed to fly through the air.

Night came. The moon was entering its first quarter, and its meager light would soon be extinguished in the mists of the horizon. Clouds were sweeping in from the east, and had already overrun one part of the sky.

The pilot had set out his running lights – an indispensible precaution in those heavily frequented seas near the approaches to land. Collisions between ships were not uncommon there, and given the speed at which she was running, the schooner would have been dashed to pieces by the slightest impact.

Fix sat dreaming in the *Tankadère*'s bow. He kept himself apart, knowing that Fogg was not by nature talkative. What's more, it disgusted him to speak with that man, whose aid he had willingly accepted. He was thinking of the future. It seemed certain, now, that Mr. Fogg would not stop in Yokohama, but would immediately take a passage on the San Francisco steamer bound for America, whose vast expanse would offer him both safety and an escape from justice. Phileas Fogg's plan now seemed perfectly straightforward.

Instead of embarking directly on a ship for the United States, like a common hoodlum, this Fogg had completed the grand tour, crossing three quarters of the globe, in order to reach more surely the American continent. There, having thrown the police

off his scent, he would enjoy the Bank's fifty-five thousand in perfect tranquility.

But what would the detective do, once Mr. Fogg arrived on U.S. territory? Would he abandon his quarry? No – a hundred times no! And what's more, he wouldn't let him out of his sight until he had obtained an act of extradition. In any case, one happy circumstance had come to pass: the Frenchman was no longer at his master's side – and it was essential, after the revelations Fix had made, that the master and the servant were never reunited.

Phileas Fogg himself had given some thought to his servant, who had disappeared in so strange a manner. All things considered, it seemed to him not unlikely that, as a result of some misunderstanding, the poor fellow had embarked on the *Carnatic* at the last minute. This was also the opinion held by Mrs. Aouda, who deeply regretted the absence of that honest servant, to whom she owed so much. It still seemed possible, therefore, that they would find him again in Yokohama, and it would be easy enough to find out if the *Carnatic* had transported him there.

Towards ten o'clock, the wind began to freshen. Perhaps it would have been prudent to reef the sails, but the pilot, having carefully observed the state of the sky, left the sails as they

were. At any rate, the *Tankadère* bore her canvas admirably well, having a deep draft, and everything was ready to be taken in quickly, should it come on to blow.

At midnight, Phileas Fogg and Mrs. Aouda went below into the cabin. Fix had preceded them, and had stretched out on one of the settees. As for the pilot and his men, they spent the whole night on deck.

By sunrise the next day, the 8th of November, the schooner had covered more than one hundred miles. The log, which was frequently cast, showed her average speed to be between eight and nine miles per hour. The *Tankadère* was on a reach, with all of her sails drawing fully, and in this point of sail she was able to achieve her maximum speed. If the wind held steady, in these conditions, she had every chance of success.

For the rest of the day, the *Tankadère* sailed no further away from the coast, remaining where the currents were favorable to her progress. The coast lay five miles at most off her port side quarter, and its irregular profile could be viewed from time to time when the weather cleared. Since the wind was coming from the land, the sea was calmer – a happy chance for the little schooner, since vessels of such a slight tonnage are hampered above all by heavy swells, which break up their run and kill their speed.

Towards noon, the wind fell slightly and veered into the southeast. The pilot sent up the topsails, but they were brought down again two hours later, because the wind was freshening once again.

Mr. Fogg and the young woman, who luckily were resistant to sea-sickness, dined with a healthy appetite on tinned food and ship's biscuits. They invited Fix to share in their meal, and he was forced to accept, knowing that stomachs require ballast just as ships do – but it vexed him. To travel at that man's expense, to feed on his personal supplies, Fogg felt, was somehow disloyal. Despite this, he ate – with little relish, to be true – but he ate.

Still, when they had finished their meal, he felt obligated to take Mr. Fogg aside.

"Sir," he said – and that 'sir' scorched his lips. He had to stop himself from grasping that 'sir' by the collar! – "sir, you have been most obliging in offering me passage aboard this ship. But, although my resources don't permit me to act with as much generosity as you, I intend to pay my share…"

"Pray let's not mention it, sir," replied Mr. Fogg.

"But I want…"

"No, sir," repeated Fogg in a tone that would admit no argument. "This falls under general expenses."

Fix nodded, choking back his rage, and went forward to

stretch out in the schooner's bow. He spoke not another word for the rest of the day.

Meanwhile, they were proceeding swiftly. John Bunsby had every hope of success. Several times he told Mr. Fogg that they would arrive on time in Shanghai. Mr. Fogg replied simply that he was counting on it. What's more, every member of the little schooner's crew was working with the utmost zeal. The bounty spurred those honest fellows on, and every single sheet on board was conscientiously tightened. Every sail was vigorously tautened. Not a single swerve or deviation was permitted by the watchful helmsman! No Royal Yacht Club regatta could have boasted stricter maneuvers.

That evening, the pilot found that they had traveled, according to the log, a distance of two hundred and twenty miles from Hong Kong, and Phileas Fogg might hope that, on arriving in Yokohama, he would have no delay to add to his itinerary. It seemed, as a result, that the first serious setback he had experienced since his departure from London would not hinder his progress in the slightest.

That night, towards the early hours of the morning, the *Tankadère* entered the Fo-kien Strait, which separates the great island of Formosa from the Chinese coast, and she crossed the Tropic of Cancer. The sea in the strait was very rough, and full of

eddies formed by counter-currents. The schooner labored. The short, choppy waves broke her momentum, and it became very difficult to remain standing on her deck.

At the break of day, the wind was freshening even more. There was in the sky every sign of an approaching gale. The barometer, too, was indicating an imminent change in the weather. Its diurnal movement was irregular, and the mercury oscillated capriciously. In the southeast, the sea was observed to be forming long swells that 'smelled of a squall'. The evening before, the sun had gone down in a red haze, in the midst of the phosphorescent scintillations of the ocean.

For a long time, the pilot sat observing the sky's unpromising aspect, and muttering unintelligibly from between his teeth. At a certain point, finding his passenger nearby, he raised his voice slightly.

"Can I speak frankly, Your Honor?"

"Certainly," replied Phileas Fogg.

"Well, we are in for a blow."

"Will it come from the north or the south?" asked Mr. Fogg.

"From the south. Look. There's a typhoon brewing!"

"All the better, since it will drive us in the right direction!" replied Mr. Fogg.

"If that's how you take it," retorted the pilot, "there's

nothing more for me to say!"

John Bunsby's premonitions had not led him astray. If it had come in an earlier part of the year, the typhoon – to use the expression of a famous meteorologist – would have passed like a luminous cascade of electric flames. But now, in the winter equinox, it was to be feared that the typhoon would unleash its violence upon them.

The pilot made sure they had taken every precaution. All the schooner's sails were furled, and the yards were brought down onto the deck. The topmasts were struck, and the bowsprit brought in. The hatches were all carefully secured and battened, so that not a drop of water could penetrate the vessel's hull. A single triangular sail – a storm jib made from heavy canvas – was raised on the forestay, in order to keep the schooner before the wind. And then they waited.

John Bunsby had advised his passengers to go below, but the thought of being imprisoned in a narrow space, more or less deprived of air, and subjected to the shock of the swells, was equally disagreeable to them. Neither Mr. Fogg, nor Mrs. Aouda, nor Fix himself would consent to leave the deck.

At about eight o'clock, a gale of wind and rain struck the ship. Though she bore no more than her storm jib, a tiny strip of canvas, the *Tankadère* was lifted like a feather by that wind,

which blew with a force that can scarcely be described. To compare it to a steam locomotive racing at four times its full speed would still be falling well below the mark.

All day long, the little ship scudded northwards, carried on by monstrous waves, and thankfully maintaining a speed equal to theirs. Twenty times it seemed that she would be buried by one of those mountains of water that rose behind her – but at the last moment, a deft movement by the pilot at the helm averted the catastrophe.

The passengers were regularly soaked from head to toe by spindrift – which, however, they received philosophically. Fix, to be sure, grumbled, but the intrepid Aouda, her eyes fixed on Mr. Fogg, whose composure she could not help admiring, showed herself worthy of her companion, and braved the tempest at his side. As for Phileas Fogg himself, it seemed as though the typhoon was merely part of his program.

Until now, the *Tankadère* had held to her northerly course – but as the evening came, the wind, veering three quarters, settled in the northwest. Now exposing her flank to the waves, the schooner was brutally shaken. The sea struck with a violence that would have terrified anyone not aware of how sturdily all the parts of a ship are secured to one another.

As night fell, the storm worsened. Seeing the darkness falling

Twenty times it seemed that she would be buried
by one of those mountains of water that rose behind her.

and the howling wind still rising, John Bunsby began to worry. He wondered if it wasn't time to give in, and he consulted his crew. Having spoken to his men, John Bunsby approached Mr. Fogg.

"I think, Your Honor, that it would be wise to head for one of the harbors on the coast."

"I think so too," replied Phileas Fogg.

"Ah!" said the pilot, "but which one?"

"I only know of one," replied Mr. Fogg calmly.

"And that is…"

"Shanghai."

At first, it took a few moments for the pilot to fully comprehend what this reply signified – what it represented in terms of obstinacy and tenacity. Then he grinned.

"Well – yes!" he cried. "Your Honor is right. To Shanghai!"

And so the *Tankadère*'s course was kept imperturbably northwards.

It was a truly terrible night. It would take a miracle for the little schooner to escape foundering. Twice she was swept by a wall of water, and everything would have gone by the board if the lashings hadn't held. Mrs. Aouda was shattered, but she uttered no word of complaint. More than once, Mr. Fogg had to scramble to protect her from the fury of the waves.

Day returned. The storm continued to rage, and had lost none of its violence. Despite this, the wind returned to the southeast – a more favorable direction. The *Tankadère* once again made headway on that broken sea, whose heavy swell crossed and collided with the waves raised by the new direction of the wind. These produced a shock of contrary forces that would have crushed a vessel less solidly constructed.

From time to time, they perceived the coast through tears in the driving cloud, but there was not another ship in sight. The *Tankadère* was the only craft upon the sea.

At noon, there appeared a few signs of respite, which became more and more distinct as the sun sank towards the horizon. The storm had been as brief as it was violent. At last the passengers, completely exhausted, were able to eat a little, and rest.

The night was relatively peaceful. The pilot ordered the sails to be set, albeit close-reefed. The speed of the vessel was considerable. At daybreak the following morning, the 11th, having made a reconnaissance of the coast, John Bunsby was able to confirm that they were some hundred miles from Shanghai.

A hundred miles – and they had less than a day to cover them! It was that very evening that Mr. Fogg needed to arrive

in Shanghai, if he was to make the departure of the steamer for
Yokohama. If it hadn't been for the storm, which had set them
back by several hours, they would have been at that moment no
more than thirty miles from the port.

The wind was falling noticeably, and at the same time the sea
grew calmer. The schooner unfurled all of her canvas. Topsails,
staysail, jib and flying jib – every sail was drawing, and the sea
was foaming around the stem.

At noon, the *Tankadère* was no more than forty-five miles
from Shanghai. She had six hours left to reach the port before
the departure of the Yokohama steamer.

Tensions were running high on board the schooner. All were
anxious to reach their destination. All – Phileas Fogg excepted,
of course – felt their hearts beating with impatience. The little
vessel would need to maintain a speed of roughly nine miles
per hour, and yet the wind continued to fall! It was now an
irregular breeze, with mild, capricious gusts coming from the
coast. After each one passed, the sea immediately smoothed its
ruffled surface.

And yet the ship was so light – and her high sails, made
from thin canvas, caught those erratic gusts so well – that, with
the aid of the current, at six o'clock, John Bunsby could count
no more than ten miles to the river of Shanghai. For the city

itself is situated at a distance of at least twelve miles upstream from the mouth of the river.

At seven o'clock, they were still three miles away from Shanghai. A formidable oath escaped the pilot's lips... It was clear now that he would not win the bounty of two hundred pounds. He looked at Mr. Fogg. Mr. Fogg appeared perfectly impassive – and yet at that moment his entire fortune hung in the balance...

And just at that moment, a long black hull, crowned with a plume of smoke, appeared upon the horizon. It was the American steamer, emerging on schedule from the harbor of Shanghai.

"Blast!" cried John Bunsby, who struck the helm in a gesture of dismay.

"Signal her!" said Phileas Fogg calmly.

A small bronze cannon stood on the foredeck of the *Tankadère*. It was used for making signals in dense fog.

The gun was swiftly loaded, but just as the pilot stepped forward to apply a glowing coal to the touch hole, Mr. Fogg intervened.

"The flag at half-mast," he said.

The flag was quickly lowered half-way down the mast. It was a well-known signal of distress, and it was to be hoped

that the American steamer, at the sight, would change course to come to their aid.

"Fire!" said Mr. Fogg.

And the boom of the little bronze cannon split the air.

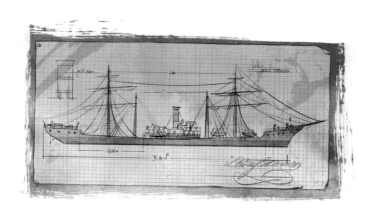

CHAPTER XXII

IN WHICH PASSEPARTOUT LEARNS THAT, EVEN AT THE ANTIPODES, IT IS ALWAYS PRUDENT TO HAVE SOME MONEY IN ONE'S POCKET

The *Carnatic*, having left Hong Kong at half past six in the evening on the 7th of November, headed at full steam towards Japan. It carried a full load of cargo and passengers. Two cabins in the stern of the ship remained empty: those reserved for Mr. Phileas Fogg.

The next morning the crew observed, not without some surprise, a passenger – with matted hair, a half-stupefied gaze and an unsteady gait – emerge from the second-class companionway and stagger across the deck to sit beneath a lifeboat.

This passenger was Passepartout himself. Here is what had transpired.

A few moments after Fix had left the opium den, two waiters had picked up Passepartout, who was in a deep sleep, and deposited him on the bed reserved for the smokers. However, three hours later, Passepartout – pursued even into his nightmares by his sense of duty – woke up and struggled against the stupefying effects of the narcotic. The thought of a task left undone shook him from his torpor. He left the drunkards' bed and, stumbling, leaning against the walls, falling and getting back up again, driven on irresistibly by a sort of instinct, he made his way out of the opium den – calling, like a man in a dream, "The *Carnatic*! the *Carnatic*!"

The steamer lay at the quay nearby, ready to depart. Passepartout had just a few more steps to make. He threw himself up the gangway and onto the foredeck, where he fell unconscious just as the *Carnatic* was casting off.

A few sailors, who were used to this type of scene, carried the poor fellow down into a second-class cabin. There Passepartout remained until the following morning, when he woke at a distance of a hundred and fifty miles from the coast of China.

That is how Passepartout came to find himself on the deck of the *Carnatic*, turning his face to the morning breeze and

taking in deep breaths. The fresh sea air sobered him. He began to gather his thoughts – no easy matter. At last, he was able to recall the events of the previous day, the revelations made by Fix, the opium den, etc.

"It's plain to see," he said to himself, "that I was abominably duped and drugged. What will Mr. Fogg say? At any rate, I haven't missed the boat, and that's the most important thing."

Then he thought of Fix.

"As for him," he said, "I hope we're rid of him now, and that with everything he said to me, he hasn't dared follow us on board the *Carnatic*. A policeman – a detective – tailing my master, and accusing him of a theft at the Bank of England! Come now! Mr. Fogg is as much a thief as I am a murderer."

Should Passepartout disclose all that he had learned to his master? Would it be proper to reveal to him the role that Fix had played in this affair? Or would it be better to wait for Mr. Fogg's arrival in London, before telling him that an agent of the Metropolitan Police had trailed him around the world? Yes, that would be best – the two of them could laugh about it then. In any case, it was something to consider. What was now most urgent was that he rejoin Mr. Fogg and apologize to him for his intolerable conduct.

So Passepartout roused himself. There was a rising swell, and

the steamer was rolling heavily. The worthy fellow, whose legs were still somewhat unsteady, made his way as best he could towards the stern of the ship.

There was no one, on the afterdeck, who resembled either his master or Mrs. Aouda.

"That's all right," he thought. "At this hour Mrs. Aouda will still be in bed. As for Mr. Fogg, he will have found some other whist players, as usual…"

With that, Passepartout went below, into the salon. Mr. Fogg wasn't there. This left Passepartout with just one option: to ask the purser which cabin was occupied by Mr. Fogg. The purser replied that he knew of no passenger by that name.

"Forgive me," persisted Passepartout. "The gentleman I'm speaking of is tall, reserved, uncommunicative, accompanied by a young woman…"

"There are no young women on board," replied the purser. "What's more, here is the list of passengers. You can check it yourself."

Passepartout checked the list… But his master's name was nowhere to be found. He stared, dumbfounded – but then he was struck with a sudden thought.

"Ah! But – am I on board the *Carnatic*?" he asked.

"Yes," replied the purser.

"En route to Yokohama?"

"Certainly."

For a moment, Passepartout had feared that he might be aboard the wrong ship! But although he was indeed on the *Carnatic*, it was certain that his master was not.

Thunderstruck, Passepartout collapsed onto a sofa. And suddenly, he understood. He remembered that the *Carnatic*'s departure time had been brought forward – that he should have warned his master – and that he had not! It was therefore Passepartout's fault that Mr. Fogg and Mrs. Aouda had missed the ship's departure!

His fault, yes – but even more so that of the traitor who, in order to separate him from his master, to keep Mr. Fogg in Hong Kong, had intoxicated him. For at last Passepartout saw through the police detective's ruse. And now Mr. Fogg would undoubtedly be ruined, his wager lost, the gentleman perhaps arrested and even imprisoned…! Passepartout tore his hair at the thought. Ah! If he should ever come across that Fix again, what a settling of accounts there would be!

When the initial shock had passed, Passepartout regained his composure and considered the situation. It did not seem promising. The Frenchman was now partway to Japan. He would arrive there, certainly, but how would he ever return?

His pockets were empty. Not a shilling; not a penny! Luckily, his passage, room and board had all been paid for in advance. He still had five or six days ahead of him in which to prepare himself. The manner in which Passepartout ate and drank during that crossing simply defies description. He ate for his master, for Mrs. Aouda, and for himself. He ate as though Japan, where he would soon step ashore, were a barren desert, stripped of every edible substance.

On the 13th, with the morning tide, the *Carnatic* entered the port of Yokohama.

This is a major port of call on the Pacific, and a regular stop for all the steamers carrying mail and passengers between North America, China, Japan, and the islands of Malaysia. Yokohama is situated in the bay of Yeddo, at a short distance from that vast metropolis, which is the secondary capital of the Japanese empire, and which was once the residence of the Taikun, in the time when that role of diplomatic emperor still existed. Yeddo is also the rival of Meaco, the great city where the Mikado, the ecclesiastical emperor and descendant of the gods, resides.

The *Carnatic* was moored at the quay of Yokohama, near the jetties of the port and the customs house, among vessels hailing from every country imaginable.

It was with little enthusiasm that Passepartout set foot on the

soil of that curious country. He had no other option than to take blind luck as his guide, and to venture out into the streets of the city.

Passepartout found himself first in a decidedly European neighborhood, which featured low-fronted houses graced with verandas and elegant peristyles, and whose streets, whose squares, whose docks and warehouses, covered all the ground from Treaty Point to the river. Here – as in Hong Kong, as in Calcutta – was a raucous throng of people of all races: Americans, Englishmen, Chinese, Dutch, merchants seeking to buy or to sell anything and everything, and among whom the Frenchman felt himself as much an alien as if he had landed in the country of the African Hottentots.

Passepartout did have one resource available to him, which was to present himself to the French or English consular agents in Yokohama. But he was reluctant to tell his story, since it was so closely intertwined with that of his master, and he wanted to explore every other possibility before it should come to that.

So, having traversed the city's European quarter without encountering any means of assistance, he entered the Japanese quarter, determined if need be to push on as far as Yeddo.

Yokohama's indigenous quarter is called Benten, after a goddess of the sea worshipped on the nearby islands. There,

Passepartout saw handsome avenues of firs and cedars, sacred gates of a singular design, bridges arching through thickets of bamboos and reeds, temples sheltering under the vast and melancholy cover of centenary cedars, and monasteries in whose depths stirred Buddhist priests and practitioners of the Confucian religion. There were endless streets where one might gather a whole harvest of rose-tinted, red-cheeked children – little characters who looked as though they had been cut from the panels of a native screen, and who played among short-legged mutts and cats of a yellowish hue, tailless, very lazy and affectionate.

The streets were swarming with people, ceaselessly coming and going: bonzes passing in procession and striking their monotonous drums, yakunins (customs officers and policemen wearing pointed hats incrusted with lacquer and carrying two sabres in their belts) and soldiers dressed in blue and white-striped cottons and armed with percussion rifles. Added to these were men-at-arms of the Mikado, splendid in their silken doublets, bearing halberds and coats of mail, and many other military men of all kinds. For, in Japan, the profession of soldier is as highly esteemed as it is scorned in China. Then there were begging friars, pilgrims in long robes, and simple civilians with hair smooth and black as ebony, with large heads, long torsos, spindly legs, a diminutive stature, and skin of a color ranging from somber, nuanced copper to a

The streets were swarming with people, ceaselessly coming and going.

matte white — but never yellow, like that of the Chinese, from whom the Japanese differ significantly. Finally, among the carts, the palanquins, the horses, the porters, the sailing wheelbarrows, the 'norimons' with lacquered sides, the supple 'kagos' — veritable litters made of bamboo — one saw passing, with small steps of their tiny feet, shod in canvas shoes, straw sandals or carved wooden clogs, a few women, not very pretty, with slanting eyes, shallow chests, teeth blackened according to the fashion of the day, but elegantly attired in the national garment, the 'kimono'. This is a cross between a robe and a silken scarf, secured with a broad belt which culminates behind the back in an extravagant knot — which today's Parisian women seem to have borrowed from their Japanese counterparts.

Passepartout strolled for several hours through this colorful crowd, browsing the curious and opulent boutiques, the bazaars where Japanese goldsmiths piled their glittering wares, the restaurants hung with banners and streamers, and which he was now forbidden to enter. He passed by those tea houses where brimming cups of hot and fragrant water are drunk along with 'sake', a liquor made from fermented rice, and those cozy smoking dens where a very fine tobacco is consumed — but where no opium is sold, as its usage is virtually unknown in Japan.

Then Passepartout found himself out in the fields, surrounded by immense rice plantations. There he found blooming, beside the flowers in all their final colors and their last perfumes, dazzling camellias – not bushes, but full-grown trees – and, within bamboo enclosures, cherry trees, plum trees and apple trees, which the locals cultivate more for their flowers than for their fruits, and which grinning scarecrows and spinners protect from the beaks of sparrows, pigeons, crows and other voracious birds. There was no majestic cedar which did not shelter some great eagle, not a weeping willow which did not cover with its foliage some heron, melancholically perched on one long leg, and everywhere there were rooks, ducks, sparrow hawks, wild geese, and great numbers of those cranes which the Japanese revere, and which for them are symbols of longevity and happiness.

As he wandered, Passepartout spotted a few violets growing among the grasses.

"Good!" he said, "Here is my supper."

But having smelled them, he found them to be odorless.

"I'm out of luck!" he thought.

As a precaution the honest fellow had, naturally, breakfasted as copiously as he was able before leaving the *Carnatic* – but after a full day of walking, he was aware of having a very empty stomach. He had noticed that sheep, goats and pigs were entirely absent from the storefronts of the local butchers and, knowing

that it is a sacrilege to kill a cow, bovines being strictly reserved
for agricultural purposes, he had concluded that meat was
a rarity in Japan. He wasn't wrong, but even if he had to do
without the usual butchers' fare, his stomach would gladly have
accommodated some quarters of boar or deer, some partridges
or quail, some fowl or fish, which the Japanese eat almost
exclusively, along with the product of the rice plantations.
But he was forced to put a good face on his ill fortune, and put
off until tomorrow the chance of finding anything to eat.

Night fell. Passepartout returned to the native quarter of
the city, and wandered down the streets, among multi-colored
lanterns, watching groups of street-performers execute their
captivating feats, and the open-air astrologers, who collected
little crowds about their telescopes. He spied the harbor in the
distance, enamelled by the fires of the fishermen, who lure their
catch with the glare of their resin torches.

At last the streets began to empty. The crowds were
succeeded by the yakunins on their rounds. These public
officers, in their magnificent costumes and surrounded by their
retinues, resemble ambassadors, and Passepartout repeated
jokingly, every time he encountered some resplendent patrol,
"Well, well! Here's another Japanese embassy departing
for Europe!"

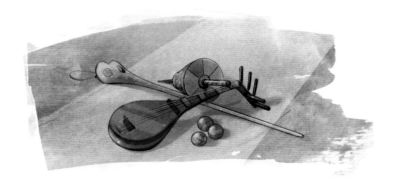

CHAPTER XXIII

IN WHICH PASSEPARTOUT'S NOSE GROWS EXCESSIVELY LONG

The following morning Passepartout, exhausted and famished, told himself that he would have to eat at any cost, and the sooner the better. He could naturally have sold his pocket watch, but he would rather have starved to death. The time had therefore come for the brave fellow to put to use that strong, if not melodious, voice with which nature had favored him.

He knew a few French and English airs, and he resolved to try them out. The Japanese certainly ought to have a taste for music, since everything in Japan is done to the sound of cymbals, the tam-tam and the drum, and they surely could not fail to appreciate

the talents of a European virtuoso.

But perhaps it was still a bit early to be organizing a concert, and even the aficionados, being woken before their time, might not have repaid the singer in the coin of the realm.

Passepartout decided therefore to wait a few hours more, but as he ambled on, he reflected that he might appear too well-dressed for an itinerant musician, and he had the idea of exchanging his clothing for an outfit more in keeping with his new position. What's more, this exchange would in principle produce some financial advantage, which he could then immediately apply to the satisfaction of his appetite.

Having decided on this course of action, it only remained for him to carry it out. After a lengthy search, Passepartout came across a second-hand clothing shop, and he went in to propose an exchange. His European suit pleased the shop's proprietor, and Passepartout soon came out again, attired in an old Japanese robe and wearing a kind of turban, faded with long use. But now, a few small coins were jingling in his pocket.

"Very well," he thought to himself, "let's just pretend I'm dressed up for Carnival!"

The first thing this newly 'Japanesed' Passepartout did was to enter a modest-looking tea house and, there, on the remnants of some wildfowl and a few handfuls of rice, to breakfast like a man

for whom dinner was a problem yet to be resolved.

"Now," he said, when he had been amply restored, "I must not lose my head. I no longer have the option of trading this coat for one even more Japanese. So I will need to find some way of leaving, as quickly as possible, this Land of the Rising Sun, which will leave me with no more than a sorry memory."

Passepartout first thought of visiting the steamers departing for America. He planned to offer his services as a cook or as a servant, asking no more payment than his passage, room and board. Once he arrived in San Francisco, he would surely find a way of getting by. The main thing was to cross those four thousand and seven hundred miles of the Pacific that stretch between Japan and the New World.

Never one to dawdle, Passepartout immediately made his way towards the port of Yokohama. But as he approached the docks, his plan, which had seemed so straightforward when the idea first struck him, appeared less and less practicable. Why would they need a cook or a servant on board an American steamer, and how could he hope to win their confidence, attired as he was? On whose recommendation would they receive him? What references could he supply?

As he pondered these matters, his gaze fell upon an enormous poster that a sort of clown was carrying through the streets of

As he pondered these matters, his gaze fell upon an enormous poster that a sort of clown was carrying through the streets of Yokohama.

Yokohama. The poster was written in English:

JAPANESE ACROBATIC TROUPE
HONORABLE WILLIAM BATULCAR, PROPRIETOR

-

FINAL PERFORMANCES
BEFORE THEIR DEPARTURE FOR THE UNITED
STATES OF AMERICA
FEATURING
THE LONG NOSES! LONG NOSES!
UNDER THE DIRECT PATRONAGE OF THE GOD
TINGOU

-

GRAND ATTRACTION!

"The United States of America!" cried Passepartout, "this is just what I was looking for...!"

He followed the man and his poster, who soon led him into the Japanese quarter. Fifteen minutes later, he stopped before a large building, adorned with placards and banners, and whose painted exterior depicted, in jarring colors and with no sense of perspective, an entire troupe of jugglers.

This was the establishment of the Honorable Batulcar, a sort of American Barnum, director of a troupe of aerialists, jugglers, clowns, acrobats, equilibrists and gymnasts which, as the advertisement stated, was giving its final performances before leaving the Empire of the Sun for the states of the Union.

Passepartout stepped in through a portico adorning the building, and asked for Mr. Batulcar. Mr. Batulcar himself appeared.

"What do you want?" he said to Passepartout, whom he mistook, at first, for a native.

"Have you any need of a servant?" asked Passepartout.

"A servant?" cried the Barnum, stroking the thick gray goatee that flourished upon his chin. "I have two servants – both obedient and loyal – who have never left me, and who work for nothing, provided that I feed them... And here they are!"

And Mr. Batulcar raised his two burly arms, criss-crossed with veins the size of the strings on a double bass.

"So then I may be of no use to you?"

"None at all."

"Drat! It's just that it would really have suited me to depart with you."

"Ah!" said the Honorable Batulcar, "You're no more Japanese than I am a monkey! But why are you dressed like that?"

"One dresses as one can!"

"True, that. You're French, aren't you?"

"Yes. A Parisian from Paris."

"So then you must know how to pull faces?"

"Humph!" replied Passepartout, annoyed to hear his nationality connected with such an assumption. "We Frenchmen may know how to pull faces, yes, but we do it no better than the Americans!"

"Right. Well, although I can't take you on as a valet, I can take you on as a clown. You understand, old fellow. In France, the clowns are foreigners – in foreign lands, the clowns are French!"

"Ah!"

"You're pretty strong, are you?"

"Especially after a good meal."

"And you know how to sing?"

"Yes," replied Passepartout, who had once been known to sing quite loudly in the streets.

"But can you sing standing on your head, with a spinning top on the ball of your left foot, and a saber balancing on the ball of your right foot?"

"*Parbleu!*" replied Passepartout confidently, recalling the gambols of his youth.

"For you see, that's what it's all about!" said the Honorable Batulcar.

And Passepartout was engaged on the spot.

At last, Passepartout had found himself a position. He had been hired as a general dogsbody for the celebrated Japanese troupe. It was not very flattering – but in less than eight days, he would be on his way to San Francisco.

The performance, announced with such extravagance by the Honorable Batulcar, was to begin at three o'clock, and soon the formidable instruments of a Japanese orchestra, complete with drummers and tam-tams, were thundering by the door. Naturally, Passepartout had not had time to learn a particular role, but he was to provide the support of his wide shoulders in the great spectacle of the 'human pyramid', executed by the Long Noses of the god Tingou. This 'grand attraction' was to be the final routine, and close the performance.

By three o'clock, the vast building had filled with spectators. Europeans and natives, Chinese and Japanese, men, women and children, filed in among the narrow benches and up into the gallery that faced the stage. The musicians had also come inside, and the complete orchestra – gongs, tam-tams, rattles, flutes, tambourines and great drums – was raising a mighty din.

The performance was what all these acrobatic exhibitions are. But one must admit that the Japanese are the very finest equilibrists in the world. One, equipped with his fan and many tiny pieces of paper, performed that graceful routine of the

butterflies and the flowers. Another, with the fragrant smoke of his pipe, traced rapidly in the air a series of bluish words, which composed a delicate compliment addressed to the audience. This one juggled flaming candles, which he blew out successively as they passed before his lips, and which he relit, one from another, without interrupting for a single moment his mesmerizing prestidigitation. That one, equipped with a series of spinning tops, executed the most unbelievable maneuvers. Beneath his hand, the droning machines seemed to take on a life of their own in their interminable gyrations. They ran along the length of pipes, along the edges of sabers, along tautened wires, no thicker than a hair, stretched from one side of the stage to the other. The tops circled the rims of great crystal vases, they climbed up bamboo ladders, they dispersed to the four corners of the room, combining their various pitches to produce harmonic effects of a strange character. The jugglers juggled with them, and they spun in the air. Using wooden racquets, they launched them like shuttlecocks, and they continued to spin. They stuck them in their pockets, and when they brought them out again, they spun still – until the moment when a hidden spring caused them to burst into a spray of fireworks!

There is no need to describe here the prodigious exercises of the troupe's acrobats and gymnasts. Their routines on the

ladder, the pole, the ball, the barrel, etc., were performed with remarkable precision. But the main attraction of the performance was the appearance of the 'Long Noses' – amazing equilibrists who are as yet unknown in Europe.

These Long Noses form a peculiar society, assembled under the direct patronage of the god Tingou. They were dressed like medieval heralds, and bore a splendid pair of wings upon their shoulders. But what made them even more remarkable was the long nose embellishing their faces, and particularly the use they made of it. These noses were nothing less than bamboo poles – five, six, or ten feet long, some straight, some curved, some smooth, and some lumpy. And it was upon these appendages (which were securely attached to their faces) that they performed all their marvelous stunts. A dozen of these followers of the god Tingou lay down on their backs, with their noses lifted straight up like so many lightning rods, and their colleagues proceeded to frolic upon these probosces, vaulting from this one to that one, and performing the most incredible tricks.

It had been specially announced to the public that, as a grand finale, they would perform a version of the human pyramid, in which some fifty Long Noses would depict the 'Car of Juggernaut'. But instead of constructing this pyramid using their shoulders as a support, the artists of the Honorable Batulcar's

troupe would use only their noses. That day, as it happened, one of those who usually helped secure the base of the pyramid had left the troupe – and, since all that was required was some strength and dexterity, Passepartout had been chosen to replace him.

Certainly, the dignified fellow felt rather pitiful when – sad to relate – he put on his medieval costume, adorned with multicolored wings, and when a six-foot nose was applied to his face! But, after all, the nose was to be his bread and butter, and so he gave in.

Passepartout went on stage and took his place alongside his colleagues who were forming the foundation of the Car of Juggernaut. They all stretched out on the ground, their noses raised in the air. A second group of equilibrists entered and balanced themselves atop these long appendages, a third group took up their positions yet one level higher, then a fourth – and so, built up from noses touching only at their points, a human monument soon rose towards the ceiling of the theater.

The audience burst into applause – but as the ovation rang around the theater, and the instruments of the orchestra erupted with a noise like a thunderstorm, the pyramid shook, and the balance was disrupted: one of the noses in the foundation dipped and vanished, and the whole of the monument tumbled down

like a house of cards…

Passepartout himself was the cause. Abandoning his post, leaping from the stage without the aid of his wings, and climbing up into the right-hand gallery, he fell at the feet of one of the spectators crying, "Ah! my master! my master!"

"You, here?"

"Yes, it's me!"

"Well then, in that case, to the steamer, my good man!…"

Mr. Fogg, Mrs. Aouda, who had accompanied him, and Passepartout rushed through the aisles and out of the building. But there, they encountered the Honorable Batulcar, furious, demanding that they pay damages. "You break it, you buy it," he said, gesturing towards the heap of acrobats behind them. Phileas Fogg appeased his rage by tossing him a handful of banknotes. And, at half past six, just as it was preparing to leave, Mr. Fogg and Mrs. Aouda set foot on the deck of the American steamer, followed by Passepartout, his wings still on his back, and on his face the six-foot nose which he had not yet had a moment to remove.

CHAPTER XXIV

DURING WHICH THE PACIFIC OCEAN IS CROSSED

What had happened within sight of Shanghai may be readily guessed. The signals made by the *Tankadère* had been spotted on board the steamer for Yokohama. The captain, on seeing a flag at half mast, had sailed towards the little schooner. A few moments later, Phileas Fogg, paying for his passage at the agreed price, had placed in the hands of the skipper John Bunsby five hundred and fifty pounds. Then the honorable gentleman, Mrs. Aouda and Fix had boarded the steamer, which promptly set course for Nagasaki and Yokohama.

On arriving that very morning, the 14th of November, at the

scheduled time, Phileas Fogg, leaving Fix to his own devices, had presented himself on board the *Carnatic* – and there he learned, to Mrs. Aouda's great joy (and perhaps his own, although if this was so he betrayed no sign of it) that the Frenchman Passepartout had indeed arrived in Yokohama the day before.

Phileas Fogg, who was to depart again that very evening for San Francisco, immediately set about searching for his servant. He visited, without success, the French and English consular agents and, having searched fruitlessly through the streets of Yokohama, he was despairing of ever finding Passepartout when chance – or perhaps a kind of presentiment – led him to step into the theater of the Honorable Batulcar. He would certainly not have recognized his servant under his eccentric disguise as a winged herald, but the Frenchman, from his reclining position on stage, spotted his master in the gallery. At this, he made an involuntary movement of the nose. It was this that upset the pyramid's equilibrium, and set off the dramatic collapse.

All this Passepartout learned from Mrs. Aouda herself, who then told him how they had made their crossing from Hong Kong to Yokohama, in the company of a man named Fix, on board the schooner the *Tankadère.*

At the mention of Fix, Passepartout made no sign of recognition. He felt that the moment had not yet come to reveal

to his master what had passed between him and the police detective. So, when he told the story of his own adventures, Passepartout put the blame on himself, apologizing for having fallen under the influence of opium in a smoking den in Hong Kong.

Mr. Fogg heard these explanations coldly, and made no response. Then, he opened a line of credit for his servant, sufficient for him to procure on board some more appropriate clothing. And indeed, an hour had not passed before the honest fellow, having doffed his nose and plucked off his wings, had nothing more about him to remind people of the god Tingou.

The steamer making the crossing from Yokohama to San Francisco was called the *General Grant*, and it belonged to the Pacific Mail Steamship Company. It was an enormous paddle steamer of two thousand and five hundred tons, well appointed and extremely fast. A great walking beam rose and fell above the deck. At one end, it was driven by a piston. The other end was attached to a connecting rod which, transforming the reciprocal movement into a rotational one, directly powered the drive shaft of the wheels. The *General Grant* was rigged as a three-masted schooner, and it benefited from a vast spread of canvas, which provided powerful assistance to the steam engine. Sailing at its average of twelve miles per hour, the steamer was expected to

cross the Pacific in no more than twenty-one days. Phileas Fogg was therefore justified in thinking that, arriving in San Francisco on the 2nd of December, he would be in New York on the 11th and in London on the 20th – thereby beating the fateful deadline of the 21st of December by several hours.

The steamer carried a full complement of passengers: some Englishmen, many Americans, a veritable emigration of coolies heading to America, and a number of officers in the British Indian Army, who were using their leave to journey around the world.

This crossing was unmarked by nautical incidents of any kind. The steamer, supported on its large wheels, carried on by its vast press of sail, rolled very little. The Pacific Ocean lived up to its name. Mr. Fogg was quite as calm, quite as uncommunicative, as ever. His young companion, increasingly, felt herself attached to him by other bonds than those of gratitude. His quiet character, which was all in all so generous, impressed her more than she realized, and it was almost unconsciously that she began to surrender to sentiments whose influence the enigmatic Fogg seemed not to feel.

Moreover, Mrs. Aouda began to take a deep interest in the gentleman's project. She worried about the many misadventures which might compromise the success of the journey. She often

chatted with Passepartout, who was able to read between the lines of Mrs. Aouda's heart. Over time, this honest fellow had come to have complete faith in his master, and so he was never short of praises for the honesty, the generosity, the devotion of Phileas Fogg. What's more, he reassured Mrs. Aouda about the outcome of the journey, reminding her that the most difficult stretch was behind them, that they had finished with those fantastical countries of China and Japan, that they were returning to the civilized countries and, finally, that a train from San Francisco to New York and a transatlantic from New York to London would undoubtedly suffice to bring to an end, within the eighty days, this impossible journey around the world.

Nine days after their departure from Yokohama, Phileas Fogg had traversed exactly half of the globe.

Indeed, on the 23rd of November, the *General Grant* crossed the one hundred and eightieth meridian – that which, in the southern hemisphere, marks the antipodes of London. Of the eighty days available to him Mr. Fogg had, it is true, used up fifty-two, and there were only twenty-eight remaining. But it should be said that, even though the gentleman had only reached the halfway mark in terms of the meridians, he had in reality completed more than two thirds of his journey. How many detours, indeed, must be made between London and Aden, Aden

and Bombay, Calcutta and Singapore, Singapore and Yokohama. If one follows a perfectly circular route along the fiftieth parallel – on which London lies – the distance around the globe is no more than some twelve thousand miles. Phileas Fogg, however, was forced, by the vagaries of his various means of locomotion, to travel twenty-six thousand miles – of which he had, on that date of the 23rd, covered around seventeen thousand and five hundred. But from now on the route ran straight ahead of him, and Fix was no longer around to raise obstacles in his path.

It also happened that, on the same 23rd of November, Passepartout made a joyful discovery. It will be remembered that the stubborn fellow had insisted on keeping his famous family watch set to London time. And, on that day, although he had never adjusted it either forwards or backwards, he found that his watch agreed perfectly with the ship's chronometers.

Passepartout's triumph and jubilation were complete. He would very much have liked to know what Fix would have said, had he been present.

"That rascal was telling me all kinds of tales about the meridians, the sun, the moon!" repeated Passepartout wherever he went. "Ha! That kind of fellow – if we took any notice of them, our horology would be in a sorry state. I was sure that one day or another the sun would come around and adjust itself to

my watch...!"

What Passepartout didn't know is this: that if the face of his watch had been divided into twenty-four hours, in the manner of Italian watches, he would have had no reason to celebrate – for the hands of his instrument, when it was nine o'clock in the morning on board the ship, would have indicated nine o'clock at night, or the twenty-first hour after midnight – a difference exactly equal to that between London and the hundred and eightieth meridian.

But although Fix might have been able to explain that purely scientific effect, it is certain that Passepartout, if not unable to understand it, would have been unable to admit its truth. And in any case, if – as was impossible – the police detective had inadvisedly showed his face on board at that very moment, it is probable that Passepartout, in his righteous fury, would have engaged him in a discourse on an entirely different topic – and in an entirely different manner.

And where was Fix at that very moment...?

Fix was, as a matter of fact, on board the *General Grant*.

Indeed, on arriving in Yokohama the detective, parting from Mr. Fogg, whom he expected to find again in the course of the day, had immediately repaired to the English consulate. There, at last, he had found waiting for him the warrant which, having

pursued him since Bombay, was now forty days old – and which had been sent from Hong Kong aboard the same *Carnatic* on which he was thought to be traveling. One can imagine the detective's disappointment! The warrant was now useless! Mr. Fogg had left the English territories behind, and an act of extradition would now be needed in order to arrest him.

"So be it," said Fix to himself, after his anger had subsided. "My warrant isn't valid here, but it will be in England. This rogue shows every sign of returning to his country, believing that he has thrown the police off his scent. Good. I'll follow him there. As for the money, God willing there'll be some left! But this fine fellow has already left more than five thousand pounds along his route, in travel costs, bounties and prizes, lawsuits, fines, elephants and expenses of all kinds. After all, the Bank is rich!"

His decision made, he immediately booked a passage on the *General Grant*. He was already on board when Mr. Fogg and Mrs. Aouda arrived, and was extremely surprised to recognize Passepartout with them in his herald's costume. He promptly hid away in his cabin, in order to avoid an encounter that might compromise all of his plans – and, thanks to the great number of passengers, he had every hope of passing unnoticed by his enemy, until the very day that he found himself face to face with

the Frenchman on the foredeck of the vessel.

Without any further explanation, Passepartout launched himself at Fix and, to the great delight of certain Americans who promptly began to bet on him, he administered a superb volley of blows to the unfortunate detective, which demonstrated the great superiority of French pugilism over that of the English.

When Passepartout had finished, he found himself feeling much calmer, and somehow unburdened.

Although he was in rather bad shape, Fix picked himself up from the deck and, regarding his adversary, said coldly, "Have you finished?"

"Yes, for the moment."

"Then come to talk to me."

"You want to…"

"Talk, yes, about your master's affairs."

Passepartout, somewhat taken aback by the detective's self-assurance, followed him forward, and the two of them sat down in the bow of the steamer.

"You've given me a thrashing," said Fix. "Very well. Now, listen to what I have to say. Until now, I've been Mr. Fogg's adversary – but from this moment I'm on his side."

"Finally!" cried Passepartout. "So you believe that he's an honest man?"

Passepartout administered a superb volley of blows to the unfortunate detective, which demonstrated the great superiority of French pugilism over that of the English.

"No," replied Fix coldly, "I believe he's a rogue... Hush! Keep still and let me speak. While Mr. Fogg was traveling through English territories, it was in my interest to slow him down while I awaited the arrival of an arrest warrant. I've done everything possible to delay him. I set the priests from Bombay against him, I drugged you in Hong Kong, I separated you from your master, I made him miss the steamer for Yokohama..."

Passepartout clenched his fists as he listened.

"But now," continued Fix, "it seems that Mr. Fogg is returning to England. Very well – I will follow him. And I'll clear any obstacles from his route with the same diligence and zeal that I once expended in accumulating them. You see, my strategy has changed as my interests have changed. And I would add that your interests align with mine, for it is only in England that you will discover whether you serve a criminal or an honest man!"

Passepartout had listened attentively, and he was convinced that Fix was arguing in good faith.

"So are we friends?" asked Fix.

"Friends, no," replied Passepartout. "Allies, yes – but on a probationary basis, for at the least sign of treason, I will wring your neck."

"Agreed," said the police detective calmly.

Eleven days later, on the 3rd of December, the *General Grant* passed through the Golden Gate and arrived in San Francisco.

Mr. Fogg had still neither gained nor lost a single day.

CHAPTER XXV

IN WHICH A QUICK SKETCH IS GIVEN OF SAN FRANCISCO
ON THE OCCASION OF A POLITICAL RALLY

It was seven o'clock in the morning when Phileas Fogg, Mrs. Aouda and Passepartout set foot on the American continent – that is, if one can apply the term to the floating dock onto which they disembarked. These docks, which rise and fall with the tide, aid greatly in the loading and unloading of vessels. Here one may find clippers of all sizes, steamers of every nationality, and those steam-boats several storeys high which serve the Sacramento River and its tributaries. And here, heaped up along the docks, are the products of a commerce that extends to Mexico, to Peru, to Chile, to Brazil, to Europe, to Asia, and to all of the islands of

the Pacific Ocean.

Passepartout, in his joy at reaching America at last, was inspired to disembark by means of a dramatic somersault. But when he landed on the worm-eaten planking of the dock, he nearly crashed through into the waters below. Put out by the manner in which he had 'set foot' in the New World, the honest fellow let out a loud cry, which startled up a multitude of the cormorants and pelicans that are the habitual residents of the floating docks.

As soon as he had disembarked, Mr. Fogg made inquiries into the departure of the next train for New York. It was scheduled for six o'clock in the evening. So Mr. Fogg had an entire day to spend in the Californian capital. He ordered a carriage for Mrs. Aouda and himself. Passepartout sat up on the box beside the coachman, and the vehicle, for a fee of three dollars, made its way to the International Hotel.

From his elevated position, Passepartout stared with much curiosity at the great American city: wide streets, low houses in straight rows, churches and temples built in an Anglo-Saxon Gothic style, vast dockyards with warehouses resembling palaces – some made of wood, others of brick. In the streets were numerous carriages, omnibuses, and tram cars, while the sidewalks were crowded, not only with Americans and

Europeans, but also with Chinese and Indian pedestrians – enough of them to make up a population of more than two hundred thousand inhabitants.

Passepartout was rather surprised by what he saw. He still had in mind the legendary San Francisco of 1849: the city of bandits, arsonists and murderers flocking in pursuit of gold nuggets; an immense confusion of all the dregs of society, where men gambled for gold dust, a revolver in one hand and a knife in the other.

But the 'good old days' were in the past. Now, San Francisco had the appearance of a great commercial city. The high tower of the town hall overlooked a vast ensemble of streets and avenues which intersected at right angles, and among which could be found lush, verdant squares, and even a little Chinatown that looked as though it had been imported from the Celestial Empire in a toy-box.

No more sombreros, no more miners' red shirts, no more feathered Indians – they had been replaced by the silk hats and black suits worn by a great number of men engaged in the all-consuming activity of business. Some streets, such as Montgomery Street – the equivalent of London's Regent Street, Paris's Boulevard des Italiens, and New York's Broadway – were lined with splendid shops, which displayed in their windows

products from around the world.

When Passepartout arrived at the International Hotel, it seemed to him that he had never left England.

The ground floor of the hotel was taken up with an immense 'bar' – a sort of open buffet provided free of charge to all comers. They could partake of cured meats, oyster soup, cheese and biscuits without ever opening their purses. They paid only for what they drank – ale, port or sherry – if they wished to refresh themselves. This seemed 'very American' to Passepartout.

The hotel restaurant was comfortable. Mr. Fogg and Mrs. Aouda installed themselves at a table and were abundantly served, in lilliputian plates, by Africans of a beautiful black hue.

When they had dined, Phileas Fogg, accompanied by Mrs. Aouda, made his way from the hotel to the offices of the English consul, in order to have his passport stamped. In the street, he encountered his servant, who asked if it might not be prudent to purchase a few dozen Enfield rifles or Colt revolvers, before taking to the Union Pacific Railroad. Passepartout had heard tell of the native Sioux and the Pawnee, who stopped trains in the manner of Spanish highwaymen. Mr. Fogg replied that this was a useless precaution, but that Passepartout was free to do as he liked. Then he continued to the offices of the consular agent.

Phileas Fogg had gone no more than two hundred steps when,

'by the luckiest of chances', he encountered Fix. The detective appeared extremely surprised. What! Had he and Mr. Fogg crossed the Pacific together on the same ship, without meeting on board? In any case, Fix was honored once again to see the gentleman to whom he owed so much and, his affairs calling him back to Europe, he would be delighted to continue his voyage in such agreeable company.

Mr. Fogg replied that the honor was all his, and Fix – who had no intention of letting him out of his sight – asked for permission to join him on his tour of this curious city of San Francisco. This was readily given.

So Mrs. Aouda, Phileas Fogg and Fix strolled together through the streets. They soon found themselves in Montgomery Street, where an enormous crowd had assembled. Countless people gathered on the sidewalks, in the middle of the road, on the tramway rails, despite the constant passage of coaches and omnibuses, in the doorways of the shops, at the windows of all the houses and even on some of the roofs. Sandwich men circulated in the throng bearing large posters. Streamers and banners floated in the breeze. Cries erupted from the crowd on all sides.

"Hurrah for Kamerfield!"

"Hurrah for Mandiboy!"

It was a political rally. This, at least, was Fix's conjecture, and he shared his thought with Mr. Fogg, adding, "It would perhaps be best, sir, if we were to avoid this commotion. There's nothing to gain here, and it could come to blows."

"Indeed," replied Phileas Fogg, "and blows, even if they are political, are blows just the same!"

Fix smiled at this observation and, in order to avoid being caught up in the melee, he, Mrs. Aouda, and Phileas Fogg took up a position on the upper landing of a stairway that led to a terrace overlooking Montgomery Street. Before them, on the other side of the street, between a coal merchant's wharf and a petrol merchant's establishment, a large platform stood in the open, and on this the various currents in the crowd seemed to be converging.

And what was the motivation behind this rally? What occasion had prompted it? Phileas Fogg had absolutely no idea. Did it concern the nomination of an important official, civil or military, or a state governor or a member of Congress? This was a reasonable conjecture, given the extraordinary passion that animated the city.

Suddenly, a considerable disturbance spread through the crowd. Everyone's hands were in the air. Some of them, closed firmly into fists, appeared to rise and fall rapidly, accompanied

by loud cries — an energetic means, no doubt, of casting a vote. Eddies formed as the dense mass surged back and forth. The banners swung to and fro, disappearing one moment and then reappearing in tatters. The undulations of this human swell propagated outward as far as the stairway, and the surface of the crowd, composed of the agitated, fleecy heads of the marchers, looked like the surface of the sea when it is struck by a squall. The number of black silk hats was visibly dwindling, and those that remained appeared to have lost their normal height.

"It's evidently a political rally," said Fix, "and the issue that's inspired it must be an important one. I wouldn't be surprised if it concerned the *Alabama* affair, even though it's already been resolved."

"Perhaps," replied Mr. Fogg simply.

"In any case," continued Fix, "there are two adversaries facing one another today: the honorable Kamerfield and the honorable Mandiboy."

Mrs. Aouda, on Phileas Fogg's arm, regarded this tumultuous scene with some surprise, and Fix was about to ask of one of his neighbors the reason behind this popular upheaval, when a more pronounced disruption began to take hold. The cheers, accompanied by curses, redoubled. The wooden handles of banners were transformed into offensive weapons. Everywhere,

open hands were replaced by fists. Blows rained down from the tops of the carriages and omnibuses hemmed in by the crowd. All kinds of objects were turned into projectiles. Boots and shoes described flat trajectories through the air, and a few revolvers were even heard to mingle their sharp reports with the din of the crowd.

The disturbance drew nearer to the stairway, and began to spill over onto the first few steps. One of the two parties was evidently being pushed back, but the spectators were unable to determine whether the advantage belonged to Mandiboy or to Kamerfield.

"I think it would be wise if we withdrew," said Fix, who would not have liked to see his quarry suffer an injury or be caught up in an unlucky incident. "If England is somehow involved in this political quarrel, and we are recognized, we could be caught up in the brawl!"

"An English citizen..." began Phileas Fogg – but the gentleman was unable to finish his sentence. Behind him, from the terrace overlooking the stairway, there erupted a series of deafening cries.

"Hurrah! Hip! Hip! For Mandiboy!" A troop of voters was charging in, outflanking the partisans of Kamerfield. Mr. Fogg, Mrs. Aouda, and Fix found themselves caught between two fires.

It was too late for them to escape. This torrent of men, armed with coshes and leaded canes, was irresistible. Phileas Fogg and Fix, in their efforts to protect the young woman, were roughly knocked about. Mr. Fogg, no less phlegmatic than usual, sought to defend himself with those weapons which nature has placed at the end of every Englishman's arms, but it was no use. An enormous ruffian with a red beard, a flushed face and broad shoulders, who appeared to be the leader of the gang, raised a massive fist to strike at Mr. Fogg, and he would have injured the gentleman severely, if Fix had not stepped in to take the blow in his place. An enormous lump formed instantly beneath the detective's silk hat, which had been transformed into a flat cap.

"Yankee!" said Mr. Fogg, flashing at his adversary a look of profound contempt.

"Englishman!" replied the other.

"We will meet again!"

"Whenever you like. Your name?"

"Phileas Fogg. Yours?"

"Colonel Stamp W. Proctor."

As these words were exchanged, the surge of combatants passed on. Fix had been knocked down, and now he picked himself up. His clothes were torn, but he had suffered no further harm. His traveling coat had been split in two unequal parts, and

An enormous ruffian raised a massive fist to strike at Mr. Fogg, and he would have injured the gentleman severely, if Fix had not stepped in to take the blow in his place.

his trousers resembled those which certain Indians, according to their fashion, deign to wear only once they have torn off the cuffs. However, Mrs. Aouda had been spared – and Fix, who was testing the throbbing lump on his head, was the only one who bore any sign of injury.

"Thank you," said Mr. Fogg to the detective when they had left the crowd behind.

"It was nothing," said Fix, "but now, come with me."

"Where?"

"To a tailor's."

Such a visit was, indeed, called for. The clothing worn by Fix and Phileas Fogg had been reduced to rags, as if those two gentlemen had truly been fighting in the cause of the honorable Kamerfield and Mandiboy.

An hour later, they were once again decently attired and neatly groomed, and they returned to the International Hotel.

There, Passepartout was waiting for his master, armed with half a dozen six-shot revolvers loaded with centerfire cartridges. When he saw Fix in Mr. Fogg's company, his face darkened. But Mrs. Aouda, in a few words, explained what had befallen them, and Passepartout soon relaxed. Fix was evidently no longer an enemy, but an ally. He was keeping his word.

After dinner, a coach was brought to convey the travelers

and their luggage to the station. As they were climbing into the vehicle, Mr. Fogg said to Fix, "You haven't seen any more of that Colonel Proctor?"

"No," Fix replied.

"I will return to America to find him," said Phileas Fogg coldly. "It would not do for an English citizen to allow himself to be treated in such a fashion."

The detective smiled and said nothing. It appeared that Mr. Fogg belonged to that race of Englishmen who, while they do not tolerate duels in their own country, will fight abroad when their honor is at stake.

At a quarter to six, the travelers arrived at the station and found the train ready to depart.

Just as Mr. Fogg was about to board, he signaled to a nearby station employee.

"Friend," he said, "was there not some disturbance today in San Francisco?"

"There was a political rally, sir," replied the employee.

"And yet, I thought I'd noticed a certain exuberance out in the streets."

"It was only a meeting organized in preparation for an election."

"The election of some executive official, no doubt?" asked

Mr. Fogg.

"No, sir, a justice of the peace."

At this, Phileas Fogg climbed into the carriage, and the train started off at full steam.

CHAPTER XXVI

IN WHICH WE RIDE ON AN EXPRESS TRAIN
BELONGING TO THE PACIFIC RAILROAD

'Ocean to ocean' is the expression used by the Americans – and those three words ought to be the official name of the 'grand trunk' which crosses the entire width of the United States of America. But, in fact, the Pacific Railroad is divided into two distinct parts: the Central Pacific between San Francisco and Ogden, and the Union Pacific between Ogden and Omaha. There, five separate lines meet, and provide frequent connections between Omaha and New York.

In this manner, New York and San Francisco are currently linked by an uninterrupted ribbon of steel no less than three

thousand, seven hundred and eighty-six miles long. Between Omaha and the Pacific, the railroad passes through a country where American Indians and wild beasts still roam — a vast expanse of territory that the Mormon people began to colonize around 1845, after they had been driven from Illinois.

In those days, under the most favorable of circumstances, it took six months to travel from New York to San Francisco. Now, it takes seven days.

It was in 1862 that, despite the opposition of the representatives of the southern states, who naturally sought a more southern route, the path of the railroad was drawn between the forty-first and forty-second parallel. President Lincoln himself, who is now so greatly missed, established the head of the new line at the city of Omaha in the state of Nebraska. Construction began immediately, and was carried out with that typically American vigor, which is neither administrative nor bureaucratic. The rapidity of the execution would not detract in any way from the quality of the completed railroad. In the prairie, the railroad advanced at a rate of a mile and a half per day. A locomotive, running on rails laid down the day before, brought up the next day's rails, and rolled along them as quickly as they could be laid.

The Pacific Railroad is joined by several branch lines along

its route, in the states of Iowa, Kansas, Colorado, and Oregon. On leaving Omaha, it follows the left bank of the Platte River to the mouth of its northern branch, then turns to follow the southern branch, then crosses the territory of Laramie and the Wahsatch Mountains, then skirts around the Great Salt Lake, arrives in Salt Lake City, the Mormon Capital. From there, it enters the Tooele Valley, crosses the American Desert, the Cedar and Humboldt mountains, the Humboldt River, and the Sierra Nevada mountains, and descends via Sacramento all the way to the Pacific, without exceeding, along the whole of the line, a gradient of one hundred and twelve feet per mile — even in the crossing of the Rocky Mountains.

This was the long artery of steel along which the trains passed in seven days, and which would permit the honorable Phileas Fogg — if all went well — to sail, on the 11th, at New York, aboard the steamer for Liverpool.

The carriage occupied by Phileas Fogg was a sort of long omnibus resting on two trucks of four wheels each, which were capable of pivoting to accommodate tighter curves along the railway line. Inside, there were no compartments: two rows of seats, one on each side, were arranged perpendicularly to the axis of the carriage, and between them passed an aisle leading to the bathrooms and other amenities, which featured in every carriage.

All the carriages along the length of the train were connected one to another by gangways, and passengers could therefore circulate freely, accessing the saloon carriage, the observation carriage, the restaurant carriage, and the café carriage. The only thing missing seemed to be a theater carriage – but this too will no doubt be added in due course.

Passing constantly from carriage to carriage were vendors of books and periodicals, hawking their wares, and vendors of food, drink, and cigars, who were rarely short of customers.

The travelers had left the station of Oakland at six o'clock in the evening. Night had already fallen – a dark, cold night, with a low sky whose heavy clouds appeared to promise an imminent snowfall. The train was not running at a very high speed. Taking into account its various stops, it advanced at no more than twenty miles per hour – a speed which, nevertheless, would enable it to cross the United States according to schedule.

There was little conversation in the carriage, and it was clear that the passengers must soon succumb to sleep. Passepartout found himself seated next to the police detective, but did not address him. Recent events had cast a notable chill over their relationship: none of the former familiarity, none of the former sympathy. Fix had not changed anything in his manner – but Passepartout, on the contrary, maintained an air of strictest

reserve, and was ready on the slightest suspicion to throttle his former friend.

One hour after their departure, the snow began to fall: a fine snow that, luckily, would in no way slow the train's progress. Through the windows, all that could be seen was a vast expanse of white, against which the steam from the locomotive unfurled in grayish billows.

At eight o'clock, a 'steward' entered the carriage and announced to the passengers that it was now time to go to bed. This carriage was a 'sleeping car' which, in just a few minutes, could be transformed into a dormitory. The backs of the seats were folded away, carefully stowed bunks were ingeniously deployed, makeshift cabins were fitted out in a matter of seconds, and each traveler soon had at his disposal a comfortable bed which was screened from view by thick curtains. The sheets were white, the pillows deep and downy. There was nothing more to do but lie down and sleep – which is precisely what each of them did, just as if they had found themselves in a comfortable cabin on board a steamship – while the train continued to run at full steam across the state of California.

The terrain in the part of the country which stretches between San Francisco and Sacramento is fairly flat. This portion of the railroad, known as the Central Pacific Railroad,

took Sacramento as its starting point, and made its way east to
meet the line coming from Omaha. From San Francisco to the
Californian capital, the line ran directly to the northeast along
the American River, which flows into the Bay of San Pablo.
The hundred and twenty miles between these two major cities
were covered in the course of six hours, and towards midnight,
while they were still deep in their first sleep, the travelers passed
through Sacramento. They saw nothing of that considerable
city, which is the seat of the legislature of the state of California:
neither its handsome quays, nor its broad streets, nor its
splendid hotels, nor its squares, nor its churches.

On leaving Sacramento, and having passed through the
stations of Junction, Roclin, Auburn and Colfax, the train
entered the range of the Sierra Nevadas. It was seven o'clock in
the morning when they passed through the station of Cisco.
One hour later, the dormitory had transformed back into an
ordinary carriage, and through the windows the passengers could
gaze upon the picturesque vistas of that mountainous country.
The railway obeyed the capricious topography of the Sierras —
now clinging to the side of the mountain, now suspended over
a precipice, evading sharp angles with its audacious curves, and
careering into narrow defiles which seemed to offer no way out.
The locomotive, shining like a reliquary, with its great headlamp

casting a fierce glare, its silvery bell glittering, its 'cowcatcher' extending like a spur, mingled its whistling and bellowing with the booming of the torrents and cascades, as its smoke billowed among the black and glossy branches of the fir trees.

There were few tunnels, or none at all, nor were there bridges along the way. The railroad climbed along the flanks of the mountains – never seeking, in a straight line, the shortest path between two points, or violating any laws of nature.

At around nine o'clock, the train entered the state of Nevada by way of Carson Valley, still following a northeasterly course. At noon, it left Reno, where the travelers had had twenty minutes in which to lunch.

From this point, the railroad, running alongside the Humboldt River, followed its course northwards for several miles. Then it swerved to the east, and continued in tandem with the watercourse until it reached, in the eastern extremity of the state of Nevada, the Humboldt Range, which was its source.

After they had dined, Mr. Fogg, Mrs. Aouda and their companions returned to their places in the carriage. Phileas Fogg, the young woman, Fix and Passepartout, seated comfortably, watched the varied landscape pass before their eyes: vast prairies, mountains finely profiled against the horizon, 'creeks' with their foamy, rushing waters. From time to time, a great herd of

bison, massing in the distance, came into view, like a moveable dam. Those numberless armies of ruminants often present an insurmountable obstacle to the passage of trains. Thousands of these animals have been known to march, in massed ranks, across the tracks. The locomotive is then forced to stop and simply wait – sometimes for several hours – until they clear the way once more.

And in fact, that is precisely what happened on this occasion. At around three o'clock in the afternoon, a herd of ten to twelve thousand head blocked the railroad. The engine, having reduced its speed, tried to push its way through the flank of that vast column, but it was forced to stop before the impenetrable throng.

The ruminants – incorrectly called 'buffalos' by the Americans – walked past at their unhurried pace, occasionally emitting formidable bellows. They were larger than European bulls, with short legs and a short tail, and prominent withers forming a muscular hump, horns widely spaced at their base, and a head, neck and shoulders covered by a thick mane of long hair. There was no point in trying to stop this migration. When the bison have set out in one direction, no force can check or modify their course. Theirs is a torrent of living flesh, which no dyke could possibly contain.

The engine, having reduced its speed, tried to push its way through the flank of that vast column, but it was forced to stop before the impenetrable throng.

The passengers, scattered along the gangways, observed this curious spectacle. But the one person who should have suffered most from this delay, Phileas Fogg, had remained in his seat, where he waited philosophically for the time when it would please the buffalos to clear the way for him. Passepartout, on the other hand, was furious at the obstruction caused by this agglomeration of animals. He was seized with a desire to discharge his arsenal of revolvers at the beasts.

"What a country!" he cried, "Where a bunch of cows can stop the trains, and continue their procession without the least sign of hurry, as though they weren't blocking traffic! *Parbleu*! I'd like to know if Mr. Fogg had planned for this setback in his itinerary! And we've got an engineer who doesn't dare drive his locomotive through a bunch of obstructive livestock!"

It is true that the engineer had not attempted to drive through the obstruction – and in this he acted prudently. The first buffalos struck by the locomotive's cowcatcher would undoubtedly have been crushed – but however powerful it might be, the engine would soon have been stopped, a derailment would inevitably have followed, and the train would have been left in severe distress. The best solution therefore was to wait patiently, and hope to make up the time lost afterwards by increasing the train's speed.

The procession of bison lasted three long hours, and it was dusk before the way was clear once again. As the last ranks of the herd crossed the rails, the first were disappearing over the horizon in the south.

It was therefore eight o'clock when the train crossed the passes of the Humboldt Range, and half past nine when it entered the territory of Utah, the region surrounding the Great Salt Lake, that curious country of the Mormons.

CHAPTER XXVII

IN WHICH PASSEPARTOUT ATTENDS, AT A SPEED OF TWENTY MILES AN HOUR, A LECTURE ON MORMON HISTORY

During the night of the 5th to the 6th of December, the train ran towards the southeast for a stretch of some fifty miles. Then it continued to the northeast for about the same distance, as it approached the Great Salt Lake.

At around nine o'clock in the morning, Passepartout stepped out to take the air on the gangways. The weather was cold, and the sky gray, but it was no longer snowing. The sun's disk, magnified by the clouds, resembled an enormous gold coin, and Passepartout was busy calculating its value in pounds sterling, when he was distracted from this useful work by the arrival of a

rather strange character.

This personage, who had boarded the train at the station in Elko, was a tall man with dark brown hair, with a black mustache, black stockings, a black silk hat, a black vest, black trousers, a white tie, and leather gloves. One might mistake him for a reverend. He was making his way from one end of the train to the other and, on the door of every carriage, he was posting a hand-written announcement.

Passepartout drew nearer and read on one of these notices that the honorable 'elder' William Hitch, a Mormon missionary, taking the opportunity offered by his presence on board the train no. 48, would deliver, between eleven o'clock and noon, in carriage no. 117, a lecture on Mormonism – and that he invited all those gentlemen interested in learning about the mysteries of the religion of the 'Latter-day Saints' to attend.

"Certainly, I'll attend," said Passepartout, who knew virtually nothing about Mormonism apart from its practice of polygamy, which forms the basis of Mormon society.

News of this attraction spread rapidly through the train, which carried roughly one hundred passengers. Of that number, thirty at most were enticed by the lecture, and at eleven o'clock they assembled on the benches of carriage no. 117. Passepartout could be found among the faithful in the very front row. Neither

his master nor Fix had bothered to attend.

At the appointed time, the elder William Hitch stood and, with a trace of irritation in his voice, as if he had already been contradicted, he began to speak.

"I, for one, can affirm that Joe Smith is a martyr, that his brother Hyrum is a martyr, and that the persecution of the prophets by the government of the Union will also make a martyr of Brigham Young! Who would dare to say any different?"

No one made so bold as to argue with the missionary, whose fervor contrasted with his naturally calm physiognomy. His anger could no doubt be explained by the fact that Mormonism was then being subjected to severe trials. And, indeed, the government of the United States had lately succeeded – not without some effort – in curtailing those fanatical independents. Having imprisoned Brigham Young on charges of rebellion and polygamy, it had taken control of Utah, and had subjected the territory to the laws of the Union. Ever since, the disciples of the prophet had redoubled their efforts and were resisting with words, if not yet by action, the authority of Congress.

As we can see, the elder William Hitch had even taken his proselytizing onto the railways.

And so, punctuating his discourse with the dramatic rise and fall of his voice and with fervent gestures, he related the history of Mormonism from Biblical times: how, in Israel, a Mormon prophet of Joseph's tribe published the annals of the new religion, and passed them down to his son Moroni. How, many centuries later, a translation of this precious book, written in Egyptian hieroglyphs, was made by Joseph Smith Jr., farmer in the State of Vermont, who revealed himself to be a mystical prophet in 1825. Finally, he related how a celestial messenger appeared to him in a luminous wood and transmitted to him the annals of the Lord.

At this, several listeners who had little interest in the missionary's historical narrative exited the carriage, but William Hitch, continuing, told how Smith Jr., being reunited with his father, his two brothers and a few disciples, founded the religion of the Latter-day Saints – a religion which, taking root not only in America, but in England, in Scandinavia, and in Germany, numbers among its adherents both artisans and numerous individuals practicing in the liberal professions. He described how a colony was founded in Ohio, how a temple was raised at a cost of two hundred thousand dollars, and a city built in Kirkland, and how Smith became an enterprising financier, and received from a simple mummy showman a papyrus scroll

containing a narrative written in the very hands of Abraham and other famous Egyptians.

The lecture proving rather long, the ranks of listeners thinned even further, and the audience now consisted of just some twenty people.

But the elder, unfazed by these desertions, related in detail how Joe Smith had gone bankrupt in 1837, how his ruined shareholders had covered him in tar and rolled him in feathers, how he had turned up a few years later, more honorable and honored than ever, in Independence, Missouri, where he was the leader of a thriving community of no less than three thousand disciples, and how, since he was nevertheless pursued by the hatred of the gentiles, he was forced to flee into the Far West.

Ten listeners remained in the carriage, and among them was the honest Passepartout, who listened attentively. So it was that he came to learn how, following lengthy persecutions, Smith ended up in Illinois and founded, in 1839, on the banks of the Mississippi, Nauvoo the Beautiful, whose population swelled to twenty-five thousand souls. And, further, he learned how Smith became the city's mayor, presiding judge, and general-in-chief, how, in 1843, he announced his candidacy for the Presidency of the United States, and how, at last, lured into an ambush in

Carthage, he was thrown into prison and assassinated by a gang of masked men.

By now, Passepartout was the only listener remaining in the carriage – and the elder, staring him in the face, mesmerising him with his words, reminded him that, two years after Smith's assassination, his successor, the inspired prophet, Brigham Young, leaving Nauvoo behind, came to settle on the edge of the Salt Lake, and that there, in that admirable territory, in the midst of that fertile country, on the route employed by the emigrants who crossed Utah to reach California, the new colony, thanks to the polygamous principles of Mormonism, grew to enormous proportions.

"And that is why," added William Hitch, "that is why the envy of Congress is turned against us! Why the soldiers of the Union have sullied the earth of Utah! Why our leader, the prophet Brigham Young, has been imprisoned in contempt of all justice! Will we give in to this aggression? Never! Driven from Vermont, driven from Illinois, driven from Ohio, driven from Missouri, driven from Utah, we will find once more some independent territory where we will raise our tent... And you, my faithful friend," the elder said, fixing his solitary listener with his wrathful gaze, "will you raise yours beneath the shadow of our banner?"

"No," Passepartout replied bravely, as he fled in turn, leaving the fanatical preacher alone in the desert.

During the whole of this lecture, the train had steamed rapidly on, and by half past noon, it had reached the northwestern point of the Great Salt Lake. From there one could take in the vast, open expanse of that inland sea, which also bears the name the Dead Sea, and into which flows an American Jordan River. It is a handsome lake, framed by wild, rocky crags with broad bases, crusted over with white salt, a superb sheet of water that once covered a much more considerable area – but over time its banks, rising little by little, have reduced its surface by increasing its depth.

The Salt Lake, some seventy miles long and thirty-five miles wide, is situated at three thousand and eight hundred feet above sea level. It is quite different from the Lake Asphaltites, or Dead Sea, whose elevation is twelve hundred feet below sea level. It is decidedly salty, and its waters contain, in solution, a quarter of their weight in solid matter. Its water has a specific gravity of 1,170, whereas that of distilled water is 1,000. Fish are unable to survive here. Those washed into the lake by the Jordan, the Weber and other creeks, soon perish, but it is not true, as is sometimes claimed, that the density of the waters is such that a man cannot dive into them.

Around the lake, the countryside was admirably cultivated, for the Mormons are skilled at working the land. Had the travelers passed in six months' time, they would have seen ranches and corrals for domesticated animals, fields of wheat, maize, and sorghum, luxuriant prairies, everywhere hedges of wild rosebushes, clumps of acacias and euphorbias – but at that moment the ground was disappearing beneath a thin layer of snow, which powdered lightly down.

At two o'clock, the travelers disembarked at the station of Ogden. Since the train would not continue on before six o'clock, Mr. Fogg, Mrs. Aouda and their two companions had time to visit the City of the Saints by the small branch line ending at the station. Two hours were sufficient for a visit to that absolutely American city, which was built according to the pattern for all the cities of the Union: a vast chess board with long, cold lines, imbued with 'the lugubrious melancholy of right angles', as the poet Victor Hugo puts it. The founder of the City of the Saints could not escape that need for symmetry which distinguishes the Anglo-Saxons. In this singular country, where the men certainly do not measure up to their institutions, all is framed in right angles – the cities, the houses, and even the follies.

At three o'clock, therefore, the travelers were strolling along the streets of the city, built between the banks of the Jordan and

the first undulations of the Wahsatch Mountains. They saw few churches, if any, but there were other monuments: the home of the prophet, the courthouse and the arsenal – and further, the houses built of bluish bricks, featuring verandahs and galleries, and surrounded by gardens bordered with acacias, palms and carob trees. A wall of clay and pebbles, erected in 1853, encircled the city. On the principal thoroughfare, where the market is held, there stood a few hotels adorned with flags, including the Salt Lake House.

Mr. Fogg and his companions did not find the city to be densely populated. The streets were practically deserted – except for the quarter near the Temple, which they reached only after passing through several neighborhoods encircled by palisades. Women were relatively numerous – a fact which can be explained by the singular composition of Mormon households. Yet it must not be thought that all Mormons are polygamous. All are free to choose, but it should be said that it is the female citizens of Utah who are particularly eager to be wed, for, according to the tenets of the local faith, the Mormon heaven does not admit single persons of the feminine sex to its blessings. These poor creatures appeared neither happy nor at ease. Some – the more wealthy among them, no doubt – wore a simple dress of black silk, hanging loosely at the waist, beneath

a bonnet or a strictly modest shawl. The others were only dressed in calico.

As for Passepartout, he could not regard these Mormon women, who were severally responsible for the happiness of a single Mormon man, without a certain dread. In his estimation, it was the husband whom he pitied the most. It seemed to him a terrible ordeal to have to shepherd so many ladies at once through the vicissitudes of life, and to conduct them like a flock of sheep all the way to the Mormon paradise, with the prospect of rejoining them there for all eternity in the company of the glorious Smith, whose presence would crown the joys of that region of delights. Indeed, he felt no calling to the Mormon faith, and he feared – or perhaps he deceived himself – that the women of Great Salt Lake City cast worrying glances his way.

Luckily for him, his visit to the City of the Saints would soon be over. At a few minutes to four o'clock, the travelers found themselves back at the station, and they took their places once more in their carriages.

The train whistle emitted a sharp blast – but just as the locomotive's wheels, spinning upon the rails, began to impart some speed to the train, an urgent cry rang out: "Stop! Stop!"

Once underway, a train cannot easily be stopped. The gentleman making these cries was evidently a tardy Mormon.

He was racing breathlessly after them. Luckily for him, the station had neither gates nor barriers. He threw himself onto the track, leapt onto the step of the final carriage, and fell, exhausted, on one of the seats inside.

Passepartout, who had followed with some excitement the course of this gymnastic exercise, came over to contemplate the stranger, and it interested him greatly to discover that this panting citizen of Utah had taken flight in such an original manner as a result of a domestic dispute.

When the Mormon had caught his breath, Passepartout ventured to ask him politely how many wives he had to himself – and, to be sure, given the hasty manner in which he had decamped, Passepartout imagined that the figure was no less than twenty.

"One, sir!" replied the Mormon, raising his hands to the heavens, "one, and that was enough!"

CHAPTER XXVIII

IN WHICH PASSEPARTOUT IS UNABLE TO MAKE PEOPLE LISTEN TO REASON

The train, leaving behind the Great Salt Lake and Ogden station, ran northwards for an hour, to the Weber River. It had now traveled roughly nine hundred miles since San Francisco. At this point, the train turned eastward again to cross the rugged chain of the Wahsatch mountains. It is in this part of the territory, extending between these mountains and the Rocky Mountains proper, that the American engineers faced their most serious difficulties. In fact, over this stretch of the railway, the expenditure of the Union government rose to forty-eight thousand dollars per mile, whereas it was just sixteen thousand

dollars on the plains. But as was said before, the engineers avoided any offense to Nature, choosing instead to surmount her obstacles with cunning and to skirt around any difficulties. Over the whole length of the railroad just a single tunnel, fourteen hundred feet long, was cut to reach the great basin.

It was at the Great Salt Lake that the track had, before now, reached its highest elevation. Since then, its profile had made an elongated curve, descending towards Bitter Creek Valley, to rise again to the watershed which divides the waters between the Atlantic and the Pacific. There were many creeks, or 'rios', to be found in this mountainous region. Trains were forced to cross, by way of culverts, the Muddy, the Green, and others.

Passepartout was growing more impatient as they drew steadily closer to their objective. But Fix, too, wished that they had already left behind this difficult country. He was wary of delays, he feared the possibility of accidents, and was in more of a hurry than even Phileas Fogg to set foot again on English soil.

At ten o'clock in the evening, the train stopped at the station in Fort Bridger, then departed again immediately. Twenty miles further, it entered the state of Wyoming – formerly Dakota – following the whole of Bitter Creek Valley, from which flow some of the waters that form the hydrographical system of the Colorado River.

The next day, the 7th of December, the train stopped for a quarter of an hour at the station in Green River. There had been an abundant fall of snow overnight, but it was mingled with rain and had partially melted, and would not hinder the train's progress. Yet this poor weather was a source of constant worry to Passepartout, for the accumulation of snow, if it were to clog the wheels of the carriages, would certainly compromise their journey.

"Really," he said, "what an idea it was to set out on this tour in the winter! Why couldn't my master have waited for finer weather to improve his chances?"

But while the honest fellow was worrying about clouds in the sky and the falling temperature, Mrs. Aouda had fallen prey to sharper fears, which stemmed from quite another source.

Indeed, several passengers had stepped down from their carriages, and were strolling along the platform of the Green River station while they waited for the departure of the train. And, gazing through the window, the young woman recognized among them Colonel Stamp W. Proctor – the American who had treated Phileas Fogg so coarsely during the political rally in San Francisco. Wishing not to be seen, Mrs. Aouda drew abruptly back from the glass.

This circumstance made a vivid impression on the young

Wishing not to be seen, Mrs. Aouda drew abruptly back from the glass.

woman. She had become attached to that man who, however coldly, showed her every day the evidence of his absolute devotion. Perhaps she did not comprehend the depth of that sentiment which her rescuer inspired in her – that sentiment which she still considered no more than gratitude – but, without her knowing, it had become something more than that. And so, when she recognized the boorish personage from whom, sooner or later, Mr. Fogg intended to demand satisfaction for his conduct, her heart sank. It was evidently no more than bad luck that had placed Colonel Proctor on that very train, but here he was – and she must, at all cost, prevent Phileas Fogg from catching sight of his adversary.

When the train had set off once more, Mrs. Aouda waited until Mr. Fogg was momentarily napping, and informed Fix and Passepartout of the situation.

"That fellow Proctor is on the train!" cried Fix. "Well, rest assured, madam, that before he can face Mr. Fogg, he'll have to deal with me! After all, it seems to me that I am the one who received the gravest insult in this affair!"

"And what's more," added Passepartout, "I'll take care of him, colonel or no colonel."

"Mr. Fix," said Mrs. Aouda, "Mr. Fogg would never permit anyone to take vengeance on his behalf. He is a gentleman,

and he has stated that he will go so far as to return to America in order to find this offender. If, therefore, he spots Colonel Proctor, we will not be able to prevent a meeting, which might have the most deplorable results. And so he must not see him."

"You are right, madam," replied Fix, "a meeting between them could ruin everything. Victor or vanquished, Mr. Fogg would inevitably be delayed, and…"

"And," finished Passepartout, "that would win the wager for the gentlemen of the Reform Club. We will reach New York in four days. So – if my master doesn't leave his carriage for the next four days, we have some chance of keeping him from coming face to face with that cursed American, the devil take him! And we can certainly find a way to stop…"

The conversation was suddenly suspended. Mr. Fogg had woken, and was gazing at the landscape through the snow-speckled windows. But later – and without being overheard by his master or by Mrs. Aouda – Passepartout spoke to the police detective.

"Would you really fight the colonel for him?"

"I will do anything to bring him back to Europe alive!" replied Fix quietly, in a tone of implacable determination.

Passepartout felt a kind of chill run down his spine, but his faith in the integrity of his master remained unshaken.

And now – was there some way of keeping Mr. Fogg in that carriage and preventing any possible encounter between him and the colonel? It shouldn't be too difficult, given the gentleman's sedentary and incurious nature. In any case, the police detective thought he had found the solution, for, a few moments later, he said to Phileas Fogg, "Do you not find, sir, that the hours we spend on board a train are often long and slow?"

"Indeed," replied the gentleman, "but they pass."

"I think," continued the detective, "that you were in the habit of playing whist when you were traveling by sea?"

"Yes," replied Phileas Fogg, "but here it would be difficult. I have with me neither cards nor partners."

"Ah! Cards can easily be purchased. All manner of things are for sale on American trains. As for partners – if, by any chance, madam…?"

"Certainly, sir," replied the young woman brightly, "I know the game. It is part of every English education."

"And I," continued Fix, "I like to think that I play the game rather well. So between the three of us and a dummy…"

"As you like, sir," replied Phileas Fogg, who was delighted to take up his favorite game again – even on the railroad.

Passepartout was sent off to find the steward, and he soon returned with two full decks of cards, scorecards, markers,

and a folding table covered with a cloth. Nothing more was required. The game began. Mrs. Aouda had a perfectly sufficient knowledge of whist, and she even received a few compliments from the stern Phileas Fogg. As for the detective, he was quite simply a player of the first order, and a worthy opponent for the gentleman.

"Now," said Passepartout to himself, "we've got him! He won't be going anywhere!"

At eleven o'clock in the morning, the train had reached the watershed between the two oceans. This was Bridger Pass, at an elevation of seven thousand, five hundred and twenty-four English feet above sea level – one of the highest points along the route traced by the railway through the Rocky Mountains. In another two hundred miles, more or less, the travelers would find themselves at last on those broad plains which extend all the way to the Atlantic, and which nature had so perfectly adapted to the construction of a railroad.

On the slope of the Atlantic basin the first rios were already forming: headwaters and tributaries of the North Platte River. The whole of the horizon to the north and to the east was covered by that immense, semi-circular curtain formed by the northern portion of the Rocky Mountains, which was dominated by Laramie Peak. Between this broad arc and the iron rails there

stretched vast, well-watered plains. On the right-hand side of the railroad rose the lower spurs of the mountain chain that curves southwards to the sources of the Arkansas River, one of the major tributaries of the Missouri.

At half past noon, for the space of an instant, the travelers spied Fort Halleck, which commands this stretch of country. In a few more hours, the crossing of the Rocky Mountains would be completed. They could now hope that no accident would mark the passage of the train through this hazardous region. The snow had stopped falling. The weather was turning cold and dry. Large birds, startled by the locomotive, flew off into the distance. Upon the plain, no wildcats, bears, or wolves were to be seen. Around them lay the desert, in its naked immensity.

After a rather comfortable lunch, served in their own carriage, Mr. Fogg and his partners had returned to their interminable whist, when they heard a series of violent blasts from the whistle. The train stopped.

Passepartout stuck his head out of the door, but saw nothing that might have caused such a delay. There was no station in sight.

Mrs. Aouda and Fix worried for a moment that Mr. Fogg might be thinking of stepping out onto the track. But the gentleman merely said to his servant, "Do go to see what it is."

Passepartout sprang from the carriage. Some forty passengers had already left their seats, and among them was Colonel Stamp W. Proctor.

The train had stopped before a signal – a red light indicating the track ahead was closed. The engineer and the conductor, having stepped down, were in heated conversation with a signalman, whom the station chief at Medicine Bow, the next station, had sent to meet the train. Some of the passengers had approached, and were taking part in the discussion – including the aforementioned Colonel Proctor, with his loud voice and imperious gestures.

Passepartout, having joined the group, heard the signalman saying, "No! There's no way for you to cross! The Medicine Bow bridge is unstable, and it wouldn't bear the weight of the train."

The bridge in question was a suspension bridge which lay across some rapids at a mile's distance from where the train had stopped. According to the signalman, it was on the point of collapse, several of its cables had already snapped, and they could not risk crossing it. So the signalman was in no way exaggerating when he stated that they could go no further. What's more, given the habitual insouciance of the Americans, one may say that, when they start behaving prudently, it would be madness not to follow suit.

Passepartout, not daring to bring this news to his master, listened with clenched teeth, still as a statue.

"Here, now!" cried Colonel Proctor, "I don't suppose that we're meant to stay here and put down roots in the snow!"

"Colonel," replied the conductor, "we've telegraphed the station in Omaha to ask for a train, but it probably won't arrive at Medicine Bow for another six hours."

"Six hours!" exclaimed Passepartout.

"That's right," replied the conductor. "And anyway, that's about the time it will take us to reach the station on foot."

"On foot!" cried the passengers together.

"But how far is the station, then?" one asked the conductor.

"It's twelve miles off, on the other side of the river."

"Twelve miles in the snow!" scoffed Stamp W. Proctor.

The colonel let loose a flood of curses, blaming the company and blaming the conductor, and the furious Passepartout was sorely tempted to join him. Here was, at last, a material obstacle that all his master's banknotes could not remove.

Indeed, their disappointment was shared by all the passengers who, not to mention the delay, were facing a fifteen-mile trek across the snow-covered plain. And so there soon arose a commotion of mingled exclamations and vociferations which would certainly have drawn the attention of Phileas Fogg, if that

gentleman had not been quite absorbed in his game.

Meanwhile, Passepartout was faced with the necessity of informing his master and he was making his way to the carriage, shaking his head, when the train's engineer – a true Yankee by the name of Forster – spoke up.

"Gentlemen, there may be a way of getting across."

"Across the bridge?" asked one passenger.

"Across the bridge."

"With our train?" asked the colonel.

"With our train."

Passepartout had stopped, and was drinking in the words of the engineer.

"But the bridge is about to fall!" repeated the conductor.

"Doesn't matter," replied Forster. "I believe that, if we can get the train up to full speed, we'll have some chance of making it across."

"*Diable!*" said Passepartout.

However, many of the passengers were immediately taken with this proposal. It was particularly pleasing to Colonel Proctor. That hothead found the project perfectly feasible. He even told how some engineers had explored the idea of crossing rivers without the use of bridges, by employing trains of a rigid construction and launching them at high speeds, etc. And so, in

the end, all those party to the discussion were brought around to the train engineer's point of view.

"We have a fifty percent chance of making it across," said one.

"Sixty," said another.

"Eighty...! Ninety percent!"

Passepartout was flabbergasted. He was prepared to try almost anything to get across Medicine Creek, but this particular scheme seemed to him rather too 'American'.

"Besides," he thought, "there's a much simpler solution to this problem, and it hasn't even occurred to these people...!"

"Sir," he said to one of the passengers, "the method proposed by the engineer seems to me somewhat hazardous, but..."

"Eighty percent chance!" replied the passenger, turning his back on the Frenchman.

"Yes, I'm sure," continued Passepartout, addressing another gentleman, "but simply consider..."

"Nothing to consider – there's no point," replied the American, shrugging his shoulders, "since the engineer is certain we'll make it across!"

"Certainly," agreed Passepartout, "we'll make it across, but it would perhaps be more prudent..."

"What! Prudent!" cried Colonel Proctor, whom this word, overheard by chance, caused to jump. "At full speed, we said!

Don't you understand? At full speed!"

"I know... I understand..." repeated Passepartout, whom no one would permit to finish a sentence, "but it would be, if not more prudent, since you find the word offensive, at the very least perfectly reasonable..."

"Who? What? How? What is that fellow going on about with this 'reasonable' business...?" the passengers cried from all sides.

The poor fellow no longer knew which way to turn to make himself heard.

"Are you afraid?" Colonel Proctor asked him.

"Me, afraid!" exclaimed Passepartout. "Then so be it! I'll show these people that a Frenchman can be just as American as they are."

"All aboard! All aboard!" shouted the train conductor.

"Yes, all aboard," repeated Passepartout, "all aboard! And right away! But you won't stop me thinking that it would have been perfectly reasonable to send us passengers safely across the bridge on foot, and to send the train afterwards!"

But no one heard this sensible proposition, nor would they have admitted that it was sound.

The passengers had returned to their carriages. Passepartout took his seat again, without saying a word about what had taken place. The players were wholly engrossed in their whist.

The locomotive whistled vigorously. The engineer, throwing the engine into reverse, backed the train along the rails for a distance of about a mile – like a hurdler giving himself a run up to a long leap.

Then, with a second blast of the whistle, they began to move ahead again. The train accelerated, and they soon reached a terrifying speed. The noise of the locomotive was a long, frenzied whinny. The pistons hammered at twenty strokes per second, and the axles of the wheels smoked inside their axle boxes. They felt as though the entire train, running at a speed of a hundred miles an hour, was hardly bearing on the rails. Their speed was devouring their weight.

And they crossed! It was over in a flash. They didn't even see the bridge. The long convoy jumped, one might say, from one bank to the other, and the engineer was unable to stop his locomotive until they had been carried five miles past the station.

But no sooner had the train crossed the river than the bridge, utterly destroyed, tumbled with a resounding crash into the rapids of Medicine Bow.

No sooner had the train crossed the river than the bridge, utterly destroyed,
tumbled with a resounding crash into the rapids of Medicine Bow.

CHAPTER XXIX

IN WHICH CERTAIN INCIDENTS ARE RELATED WHICH ARE ONLY TO BE MET WITH ON THE RAILROADS OF THE UNION

That very evening, the train continued along its route without any further obstacles. It passed by Fort Saunders, traversed the Cheyenne Pass and arrived at the Evans Pass. In this place, the railroad reached the highest point on its route, of eight thousand and ninety-one feet above sea level. The passengers now had only to descend to the Atlantic along those limitless plains so perfectly graded by nature herself.

Here, a branch of the grand trunk led away to Denver City, the capital city of Colorado. That territory is rich in gold and silver mines, and more than fifty thousand inhabitants have

already made it their home.

At that point, over the course of three days and three nights, they had traveled thirteen hundred and eighty-two miles from San Francisco. Phileas Fogg was therefore still perfectly on schedule.

During the night, they passed Camp Walbach on their left. Lodge Pole Creek ran parallel to the railway, following the straight line of the border between the states of Wyoming and Colorado. At eleven o'clock, they entered Nebraska, passing near Sedgwick, and stopping briefly at Julesburg, situated on the southern branch of the Platte River.

It was there that the Union Pacific Railroad, under the direction of the head engineer Major General G. M. Dodge, was inaugurated on the 23rd of October, 1867. There stopped the two powerful locomotives, drawing nine carriages full of guests, among whose number was the vice-president, Mr. Thomas C. Durant. There, the cheers rang out, there, the Sioux and the Pawnee staged the spectacle of an Indian skirmish, there, the fireworks burst in the air, and there, finally, was published, by means of a portable printing press, the first issue of the Railway Pioneer newspaper. Such was the inaugural celebration of that great railroad, instrument of progress and of civilization, thrown across the desert and destined to link together all the towns

and cities which had not yet been built. The whistle of the locomotive, more powerful than the mythical Amphion's lyre, would soon bring them surging out of the American soil.

At eight o'clock in the morning, they were leaving behind them Fort MacPherson, situated three hundred and fifty-seven miles from Omaha. The railroad was following the capricious sinuosities of the southern branch of the Platte River, keeping to its left bank. At nine o'clock, they reached the large city of North Platte, built between the two arms of that great waterway, which curve around it to join together into a single artery – a considerable tributary whose waters mingle with those of the Missouri, some distance north of Omaha.

They had crossed the hundred and first meridian.

Mr. Fogg and his partners had resumed their game. None of them complained about the length of the journey – not even the dummy. Fix had begun by winning a few guineas, which he was now in the process of losing, but he was no less passionate a player than was Mr. Fogg. In the course of the morning, chance had singularly favored this gentleman. Trumps and honors poured through his hands. At one point, having concocted an audacious stroke, he was about to play spades when, from behind his seat, a voice was heard.

"Me, I would play diamonds," the voice said.

Mr. Fogg, Mrs. Aouda, and Fix raised their heads. Colonel Proctor stood beside them.

Stamp W. Proctor and Phileas Fogg recognized one another at once.

"Ah! So you're the one, Mister Englishman," cried the colonel, "you're the one who means to play spades!"

"And who plays it," replied Phileas Fogg coldly, laying down a ten of that suit.

"Well, I prefer that it be diamonds," rejoined Colonel Proctor with irritation in his voice – and he moved as if to seize the card Fogg had played, adding, "You understand nothing about this game."

"Perhaps I will prove more skilled at another," said Phileas Fogg, standing.

"It's up to you if you want to try one, you son of John Bull!" replied that coarse personage.

Mrs. Aouda turned pale, and her blood ran cold. She had seized Phileas Fogg's arm, but he gently removed her hand. Passepartout was ready to spring upon the American, who regarded his adversary with the most insulting expression. But Fix had risen and, stepping over to Colonel Proctor, he told him, "You forget that it is me whom you should answer to, sir – me, whom you have not only insulted, but struck!"

"Mr. Fix," said Mr. Fogg, "I beg your pardon, but this affair concerns me alone. By claiming that I was wrong to play spades, the colonel had insulted me yet again, and he will offer me satisfaction."

"Any time you like, and any place you like," replied the American, "and with whatever weapon you like!"

Mrs. Aouda tried in vain to restrain Mr. Fogg. The detective tried fruitlessly to reclaim the quarrel as his own. Passepartout wanted to throw the colonel out of the door, but a sign from his master stopped him short. Phileas Fogg left the carriage, and the American followed him onto the gangway.

"Sir," said Mr. Fogg to his adversary, "I am in a great hurry to return to Europe, and a delay of any kind would seriously prejudice my affairs."

"And so? What's that to me?" replied Colonel Proctor.

"Sir," continued Mr. Fogg politely, "following our encounter in San Francisco, I had formed the project of returning to America in order to find you, as soon as I had seen to the affairs which now demand my presence in England."

"Really!"

"Will you agree to meet with me again in six months' time?"

"Why not in six years?"

"I say six months," replied Mr. Fogg, "and I will be punctual

to our rendezvous."

"This is just an evasion!" cried Stamp W. Proctor. "It's right away or never."

"Very well," replied Mr. Fogg. "You are going to New York?"

"No."

"To Chicago?"

"No."

"To Omaha?"

"What difference is it to you? Do you know Plum Creek?"

"No," replied Mr. Fogg.

"It's the next station. The train will be there in an hour. It'll stop at the station for ten minutes. In ten minutes' time, we can easily exchange a few pistol shots."

"Very well," replied Mr. Fogg. "I'll stop at Plum Creek."

"And I'd go so far as to say that you'll stay there!" added the American with unparalleled insolence.

"Who knows, sir?" replied Mr. Fogg, and he returned to his carriage, as cold as ever.

There, the gentleman began by reassuring Mrs. Aouda that braggarts are never to be feared. Then he asked Fix to serve as a second in the encounter that was to take place. Fix could not refuse. Then, Phileas Fogg calmly continued his interrupted game, playing spades with perfect equanimity.

At eleven o'clock, the locomotive's whistle announced their approach to Plum Creek station. Mr. Fogg rose and, followed by Fix, stepped out onto the gangway. Passepartout accompanied them, carrying a pair of revolvers. Mrs. Aouda had remained in the carriage, pale as a corpse.

At that moment, the door to the next carriage opened, and Colonel Proctor also appeared on the gangway, followed by his second, a Yankee cut from the same cloth. But just as the two adversaries were preparing to step onto the track, the conductor ran up to them.

"No one is to get off, gentlemen!"

"And why not?" asked the colonel.

"We are twenty minutes behind schedule, and the train isn't stopping."

"But I need to fight with this gentleman."

"I do apologize," the employee replied, "but we are departing immediately. There's the bell!"

The bell was indeed ringing, and soon the train was underway again.

"I really am very sorry, gentlemen," the conductor said. "In different circumstances, I would have been able to oblige you. But, after all, since you haven't had time to fight here, who is stopping you from fighting en route?"

"It might not be to this gentleman's liking!" said Colonel Proctor in a mocking tone.

"It suits me perfectly," replied Phileas Fogg.

"Well now, we really are in America!" thought Passepartout, "and this train conductor is the very best of gentlemen!"

And with this, he followed his master.

The two combatants and their seconds, preceded by the conductor, made their way, by passing from one carriage to the next, to the rear of the train. The last carriage was occupied by no more than ten passengers. The conductor asked them if they would mind ceding their carriage, for a few moments, to two gentlemen who wished to settle an affair of honor.

But of course! The passengers were only too happy to oblige the two gentlemen, and they withdrew to the gangways.

This carriage, roughly fifty feet long, was very well suited to the circumstance. The two opponents could walk towards one another between the two rows of seats and pistol one another at their leisure. Never was a duel easier to organize. Mr. Fogg and Colonel Proctor, each equipped with two six-shot revolvers, entered the carriage. Their seconds, remaining outside, shut them in. At the first blast of the locomotive's whistle, they were to begin firing... Then, after a lapse of two minutes, whatever remained of the two gentlemen would be removed

from the carriage.

Indeed, nothing simpler. It was in fact so simple, that Fix and Passepartout could feel their hearts beating as if they were about to burst.

All were therefore awaiting the agreed-upon blast of the whistle when, suddenly, there rang out a series of savage cries. They were accompanied by loud shots – but these did not come from the duellists' carriage. The shots echoed, on the contrary, along the full length of the train. Cries of terror were heard from inside the forward carriages.

Colonel Proctor and Mr. Fogg, revolvers in their hands, promptly exited the carriage and rushed forward, where the cries and shots were ringing out even more loudly. They had understood that the train was being attacked by a party of Sioux.

It was not the first time that these daring American Indians had made such an attempt. They had, more than once, succeeded in stopping entire trains. According to their habit, while the train continued at speed, nearly a hundred natives had launched themselves onto the steps of the carriages, and were clambering aboard in the manner of a clown mounting a horse at full gallop.

The Sioux were armed with guns. These were the source of the shots to which the passengers – almost all of whom carried revolvers – were now returning fire. Almost immediately, the

Indians had rushed towards the engine. The fireman and the train engineer were rendered nearly unconscious with blows from Sioux war clubs. A Sioux chieftain, seeking to stop the train, but not knowing how to operate the regulator, had fully opened the steam valve instead of closing it, and the locomotive, out of control, was now hurtling on at a terrifying speed.

In the meantime, the Sioux had overrun the carriages. They scrambled like furious monkeys across the upholstery, they beat in the doors, they grappled hand to hand with the passengers. The baggage car had been forced open and pillaged, and packages were hurled out onto the tracks. Cries and shots rang out continuously.

And yet, the passengers put up a courageous defense. Some carriages were barricaded, and were besieged like veritable moving fortresses, carried along at a speed of a hundred miles an hour.

From the first moments of the attack, Mrs. Aouda had behaved most courageously. A revolver in her hand, she defended herself heroically, firing through the broken windows whenever some savage came within range. Some twenty Sioux, mortally wounded, had fallen upon the track, and the wheels of the carriages crushed like worms all those who slipped from the gangways onto the rails.

Several passengers, grievously wounded by Sioux bullets or war-clubs, lay motionless upon the seats.

And yet they had to find some way to end the struggle. The battle had been raging for ten minutes, and if the train didn't stop, it would certainly result in victory for the Sioux. Indeed, the station at Fort Kearney was now less than two miles away. This was an American military post – but once they passed beyond it, between Fort Kearney and the following station, the Sioux would win control of the train.

The conductor was fighting by Mr. Fogg's side when a bullet knocked him down. As he fell, the man cried, "We are lost, if the train doesn't stop within five minutes!"

"It will stop!" said Phileas Fogg, preparing to rush from the carriage.

"Stay here, monsieur!" Passepartout called to him, "I'll see to it!"

Before Phileas Fogg could act to stop him, the brave fellow opened a door and, unseen by the Indians, managed to slip beneath the carriage. And so, while the fighting continued unabated, and bullets crossed above his head, rediscovering the agility and flexibility of his days as an acrobat, working his way along beneath the carriages, dangling from the chains, clinging to the brake levers and the girders of the trucks, crawling from

one carriage to the next with remarkable dexterity, Passepartout reached the front of the train. He hadn't been spotted; he could not have been.

There, suspended by one hand between the baggage car and the tender, he used his free hand to uncouple the safety chains. But due to the traction operating on the carriages, he could never have succeeded in freeing the drawbar, if a sudden juddering in the engine had not sprung it loose – and the train, now detached, fell behind little by little, while the locomotive surged ahead at even greater speed.

Carried on by its momentum, the train continued along the rails for several minutes more, but the brakes were applied from within the carriages, and the convoy stopped at last no more than a hundred steps from Kearney station.

There, the soldiers garrisoned at the fort, drawn by the sound of gunfire, rushed to the scene. The Sioux had not awaited their arrival and, before the train had fully stopped, the entire war party had decamped.

But when the passengers counted themselves upon the platform at the station, they found that several people were still missing, and among them was numbered the courageous Frenchman whose devotion had saved them all.

CHAPTER XXX

IN WHICH PHILEAS FOGG SIMPLY DOES HIS DUTY

Three passengers, including Passepartout, had disappeared. Had they been killed in the skirmish? Were they prisoners of the Sioux? It wasn't yet possible to say.

There were many wounded, but it appeared that no passenger had been mortally injured. One of the most grievously wounded was Colonel Proctor, who had fought bravely, and who had been knocked down by a bullet to the groin. He was carried into the station with several other passengers whose condition required immediate medical attention.

Mrs. Aouda was safe. Phileas Fogg, despite being in the thick

of the fight, had not received a scratch. Fix was wounded, lightly, in the arm. But Passepartout was missing, and tears were running down the young woman's cheeks.

Meanwhile, all the passengers had left the train. The wheels of the carriages were stained with blood. Shapeless scraps of flesh dangled from the hubs and spokes. The white plains were marred with streaks of red stretching back into the distance along the line. The last of the Indians were disappearing into the south, towards Republican River.

Mr. Fogg, his arms crossed, stood motionless. He had an important decision to make. Mrs. Aouda, standing beside him, regarded him without breathing a word... And he understood what was in her eyes. If his servant had indeed been taken prisoner, was it not his duty to risk all and tear him from the Indians' grasp...?

"I will find him, dead or alive," he told Mrs. Aouda simply.

"Oh! Mr. ... Mr. Fogg!" cried the young woman, grasping her companion's hands, which were wet with her falling tears.

"Alive," added Mr. Fogg, "if we don't lose a minute!"

In taking this course of action, Phileas Fogg was sacrificing everything. He had just pronounced his own ruin. A delay of a single day would cause him to miss the steamer in New York.

His wager was irredeemably lost. But faced with the thought, "It is my duty!" he had not hesitated.

The captain in command of Fort Kearney had arrived. His soldiers – roughly one hundred men – had set up a defensive perimeter in case the Sioux tried to mount a direct attack on the station.

"Sir," said Mr. Fogg to the captain, "three passengers have disappeared."

"Killed?" asked the captain.

"Killed or taken prisoner," replied Phileas Fogg. "That is an uncertainty which must be resolved. Is it your intention to pursue the Sioux?"

"That is a grave matter, sir," said the captain. "The Indians may flee well beyond Arkansas! I cannot abandon the fort which I command."

"Sir," continued Mr. Fogg, "three men's lives are at stake."

"Undoubtedly... but can I risk the lives of fifty to save just three?"

"I don't know if you can, sir, but you ought to."

"Sir," retorted the captain, "no one here need tell me where my duty lies."

"So be it," said Phileas Fogg coldly. "I will go alone!"

"You, sir!" cried Fix, who had drawn near, "go alone in pursuit of the Indians!"

"Would you ask me to let that poor fellow perish, to whom all those present owe their lives? I will go."

"Well then, no – you will not go alone!" cried the captain, moved despite himself. "No! You have a gallant heart! … Give me thirty volunteers," he added, turning towards his troops.

The entire company stepped forward as one. The captain had only to choose as he pleased among those brave men. Thirty soldiers were selected, as well as an old sergeant to lead them.

"Thank you, Captain," said Mr. Fogg.

"Will you permit me to accompany you?" Fix asked the gentleman.

"You must do as you please, sir," replied Phileas Fogg. "But you would be doing me a service if you were to stay with Mrs. Aouda. If something should happen to me…"

The police detective turned suddenly pale. Could he part from the man whom he had followed so closely, for so long, and with such persistence? Could he simply let him vanish across that deserted plain? For a moment Fix looked hard at the gentleman – and, despite all his suspicions, despite the struggle that raged within him, he dropped his eyes before that calm and open gaze.

"I'll stay," he said.

A few moments later, Mr. Fogg had pressed the hand of the young woman. Then, having left his precious overnight bag in her care, he departed with the sergeant and his little troop.

But before they left, he had told the soldiers, "My friends, you will have a thousand pounds if we can save the prisoners!"

It was then a few minutes past noon.

Mrs. Aouda had retired to a room in the station, and there, alone, she waited, thinking of Phileas Fogg, of that great and simple generosity, of that tranquil courage. Mr. Fogg had sacrificed his fortune, and now he was risking his life – and all without hesitation or debate, and out of a deep sense of duty. In her eyes, Phileas Fogg was a hero.

Detective Fix did not share this view, and he could hardly contain his agitation. He paced feverishly up and down the platform. He had been momentarily enthralled – but now he was himself again. Now that Fogg had departed, he saw the folly of letting him go. What! Had he really agreed to let out of his sight the man he had just followed around the world? His true nature reasserted itself, and he blamed himself, he leveled accusations, he raged at himself like a police commissioner berating an officer guilty of the most basic naivety.

"I've bungled it!" he thought, "His servant will have told him

who I am. He has gone, and he won't come back! Where can I hope to find him again? How could I let him beguile me – me, Fix, when I've got a warrant for his arrest in my very pocket! Really, I'm no better than a dumb beast."

This is what ran through the police detective's mind as the hours crawled slowly by. He didn't know what to do. At times, he was gripped by the urge to reveal everything to Mrs. Aouda. But he knew how the young woman would receive such accusations. What course of action could he take? He was tempted to start off across the wide white plains in pursuit of Mr. Fogg. It still seemed possible that he might be found. The footprints of the rescue party were still visible in the snow…! But a fresh layer of snow was falling rapidly, and soon the trail had vanished.

Fix was truly disheartened. He felt an overwhelming desire to give up his chase. And in fact, an opportunity to leave Fort Kearney station and continue his journey – until now so rich in disappointments – presently arose.

At around two o'clock, as the snow fell in heavy flakes, a series of long whistles was heard coming from the east. An immense shadow, preceded by a fierce glare, advanced slowly, considerably magnified by the mist, which gave it a fantastical aspect.

Strangely enough, no train was expected from the east. The aid requested by telegraph could not have arrived so quickly, and the train running from Omaha to San Francisco was meant to pass only the following day. But the mystery was soon cleared up.

This locomotive, proceeding slowly and emitting long blasts of its whistle, was that which, having been detached from the rest of the train, had continued on its way at such a terrible speed, carrying off the unconscious engineer and fireman. It had run along the rails for several miles, and then its fires had died down due to a lack of fuel. The steam pressure had fallen, and one hour later, having slowed little by little, the engine had stopped at twenty miles' distance from Fort Kearney.

Neither the engineer nor the fireman had perished and, after a rather lengthy period, they both regained consciousness.

The engine was still and cold. When he found himself in the wilderness, on board the locomotive but with the carriages nowhere to be seen, the engineer understood what had happened. He could not guess how the locomotive had been detached from the train, but he was certain that the train, left behind, would be in distress.

The engineer had no doubts about what he had to do. Continuing in the direction of Omaha was prudent. Returning

towards the train, which the Indians might still be pillaging, was dangerous… But no matter! Lumps of coal and wood were crammed into the furnace, the fires roared back to life, the steam pressure rose again, and towards two o'clock the locomotive was running backwards towards Fort Kearney station. This was the source of the whistles in the mist.

It was a great satisfaction to the passengers to see the locomotive rejoining the front of the train. They would be able to continue the voyage that had been so tragically interrupted.

As the locomotive arrived, Mrs. Aouda had stepped out of the station and addressed the conductor.

"Are you planning to leave?" she asked him.

"Immediately, madam."

"But the prisoners… our unfortunate companions…"

"I cannot delay the service," replied the conductor. "We are already three hours behind schedule."

"And when will the next train from San Francisco pass?"

"Tomorrow evening, madam."

"Tomorrow evening! But that will be too late. You must wait…"

"It's impossible," insisted the conductor. "If you wish to depart, you must board now."

"I'll stay," replied the young woman.

Fix had overheard this conversation. Just a few moments before, when he had lacked any means of locomotion, he had been determined to leave Fort Kearney, and now that the train was there, ready to depart, and he had only to take his place in the carriage, an irresistible force held him back. The station platform burned his feet, but he couldn't lift them from the ground. The struggle began again inside of him. Rage at his own failure rose in his throat. He wanted to fight on until the end.

Meanwhile, the passengers and some of the wounded – Colonel Proctor among them, whose condition remained serious – had boarded the carriages. The locomotive's overheated boiler hummed audibly, and steam was billowing from the safety valves. The engineer blew his whistle, the train began to move, and it soon disappeared, mingling its white smoke with the swirling snow.

Detective Fix had stayed behind.

Several hours passed. The weather was very bad, and it was bitingly cold. Fix, seated on a bench in the station, remained perfectly still. One might have thought that he was asleep. Mrs. Aouda, despite the blowing snow, was constantly leaving the room that had been placed at her disposal. She would walk to the end of the platform, trying to see through the blizzard, wanting to pierce the mist that drew the horizon in around her,

The engineer blew his whistle, the train began to move, and it soon disappeared, mingling its white smoke with the swirling snow.

listening for any sound from beyond the curtain of snow. But there was nothing. So she would return, numb with cold, only to venture forth again a few moments later – and always fruitlessly.

By evening, the little detachment still had not returned. Where were they at that moment? Had they caught up with the Indians? Had a fight taken place, or were those soldiers, lost in the mist, wandering at random? The captain at Fort Kearney was deeply worried, although he tried not to show any sign of concern.

Night came, and with it the snow fell less heavily, but the cold intensified. Even the most intrepid gaze could not have regarded that black immensity without some sense of horror. Absolute silence reigned upon the plain. Neither the flight of a bird, nor the passage of a beast, troubled that infinite calm.

Throughout the night, her mind filled with sinister presentiments, her heart filled with anxiety, Mrs. Aouda paced at the threshold of the prairie. Her imagination carried her far across it, and showed her a thousand different dangers. It would be impossible to express what she suffered during those long hours.

Fix remained where he was, motionless – but he, too, was unable to sleep. At one point, a man had approached him, and

had even spoken to him, but the detective sent him away, having responded to his words with a sign of refusal.

So the night passed. At dawn, the half-extinguished disk of the sun rose above a misty horizon. One could see for a distance of about two miles across the plains. Phileas Fogg and the detachment of soldiers had headed south... To the south there was nothing to be seen. It was seven o'clock in the morning.

The captain, now extremely concerned, was weighing his options. Should he send a second detachment to the aid of the first? Could he sacrifice more men, with so little chance of saving those who had been sacrificed before them? But he did not hesitate for long – and summoning one of his lieutenants with a gesture, he was giving the order to pursue a reconnaissance towards the south, when the sound of shots broke out in the distance. Was it a signal? The soldiers rushed out of the fort, and half a mile away they spotted a small troop returning in good order.

Mr. Fogg marched at the head of the column, and with him were Passepartout and the two other passengers, who had been freed from the grasp of the Sioux.

At a distance of ten miles south of Fort Kearney, a skirmish had taken place. A few moments before the detachment had caught up to them, Passepartout and his two companions had

begun the fight against their captors, and the Frenchman had knocked out three Indians with his bare fists, when his master and the soldiers had rushed to their aid.

All of them – the rescued and the rescuers – were welcomed with shouts of joy, and Phileas Fogg distributed to the soldiers the bounty which he had promised them, as Passepartout muttered to himself, not without good reason, "To be sure, one must admit that I have cost my master a great deal of money...!"

Fix, without letting slip a single word, stared at Mr. Fogg, and it would have been difficult to analyze the feelings that were battling within him. As for Mrs. Aouda, she had taken the gentleman's hand, and she pressed it tightly in hers, unable to say anything more!

No sooner had they arrived, however, than Passepartout had gone to search for the train at the station. He had expected to find it there, ready to race on towards Omaha, and he was still hoping that they could make up the time they had lost.

"The train, the train!" he cried.

"Gone," replied Fix.

"And the next train – when will it come by?" asked Phileas Fogg.

"Not before this evening."

"Ah!" replied the impassive gentleman.

CHAPTER XXXI

IN WHICH DETECTIVE FIX TAKES
PHILEAS FOGG'S INTERESTS VERY SERIOUSLY

Phileas Fogg was now running twenty hours behind schedule. Passepartout, the involuntary cause of that delay, was in despair. He had undoubtedly ruined his master!

At that moment, the detective approached Mr. Fogg and, gazing keenly into his face, he said, "Sir, let us be perfectly frank. You are really in a serious hurry?"

"Very serious," replied Phileas Fogg.

"I must insist," pressed Fix. "Is it essential to your interests that you be in New York on the 11th, before nine o'clock in the evening, the departure time of the steamer for Liverpool?"

"Absolutely essential."

"And if your journey had not been interrupted by this Indian attack, you would have arrived in New York on the morning of the 11th?"

"Yes, with an advance of twelve hours on the departure of the steamship."

"Good. So you are twenty hours behind your original schedule. The difference between twenty and twelve is eight. So you need to make up a delay of eight hours in order to catch the steamer. Do you wish to try it?"

"On foot?" asked Mr. Fogg.

"No, by sledge," replied Fix. "A sledge with sails. A man suggested this mode of transportation to me."

This was the man who had spoken to the police detective during the night, and whose offer Fix had refused.

Phileas Fogg did not respond, but Fix pointed out the man in question, who was walking before the station, and the gentleman approached him. A moment later, Phileas Fogg and the American, by the name of Mudge, together entered a hut situated next to the fort.

Within, Mr. Fogg examined a rather singular vehicle: a sort of chassis, built upon two long beams, raised slightly at the front, like the runners of a sledge, and upon which five or six people

could be accommodated. A very tall mast rose from the chassis. It was positioned a third of the way from the front, and rigged to bear a vast spread of sail. From the mast, which was firmly secured by metallic shrouds, there stretched an iron stay which served to hoist an immense jib. Behind, a sort of rudder or steering oar made it possible to steer the contraption.

It was, clearly, a sledge rigged as a sloop. During the winter, on the icy plain, when the trains have been stopped by heavy snow, these vehicles make extremely swift crossings from one station to the next. They are, in fact, prodigiously canvassed – bearing far more sail than does a racing cutter, which runs the risk of capsizing – and, with a following wind, they glide along the surface of the prairies with a speed equal, if not superior, to that of an express train.

In a few moments, a deal had been struck between Mr. Fogg and the master of that terrestrial craft. The wind was favorable. It was blowing strongly from the west. The snow had hardened, and Mudge was certain he could convey Mr. Fogg to the station at Omaha in just a few hours. There, the gentleman would find an abundance of trains serving various routes to Chicago and New York. It was possible that the lost time could be made up. There was no reason, therefore, not to embark on this adventure.

Mr. Fogg, not wanting to expose Mrs. Aouda to the sufferings

of a crossing in the open air, in freezing temperatures which their speed would render even more intolerable, proposed to her that she remain under the care of Passepartout in the station at Fort Kearney. The honest fellow would be charged with accompanying the young woman to Europe along a more favorable route, and under more acceptable conditions.

Mrs. Aouda refused to be separated from Mr. Fogg, and her decision made Passepartout very happy indeed – for nothing on earth would bring him to part from his master now, knowing that Fix would accompany him.

As for the police detective, it would be difficult to describe his thoughts at that very moment. Had his suspicions been shaken by the return of Phileas Fogg, or did he still believe him to be an extremely canny rogue – who, having completed his journey around the world, would think himself perfectly safe in England? Perhaps Fix's opinion of Phileas Fogg had indeed evolved. But he was no less determined to do his duty and, more impatient even than his companions, to hasten as much as possible their return to England.

At eight o'clock, the sledge was ready to depart. The travelers – one might be tempted to call them passengers – took their places and wrapped themselves tightly in their traveling rugs. The two immense sails were raised and, with the impetus of the

wind, the craft ran across the hardened snow at a speed of forty miles per hour.

The distance which separates Fort Kearney from Omaha is, in a straight line – as the bee flies, according to the American expression – no more than two hundred miles. If the wind held, they could cover that distance in the space of five hours. If no incident occurred along the route, the sledge should reach Omaha by one o'clock in the afternoon.

What a crossing! The travelers, huddled closely together, could not speak. The cold was intensified by their speed, and would have frozen the words in their mouths. The sledge glided across the surface of the plain as lightly as a boat on the water, and without the rocking of the swells. Whenever a gust of wind came sweeping past, it seemed as if the sledge was lifted from the earth by its sails – vast wings of a breathtaking span.

Mudge, at the helm, maintained a steady course and, with a stroke of the steering oar, would correct the occasional swerving of the craft. Every foot of canvas was drawing. The jib had been set so that it was no longer sheltered by the mainsail, and the craft was running wing and wing before the wind. A topmast had been hoisted, and a topsail was raised to add its propulsive force to that of the other sails. Although it could not be precisely calculated, the speed of the sledge was certainly no less than

forty miles per hour.

"If nothing breaks," Mudge remarked, "we'll make it!"

And this would indeed be in Mudge's best interests – for Mr. Fogg, true to form, had offered him a hefty reward should they reach their destination in time.

The prairie, across which the sailing sledge cut a long, straight line, was flat and featureless as a sea. One might have taken it for an immense, frozen lake. The railroad that served this part of the territory ran, from the southwest to the northwest, via Grand Island, Columbus – one of Nebraska's major cities – Schuyler, Fremont, and then Omaha. The entirety of its route followed the right bank of the Platte River. The sledge took a shorter and more direct route, cutting straight across the long arc described by the railroad. Mudge had no fear of being stopped by the Platte River, at the little crook it makes before Fremont, since its waters were now frozen. The way was entirely clear of obstacles, and Phileas Fogg had therefore only two circumstances to fear: that the craft sustain some damage, or that a change take place in the force or direction of the wind.

But the wind did not fall. On the contrary, it blew so hard it curved the mast, which the iron shrouds nevertheless held securely in place. These metal wires, which resembled the strings of an instrument, resonated as if a bow were drawn across them.

The sledge sailed on, surrounded by their plaintive harmony, which had a most particular intensity.

"These strings are sounding the fifth and the octave," commented Mr. Fogg. And these were the only words he spoke for the entirety of the crossing.

Mrs. Aouda, carefully enveloped in furs and traveling rugs, was protected, insofar as was possible, from the effects of the cold. As for Passepartout, whose face was as red as the disk of the sun setting in mist, he happily breathed in that biting air. Drawing on his natural store of imperturbable confidence, he had begun to hope again. Instead of arriving in New York in the morning, they would arrive in the evening – but they still had a chance of reaching the city before the departure of the steamer for Liverpool.

For a moment, Passepartout had even felt a strong desire to shake the hand of his ally, Fix. He wouldn't soon forget that it was the detective himself who had procured the sailing sledge and, thereby, offered them their only chance of reaching Omaha in time. However, as if by some vague premonition, he maintained his habitual reserve. In any case, one thing that Passepartout would never forget was the sacrifice that Mr. Fogg had made, without hesitation, to tear him from the grasp of the Sioux. For this, Mr. Fogg had risked his fortune and his life. No!

His servant would not forget it!

While each of the travelers sat absorbed in their individual reveries, the sledge flew on across the immense carpet of snow. It may have traversed several streams – tributaries or branches of the Little Butte Creek – but these crossings went unnoticed. The fields and watercourses had disappeared beneath a uniform whiteness. The plain was absolutely deserted. Stretching from the Union Pacific railroad to the branch line that connects Fort Kearney with St. Joseph, it formed a kind of vast and uninhabited island. Not a single village, not a single station, not even a fort.

From time to time, they saw some single, looming tree pass like a flash, its white skeleton twisting in the wind. Sometimes, groups of wild birds would startle up into flight. And sometimes, packs of prairie wolves – gaunt, famished, driven by ferocious need – raced silently after the speeding sledge. Then, Passepartout, a revolver in his hand, would ready himself to fire on those that drew nearest. If any accident should then have stopped the sledge, the travelers, attacked by those fierce carnivores, would have run the greatest of risks. But the sledge held its course, and gradually outstripped its pursuers, and soon enough the whole pack was left howling in the distance.

Sometimes, packs of prairie wolves – gaunt, famished, driven by
ferocious need – raced silently after the speeding sledge.

At noon, Mudge recognized by certain signs that they were crossing the frozen surface of the Platte River. He said nothing, but he was already certain that, in another twenty miles, he would have reached the station in Omaha.

And indeed, before an hour had passed, the able skipper abandoned the helm, swiftly loosed the halyards, and furled the sails. Driven on by its irresistible momentum, the sledge covered another half a mile with bare poles. At last, it came to a stop, and Mudge, indicating a group of snow-covered roofs, declared: "We've arrived."

Arrived! Arrived, indeed, at that station which, by way of numerous trains, is in daily contact with the eastern United States. Passepartout and Fix had jumped down and were shaking the stiffness from their limbs. They helped Mr. Fogg and the young woman to descend from the sledge. Phileas Fogg generously settled his accounts with Mudge, who also received a warm and friendly handshake from Passepartout, and then the travelers hurried towards the station of Omaha.

It is here, in Nebraska's largest city, that the Pacific railroad properly speaking – the railroad connecting the basin of the Mississippi with the great ocean – comes to an end. To travel on from Omaha to Chicago, one takes the Chicago and Rock Island Railroad, which heads directly east, stopping at fifty stations.

A train was ready to depart. Phileas Fogg and his companions had just time enough to spring into a carriage. They had seen nothing at all of Omaha, but Passepartout had to admit to himself that there was no cause for regret, and that visiting was hardly the point.

The train passed very quickly through the state of Iowa, by way of Council Bluffs, Des Moines, and Iowa City. During the night, it crossed the Mississippi at Davenport, and it entered Illinois via Rock Island. The next day, the 10th, at four o'clock in the evening, the train arrived in Chicago, already built up from the ruins of its Great Fire, and seated more proudly than ever on the edge of its fair Lake Michigan.

Nine hundred miles separate Chicago from New York. There were plenty of trains to be had at Chicago. Mr. Fogg transferred immediately from one to another. The sparkling locomotive of the Pittsburgh Fort Wayne Chicago Railroad set off at top speed, as if it had understood that the honorable gentleman had no time to lose. It went like a flash, crossing Indiana, Ohio, Pennsylvania, and New Jersey, passing through cities with ancient names, some of which already had both streets and tramways, but were still lacking houses. Finally, the Hudson came into view and, on the 11th of December, at a quarter past eleven in the evening, the train stopped in the

station, on the right bank of the river, directly before the pier serving the steamers of the Cunard Line, also known as the British and North American Royal Mail Steam Packet Co.

The *China*, bound for Liverpool, had set sail forty-five minutes earlier!

CHAPTER XXXII

IN WHICH PHILEAS FOGG ENGAGES IN A
DIRECT STRUGGLE WITH BAD FORTUNE

With its departure, the *China* seemed to have taken away Phileas Fogg's last hope of success.

Indeed, none of the other steamers providing a direct service between America and Europe – neither the French transatlantic vessels, nor the ships of the White Star Line, nor the steamers of the Imman Line, nor those of the Hamburg Line, nor any others – could be of any use to the gentleman in his project.

As it happened, the *Pereire*, of the French Transatlantic Company – whose admirable vessels equal in speed and surpass in comfort all those of other lines, without any exception –

would not depart before the 14th of December. And, like
the vessels of the Hamburg Line, it would not sail directly
to Liverpool or to London, but to Le Havre. The additional
crossing from Le Havre to Southampton, adding further delay to
Phileas Fogg's journey, would have nullified his final efforts.

It is true that one of the Imman Line steamers, the *City of
Paris*, was scheduled to set sail the following day, but it would be
of little assistance. It belonged to a class of ships devoted to the
transportation of emigrants. Their engines are underpowered,
and as they rely more on sail than on steam, their speed is
mediocre at best. It would take the *City of Paris* more time to
cross from New York to England than was left for Mr. Fogg to
win his wager.

All of this was made perfectly clear to the gentleman when he
consulted his Bradshaw's Guide, which set out, day by day, an
account of the movements of every transoceanic vessel.

Passepartout was utterly devastated. It killed him to have
missed the steamer by forty-five minutes. It was his fault –
his alone – who, instead of assisting his master, had again
and again strewn obstacles in his path! And when he called
to mind the incidents of their journey, when he reckoned all
the sums of money that had been lost purely on his account,
when he considered that this enormous wager, combined with

the considerable costs of their now-fruitless journey, would completely ruin Mr. Fogg, he heaped curses upon his own head.

Mr. Fogg, however, made no reproach and, leaving the transatlantic pier, he spoke no more than a few words.

"We will consider our options tomorrow. Come."

Mr. Fogg, Mrs. Aouda, Fix, and Passepartout crossed the Hudson in the Jersey City ferry boat, and stepped into a hackney cab which transported them to the Saint Nicholas Hotel, on Broadway. Rooms were placed at their disposal, and the night passed quickly for Phileas Fogg, whose sleep was undisturbed, and very slowly for Mrs. Aouda and her companions, whose anxiety would not permit them any rest.

The following day was the 12th of December. Between seven o'clock on the 12th and eight forty-five on the evening of the 21st, there remained nine days, thirteen hours, and forty-five minutes. If Phileas Fogg had departed the night before on board the *China*, one of the Cunard Line's fastest steamers, he would easily have arrived in Liverpool, and then in London, within the allotted time!

Mr. Fogg left the hotel, alone, having told his servant to wait for him and to inform Mrs. Aouda that she should be ready to depart at any moment. He made his way to the banks of the Hudson, where he searched carefully, amongst the vessels

moored at the quay or anchored in the river, for one that might be ready to sail. A number of ships were flying their departure signal, and were preparing to take to the sea on the morning tide, for in that vast and admirable port of New York, no day goes by without some hundred vessels setting out for every corner of the globe, but the majority of them were sailing ships, and consequently of no use to Phileas Fogg.

It was beginning to look as though the gentleman must fail in his final attempt, when at last he spotted, laying at anchor before the Battery, at no more than a cable's length, a trading vessel with elegant lines and a screw propeller, whose funnel, emitting great puffs of smoke, indicated that she was preparing to put out to sea.

Phileas Fogg hailed a shoreboat, stepped in, and with a few strokes of the oars, he found himself at the side-ladder of the *Henrietta*, a steamer with an iron hull and wooden superstructure. The captain of the *Henrietta* was on board. Phileas Fogg climbed onto the deck and asked to see him. He appeared forthwith.

The captain was a man of some fifty years – the very type of the grizzled sea-wolf – and he appeared disinclined to be helpful. He had large eyes, a coppery complexion, red hair, and a thick neck. In no way did he resemble a man of the world.

"The captain?" inquired Mr. Fogg.

"That's me."

"I am Phileas Fogg, of London."

"And I'm Andrew Speedy, of Cardiff, New York."

"You are departing...?"

"Within the hour."

"And your destination...?"

"Bordeaux."

"Your cargo?"

"Stones in the hold. No freight. I'm sailing on ballast alone."

"Do you have any passengers?"

"No passengers. Never any passengers. They make the most inconvenient cargo."

"Your ship is a swift one?"

"She can do between eleven and twelve knots. The *Henrietta*. Ask anyone."

"Would you transport me to Liverpool, myself and three other people?"

"To Liverpool? Why not to China?"

"I say Liverpool."

"No!"

"No?"

"No. I'm setting out for Bordeaux, and that's where I'll go."

"And money is no object?"

"Money is no object."

The captain spoke with a tone that would admit no reply.

"But the *Henrietta*'s owners..." Phileas Fogg insisted.

"I am the owners," replied the captain. "The vessel is mine."

"I'll charter her."

"No."

"I'll buy her."

"No."

Phileas Fogg didn't blink. And yet the situation was serious. New York wasn't like Hong Kong, nor was the captain of the *Henrietta* like the master of the *Tankadère*. Until now, the gentleman's money had always surmounted the obstacles in his path. This time, it seemed that money had failed.

And yet, he had to find some way to cross the Atlantic by boat – unless he were to cross it by balloon, which would have been quite the adventure, but was, after all, not feasible.

It seems, however, that Phileas Fogg was struck by an idea, for he said to the captain, "Well, then, would you take me to Bordeaux?"

"No, not even if you paid me two hundred dollars!"

"I'll pay you two thousand."

"Per passenger?"

"Per passenger."

"And there are four of you?"

"Four."

Captain Speedy scratched his head roughly, as if he were trying to scrape away his skin. Here were eight thousand dollars to be won, without his changing his journey in any way — and they seemed well worth his setting aside his pronounced antipathy towards all manner of passengers. In any case, passengers at two thousand dollars apiece weren't really passengers — they were precious cargo.

"I sail at nine o'clock," Captain Speedy said plainly, "and if you and yours can make it…"

"We will be on board at nine o'clock," replied Mr. Fogg no less plainly.

It was half past eight. With the unvarying calm that accompanied him in every circumstance, the gentleman went ashore, stepped into a cab, returned to the Saint Nicholas Hotel, and gathered together Mrs. Aouda, Passepartout, and even the inseparable Fix, to whom he graciously offered the passage to England.

The moment the *Henrietta* weighed anchor, all four were safely on board.

When Passepartout learned what this final crossing would

cost, he let slip an extended "Oh!" that ran through every interval of the descending chromatic scale!

As for Detective Fix, he muttered to himself that, decidedly, the Bank of England would not come out of this affair without some loss. Indeed, at their arrival, more than seven thousand pounds would have been dispensed from the overnight bag full of banknotes – that is, if Mr. Fogg didn't toss a few more handfuls overboard along the way!

CHAPTER XXXIII

IN WHICH PHILEAS FOGG PROVES HIMSELF EQUAL TO THE OCCASION

One hour later, the steamer *Henrietta* was passing the lightship that marks the mouth of the Hudson, rounding the point of Sandy Hook, and heading out on the open sea. In the course of the day, she followed the coast of Long Island, passed Fire Island, and sailed rapidly eastwards.

The following day, the 13th of December, when the sun was at its highest, a man stepped onto the bridge to take the noon sight. One would necessarily assume that this man was Captain Speedy! But not at all. It was Phileas Fogg, Esquire.

As for Captain Speedy, he was in fact locked up in his cabin,

where he produced shouts indicative of a perfectly justifiable fury which was now bordering on a paroxysm.

What had happened was very simple. Phileas Fogg wished to go to Liverpool, and the captain had refused to take him there. Phileas Fogg had instead accepted a passage to Bordeaux and, in the course of the thirty hours which he had so far spent on board, had so deftly applied his banknotes that the sailors and stokers – a somewhat shady crew, which found itself on rather poor terms with the captain – soon belonged to him. And that was why Phileas Fogg was in command instead of Captain Speedy, and why the captain was locked up in his cabin, and why, finally, the *Henrietta* was making her way towards Liverpool. What's more, it was clear from the manner in which Mr. Fogg handled the vessel, that the mysterious Englishman had once been a sailor.

It was now anyone's guess what the outcome of this adventure would be. Mrs. Aouda continued to worry, without saying a word. Fix was stunned by this latest turn of events. As for Passepartout, he found the affair quite simply delightful.

"Between eleven and twelve knots," Captain Speedy had said – and indeed the *Henrietta* easily maintained this average speed.

If – and what an if! – the sea remained calm, if the wind didn't turn into the east, if the vessel did not sustain any

As for Captain Speedy, he was in fact locked up in his cabin, where he produced shouts indicative of a perfectly justifiable fury which was now bordering on a paroxysm.

damage, and if the engine did not break down, the *Henrietta*,
in the nine days between the 12th of December and the 21st,
could cross the three thousand miles separating New York from
Liverpool. It is true that, once they arrived, the affair onboard
the *Henrietta*, combined with the affair of the Bank of England,
might still pose more of a problem to the gentleman than he
might like.

For the first few days, the cruise proceeded under excellent
conditions. The sea was not too choppy, the wind appeared
to be fixed in the northeast, the sails were set and, with her
fore- and mainsails drawing, the *Henrietta* was going like a real
transatlantic liner.

Passepartout was enchanted. This latest exploit of his master's
– whose consequences he did not wish to consider – filled him
with enthusiasm. The crew had never seen a jollier, or a more
agile fellow. He was immediately on the friendliest terms with
the sailors, and astonished them with his feats of acrobatics.
He gave them nicknames, and brought them refreshments. In
his view, they handled the ship like gentlemen, and the stokers
stoked her furnace like heroes. His good humor was infectious,
and soon spread to everyone. He had forgotten about the past,
all worries, and any dangers. He thought only of their goal,
now so close to being achieved, and he sometimes boiled with

impatience, as if he himself were fired by the furnaces of the *Henrietta*. Often, too, when the dignified fellow passed Fix on deck, he regarded him with a look that spoke volumes! But he never spoke out loud, for there remained no shred of intimacy between the two former friends.

As for Fix, it must be said that this entire situation was beyond him. The conquest of the *Henrietta*, the bribing of her crew, this fellow Fogg who handled her like a consummate mariner – all these developments left him utterly stunned. He no longer knew what to think! But, after all, a gentleman who started off by stealing fifty-five thousand pounds might very well finish by stealing a ship. And Fix, naturally, was inclined to believe that the *Henrietta*, with Fogg at the helm, would not go to Liverpool at all, but rather to some other part of the world where the thief, turned pirate, would quietly seek refuge! It must be admitted that this hypothesis was perfectly plausible, and the detective was beginning to regret very seriously his having involved himself in this affair.

As for Captain Speedy, he continued to shout in his cabin – and Passepartout, who was tasked with providing him with his meals, would do so only while taking the greatest precautions, however strong he might be. On the other hand, Mr. Fogg himself behaved as if no other captain had ever been on board.

On the 13th, they crossed the outer edge of the Grand Banks of Newfoundland. These are dangerous waters – especially in the winter, when they are plagued by frequent fogs, and violent gusts of wind. The barometer, which had begun a rapid decline the previous evening, foretold a change in the atmosphere. And indeed, the temperature fell throughout the night: the cold was even sharper, and at the same time the wind jumped into the southeast.

This was a setback. In order not to deviate from his route, Mr. Fogg was obliged to take in his sails, and to increase the steam pressure. And despite this, the vessel's speed was checked by the condition of the sea, whose long swells broke against her bow. She was pitching violently, and this movement slowed her considerably. The wind was building little by little into a hurricane, and it seemed likely that the *Henrietta* could not stand up to the force of the waves for much longer. And, if they had to run before the storm, they would be taking their chances with the unknown.

Like the sky, Passepartout's expression grew gradually stormier. For the space of two days, the honest fellow was on tenterhooks. But Phileas Fogg was an experienced seaman, who knew how to face down a storm, and he held his course, without once having to reduce steam. When the *Henrietta* was unable

to rise above the waves, she passed through them. Her deck was swept from stem to stern, but she passed through. Sometimes, when a mountain of water lifted her stern out of the depths, the ship's propeller emerged and beat the air with its furious blades – but she continued to make headway.

In the end, the wind did not blow as hard as one might have feared. It was not one of those hurricanes which pass at a speed of ninety miles per hour. It grew no worse than a moderate gale, but unfortunately, it continued to blow steadily from the south-east, and would not permit them to set any sails. And indeed, as we shall see, any such assistance to the steam-powered engine would have been most useful!

The 16th of December was the seventy-fifth day since their departure from London. Overall, the *Henrietta* was not so far behind schedule as to cause any alarm. Roughly half of the crossing was behind them, and they had passed through the most dangerous waters. In the summertime, they would have been assured of success. In winter, they remained at the mercy of the season. Passepartout would not yet declare victory. He was inwardly hopeful and, although the wind was against them, he felt at least that he could rely on steam.

Yet that very day, the engineer, having come on deck, engaged Mr. Fogg in an animated discussion.

Without knowing why – some obscure foreboding, no doubt – Passepartout suddenly felt a vague apprehension creep over him. He would have given one of his ears to listen with the other to what was being said. Still, he was able to pick up a few words – these ones, among others – spoken by his master:

"You are certain of what you say?"

"Certain, sir," replied the engineer. "Don't forget that, since our departure, we've kept all our furnaces blazing, and although we had enough coal to travel on short steam from New York to Bordeaux, we don't have enough to travel at full steam from New York to Liverpool!"

"I will consider the matter," replied Mr. Fogg.

Passepartout understood. He was seized with dread.

They were running out of coal!

"Ah! If my master can find a way out of this one," he said to himself, "then he really is a remarkable man!"

And, encountering Fix on deck, he could not resist informing him of the situation.

"So," replied the detective through clenched teeth, "you still believe that we are going to Liverpool!"

"*Parbleu!*"

"Imbecile!" replied the detective, walking off with a shrug.

Passepartout was about to reply in the strongest terms to that

insult – whose full meaning he did not, in fact, understand – but he reminded himself that the unfortunate Fix must be very disappointed, and that his self-esteem must have suffered, now that it was clear he had been on a wild goose chase around the world, and so he restrained himself.

Now, what course of action would Phileas Fogg pursue? It was difficult to imagine what, if anything, he could do. Yet the phlegmatic gentleman seemed to have come to a decision, for that very evening he summoned the engineer.

"Stoke the fires," he ordered, "and keep stoking until you have used up all of the fuel."

A few moments later, the *Henrietta*'s funnel was spewing forth torrents of smoke.

The vessel carried on at full speed – but two days later, on the 18th, the engineer reported that, as he had warned, their supply of coal would run out before nightfall.

"Do not let the fires die down," replied Mr. Fogg. "On the contrary. Keep the valves filled."

That day, at around noon, having taken a sighting and calculated the vessel's position, Phileas Fogg summoned Passepartout and gave him the order to bring up Captain Speedy. It was as if the poor fellow had been ordered to go unchain a tiger, and as he went below, he muttered, "No doubt about it,

he'll be furious!"

Indeed, a few minutes later, accompanied by shouts and curses, a bomb crashed onto the quarterdeck. That bomb was Captain Speedy, and it was clear that he was about to explode.

"Where are we?" – These were the first words that he uttered from amidst the gasps and suffocations of his rage, and certainly, if the poor man had chanced to be apoplectic, he would never have recovered himself from this attack.

"Where are we?" he repeated, his face flushed.

"Seven hundred and seventy miles from Liverpool," replied Mr. Fogg, imperturbably calm.

"Pirate!" cried Andrew Speedy.

"I have summoned you, sir..."

"Buccaneer!"

"...sir," continued Phileas Fogg, "in order to ask that you sell me your ship."

"No! By all the devils, no!"

"You see, I shall be obliged to burn her."

"Burn my ship!"

"Yes – her superstructure, at any rate, for we are out of fuel."

"Burn my ship!" cried Captain Speedy, who was barely able to get out the syllables. "A ship worth fifty thousand dollars!"

"Here are sixty thousand!" replied Phileas Fogg, offering the

captain a bundle of banknotes.

This gesture had a prodigious effect on Andrew Speedy. One cannot be American without feeling somewhat emotional at the sight of sixty thousand dollars. For a moment the captain forgot his anger, his imprisonment, and all the grievances he held against his passenger. His vessel was twenty years old. This could be the deal of a lifetime…! The bomb could no longer explode. Mr. Fogg had whipped out the fuse.

"And the iron hull will be returned to me," he said in a distinctly gentler tone of voice.

"The iron hull and the engine, sir. Are we agreed?"

"Agreed."

And Andrew Speedy, seizing the bundle of banknotes, counted them and thrust them into his pocket.

Passepartout observed this scene with a white face. As for Fix, he came close to suffering a stroke. Nearly twenty thousand pounds spent – and that fellow Fogg was even planning to relinquish the hull and the engine to the seller, which constituted nearly all of the value of the vessel! But it was true, of course, that the sum he had stolen from the bank was no less than fifty-five thousand pounds.

When Andrew Speedy had pocketed the money, Mr. Fogg addressed him.

"Sir," he said, "Don't let any of this surprise you. If I have not returned to London on the 21st of December, at eight forty-five in the evening, I stand to lose twenty thousand pounds. And since I had missed the steamer in New York, and you were refusing to convey me to Liverpool..."

"And I was right to refuse, by the fifty thousand devils in Hell," cried Andrew Speedy, "since I'm making a profit of at least forty thousand dollars."

Then, more calmly, he added, "Do you know what, Captain...?"

"Fogg."

"Captain Fogg, well, there's a bit of Yankee about you."

Having made what he thought was a compliment to his passenger, he was walking off when Phileas Fogg called him back.

"This vessel now belongs to me?"

"Certainly. From the keel to the truck of the masts, anything made of wood is yours!"

"Good. Have the interiors demolished, and use the debris to stoke the fires."

One can imagine how much dry wood was required to keep the steam at a sufficiently high pressure. That day, the poop deck, the deckhouses, the cabins, the bulkheads, the lower deck – everything went into the fire.

The next day, the 19th of December, they burned the masts, the lifeboats, and the spars. They chopped down the masts, and cut them up with axes. The crew went about their work with incredible zeal. Passepartout, chopping, cutting, sawing, accomplished the work of ten men. It was a festival of demolition.

The day after that, the 20th, the ship's rails, the bulwarks, the upperworks, and most of the deck were devoured. The *Henrietta* was no more than a stripped and naked vessel, like a pontoon.

That day, they came in sight of the coast of Ireland and the Fastnet Light.

However, by ten o'clock that night, the ship was still only passing Queenstown. Phileas Fogg had just twenty-four hours left in which to get himself to London – precisely the time it would take for the *Henrietta* to reach Liverpool, even going at full steam. And the steam was finally running out for that audacious gentleman!

"Sir," said Captain Speedy, who had begun to take an interest in this wild project, "I rather feel for you. Everything's against you! We've only made it as far as Queenstown."

"Ah!" said Mr. Fogg, "is that Queenstown, the city whose lights we can see there?"

"Yes."

"Can we enter the harbor?"

"Not for another three hours. Only at high tide."

"Let us wait," Phileas Fogg replied calmly – without betraying any sign that, through a supreme stroke of inspiration, he would try once more to overcome his contrary fortunes!

Indeed, Queenstown is a harbor on the coast of Ireland into which the transatlantic steamers coming from the United States toss, as they go by, their mail bags. The letters are transported to Dublin by express trains which are always waiting, ready to depart. From Dublin, they reach Liverpool on board steamers of phenomenal speed – thus gaining an advance of twelve hours on even the fastest vessels of the transatlantic companies.

Those twelve hours gained by the American post, Phileas Fogg intended to gain for himself. Instead of arriving in Liverpool the following evening on board the *Henrietta*, he would be there at noon and, as a result, would have time to get to London before eight forty-five in the evening.

At around one o'clock in the morning, the *Henrietta* sailed into the harbor of Queenstown on the high tide, and Phileas Fogg, having received a vigorous handshake from Captain Speedy, left him behind on the naked carcass of his vessel – which was still worth half of its price of sale!

The passengers immediately disembarked. Fix, at that

moment, was seized with a ferocious urge to arrest Mr. Fogg. And yet, he did not do so. Why not? What struggle was taking place within him? Had he changed his mind about Mr. Fogg? Had he realized his mistake at last? At any rate, Fix did not let his quarry go. With Mr. Fogg, with Mrs. Aouda, with Passepartout — who hardly gave himself time to breathe — he stepped onto the Queenstown train at one thirty in the morning, arrived in Dublin at the break of day, and promptly embarked on one of those swift steamers — real iron rockets, entirely machine-powered — which, not deigning to climb over the waves, invariably pass right through them.

At twenty minutes before noon, on the 21st of December, Phileas Fogg at last disembarked in the harbor of Liverpool. He was no more than six hours from London.

But at that very moment, Fix approached. He placed a hand on Mr. Fogg's shoulder and, displaying his warrant, said, "You are indeed Mr. Phileas Fogg?"

"Yes."

"I arrest you, in the name of the Queen!"

Mr. Phileas Fogg? I arrest you, in the name of the Queen!"

CHAPTER XXXIV

WHICH AFFORDS PHILEAS FOGG THE OPPORTUNITY OF MAKING A SUDDEN MOVEMENT

Phileas Fogg was in prison. He had been shut up in the Liverpool customs house, where he was to spend the night before his transfer to London.

At the moment of the arrest, Passepartout had tried to spring upon the detective. Several policemen held him back. Mrs. Aouda, shocked by the brutality of this new development, and unaware of the details, could not understand what had transpired. Passepartout explained the situation to her. Mr. Fogg, that honest and courageous gentleman to whom she owed her life, had been arrested as a common thief. The young woman

protested against such an allegation. Her heart overflowed with indignation, and tears streamed from her eyes when she realized there was nothing she could do, nothing she could attempt, to rescue her rescuer.

As for Fix, he had arrested the gentleman because his duty required him to make the arrest — whether the gentleman was guilty or not. The law would decide the matter.

But then Passepartout was struck by a sudden thought: the appalling thought that he was, in fact, the cause of all this misery! Indeed, why had he kept this matter from Mr. Fogg? When Fix had announced himself as a police detective, and revealed the true purpose of his mission, why had Passepartout not alerted his master? Had he been warned, Phileas Fogg would undoubtedly have offered Fix some proof of his innocence. He would have demonstrated to him the error of his accusations, and at any rate he would not have ferried half-way around the world, and at his own expense, a misguided agent whose primary aim was to arrest him the moment he set foot on the soil of the United Kingdom. As he considered all his failings, all his carelessness, the poor fellow was filled with irresistible remorse. He wept, and it was pitiful to see him. He wanted to throw himself from the quay!

He and Mrs. Aouda had remained, despite the cold, beneath

the portico of the customs house. Neither of them would consent to leave the place. They wanted to see Mr. Fogg one more time.

As for that gentleman, he was well and truly ruined – and at the very moment when his objective was within his grasp. This arrest would doom his project. Having arrived in Liverpool at eleven forty in the morning, on the 21st of December, he had until eight forty-five to present himself at the Reform Club – that is, nine hours and fifteen minutes. It should have taken him no more than six hours to reach London.

If anyone had entered the customs house at that moment, they would have found Mr. Fogg, immobile, seated on a wooden bench, imperturbable and devoid of anger. Perhaps it would be wrong to say he appeared resigned, but this latest blow had not, as far as could be seen, moved him in the slightest. Was there, building inside of him, one of those secret furies, terrible because they are contained, which only erupt at the very last moment with irresistible force? It is impossible to say. But there was Phileas Fogg: calmly waiting... for what? Had he preserved some final hope? Did he still believe he could succeed, even when the door of that prison had been shut upon him?

Whatever the case might be, Mr. Fogg had carefully placed his watch upon a table, and he was watching the hands move across

the dial. Not a word escaped his lips, but his gaze appeared
singularly fixed.

It was a terrible situation – and, for all those who could not
read that inscrutable mind, it could be summed up as follows:

If he was an honest man, Phileas Fogg was ruined.

If he was a dishonest man, he was caught.

Did he think at all of escaping? Did it occur to him to
examine whether his prison offered any practicable way out? Did
he consider flight? It is tempting to think so, for, at one point,
he took a turn about the room. But the door was solidly shut,
and the window equipped with iron bars. So he sat down again,
and he drew from his pocketbook the itinerary of his voyage.
To the line inscribed with these words:

"21st of December, Saturday, Liverpool,"

he added

"80th day, 11:40 in the morning,"

and he waited.

The customs house clock struck one o'clock, and Mr. Fogg
noted that his own watch had an advance of two minutes upon
that timepiece.

Two o'clock! If he could, at that very moment, step onto
an express train, he would still arrive in London and reach the
Reform Club before eight forty-five in the evening. His brow

furrowed slightly...

At two thirty-three, a disturbance could be heard outside – a noise of doors opening. Passepartout's voice rang out, as did that of Fix.

For a moment, Phileas Fogg's gaze brightened.

The door to his cell was opened, and he saw Mrs. Aouda, Passepartout, and Fix, who all rushed in to him.

Fix was out of breath, his hair disheveled... He could barely speak!

"Sir," he babbled, "sir – forgive me – an unfortunate resemblance – thief arrested three days ago – you – free!"

Phileas Fogg was free! He strode across to the detective. He looked him squarely in the face. Then, making the one sudden movement that he ever had or ever would make in his life, he drew back his arms and, with the precision of an automaton, he struck the poor detective with both his fists.

"Well struck!" cried Passepartout, adding, "*Parbleu*! That's what I call a proper application of English fists."

Fix, stretched out on the ground, did not speak a word. He had got no more than he deserved. Immediately, Mr. Fogg, Mrs. Aouda and Passepartout left the customs house. They sprang into a carriage and, in a few minutes, arrived at the Liverpool train station.

Phileas Fogg inquired whether there was an express ready to depart for London…

But it was twenty to three… and the express had departed thirty-five minutes earlier.

Phileas Fogg chartered a special train.

There were several high-speed locomotives ready to depart – but, due to the demands of the service, no special train could depart from the station before three o'clock.

At three o'clock, Phileas Fogg, having spoken a few words to the driver about a certain prize which might be won, was speeding towards London in the company of the young woman and his loyal servant.

He had to cross, in five and a half hours, the distance between Liverpool and London – a perfectly manageable undertaking, when the way is clear along the whole length of the route. But they met with unavoidable delays and, when the gentleman arrived at the station, every clock in London showed the time as ten to nine.

Phileas Fogg, having completed his journey around the world, was arriving five minutes behind schedule…!

He had lost.

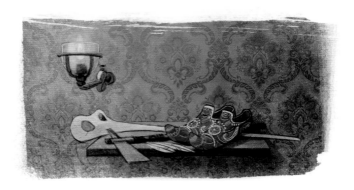

CHAPTER XXXV

IN WHICH PASSEPARTOUT DOESN'T NEED TO BE
TOLD TWICE TO OBEY HIS MASTER'S COMMAND

The following day, residents of Savile Row would have been astounded to hear that Mr. Fogg had returned to his home. Its doors and windows were tightly shut. No change could be seen on the outside of the house.

But indeed, it was so: after leaving the station, Phileas Fogg had ordered Passepartout to purchase a few provisions, and had then gone home.

The gentleman had received with his usual impassivity the blow that fell upon him. He was ruined – and all because of that clumsy police detective! After so long and so deftly managed a

campaign, after having overcome a thousand obstacles, braved a thousand dangers, and even having found time to do some good along the way, to fail at the last step due to such brutal interference, which he could not have predicted, and which he could not resist – that was terrible.

Of the considerable sum which he had brought with him at his departure, there remained only some insignificant odds and ends. His fortune consisted now of nothing more than the twenty thousand pounds deposited at Baring Brothers, and he owed those twenty thousand pounds to his colleagues at the Reform Club. Because he had had to spend so much money on his expenses along the way, winning his wager would certainly not have made Phileas Fogg any richer – and indeed, it is probable that he had not sought to enrich himself, being one of those men who wager for the sake of honor – but the loss of his wager would totally ruin him. And now, he had decided on a course of action. He knew what he would have to do.

One of the bedrooms in the house on Savile Row had been set aside for Mrs. Aouda's use. The young woman was in absolute despair. Based on certain words uttered by Mr. Fogg, she was convinced that he was contemplating some fatal act.

And indeed, it is well known to what deplorable lengths those English monomaniacs can sometimes go when they are in the

grip of an obsession. That is why Passepartout, without at all seeming to, was watching his master carefully.

But – first things first – the honest fellow had gone up to his room and had extinguished the gas burner, which had been blazing brightly for the past eighty days. He had found, in the letterbox, a bill from the gas company, and he thought it was high time he put a stop to the charges for which he was accountable.

The night passed. Mr. Fogg had gone to bed – but had he slept? As for Mrs. Aouda, she did not have a moment's rest. And Passepartout had sat awake like a guard dog at his master's door.

In the morning, Mr. Fogg sent for him and requested, in the briefest of terms, that he attend to Mrs. Aouda's breakfast. As for himself, he would be satisfied with a cup of tea and a piece of toast. If Mrs. Aouda would please excuse him, he would be unable to join her for lunch or dinner; all his time would be taken up with putting his affairs in order. In the evening, however, he would ask Mrs. Aouda's permission to speak with her for a few moments.

Passepartout, having received his orders for the day, had nothing more to do but carry them out. But he looked at his master, impassive as ever, and suddenly he could not bring himself to leave. His heart was heavy, his conscience plagued

with regrets, for he blamed himself more than ever for this irreparable disaster. Yes! If he had warned Mr. Fogg – if he had revealed the detective's plans – Mr. Fogg would certainly not have dragged Fix all the way to Liverpool, and then...

Passepartout could restrain himself no longer.

"Master! Mr. Fogg!" he cried, "Why don't you curse me? It is my fault that..."

"I blame no one," replied Phileas Fogg in the calmest of tones. "Go."

Passepartout left the room and went to find the young woman, to whom he relayed his master's intentions.

"Madame," he added, "I can do nothing myself – nothing at all! I have no influence over my master's state of mind. But you, perhaps..."

"What influence could I possibly have?" replied Mrs. Aouda. "Mr. Fogg cannot be swayed! Has he never seen that my gratitude to him is ready to overflow? Has he never read what is in my heart...? Dear friend, we must not leave him alone – not for one moment. You say that he intends to speak with me tonight?"

"Yes, madame. It must have to do with securing your situation in England."

"We shall see," replied the young woman, who remained deep

in thought.

So, for the whole of that Sunday, the house on Savile Row remained, for all appearances, uninhabited – and, for the first time since he had occupied the house, when half-past eleven rang from the clock tower at Parliament, Phileas Fogg did not depart for his club.

Why, after all, would the gentleman present himself at the Reform Club? His colleagues were no longer expecting him. Since Phileas Fogg had not appeared, the night before, in the salon of the Reform Club, before that fateful deadline of Saturday the 21st of December, at a quarter to nine, his wager had been lost. It was not even necessary for him to visit his banker to withdraw the sum of twenty thousand pounds. His adversaries had, in their possession, a check signed by him, and a brief note sent to Baring Brothers was all that was needed for the twenty thousand pounds to be transferred to their account.

Mr. Fogg had therefore no reason to go out, and he did not go out. He remained in his bedroom and put his affairs in order. Meanwhile, Passepartout ceaselessly climbed and descended the stairs of the house on Savile Row. The hours were crawling by for that poor fellow. He listened at his master's door – without, in doing so, feeling that he committed the slightest indiscretion.

He peered through the keyhole, and felt perfectly within his rights to do so. Passepartout feared that some catastrophe might strike at any moment. From time to time, he thought of Fix, but a kind of reversal had taken place in his mind. He no longer bore a grudge against the police detective. Fix, like everyone else, had been mistaken about Phileas Fogg, and, by following him, and by arresting him, he had only done his duty – whereas in contrast, Passepartout... This reflection overwhelmed him, and he felt himself to be the meanest and most miserable of all people.

When, at last, Passepartout was too unhappy to be alone, he knocked at Mrs. Aouda's door, entered her room, sat down in a corner without saying a word, and watched the young woman, who was still lost in thought.

At about half past seven in the evening, Mr. Fogg sent word to Mrs. Aouda inquiring whether she would receive him. A few moments later, he and the young woman were alone in her room.

Phileas Fogg took a chair and sat near the fireplace, facing Mrs. Aouda. No emotion could be read upon his features. The Fogg who returned was exactly the same as the Fogg who had departed – the same calm, the same impassivity.

For five minutes, he did not speak a word. Then, he lifted his gaze to Mrs. Aouda.

"Madam," he said, "will you forgive me for having brought

you to England?"

"Mr. Fogg…!" replied Mrs. Aouda, suppressing the beating of her heart.

"Please, allow me to finish," continued Mr. Fogg. "When I had the idea of taking you far away from that country, which had become so dangerous to you, I was wealthy, and I intended to place part of my fortune at your disposal. Your existence would have been one of happiness and freedom. Now, I am ruined."

"I know it, Mr. Fogg," replied the young woman, "and now, in turn, I must ask of you: Will you forgive me for having accompanied you and — who knows? — for having perhaps contributed to your ruin, because I delayed your journey?"

"Madam, you could not remain in India, and your safety could only be assured if you were far enough away that those fanatics could never recapture you."

"And so, Mr. Fogg," Mrs. Aouda continued, "not content with rescuing me from a horrible death, you feel you are also obliged to secure my happiness in a foreign country?"

"Yes, madam," replied Mr. Fogg, "but events did not turn in my favor. And yet, I ask your permission to employ the little that remains to me in your interests."

"But what about you, Mr. Fogg — what will become of you?" asked Mrs. Aouda.

"Madam," the gentleman coldly replied, "I need nothing."

"But how, sir, will you endure the fate which awaits you?"

"As one ought to do," replied Mr. Fogg.

"In any case," Mrs. Aouda began again, "it is not possible that destitution should strike a man like yourself. Your friends…"

"I have no friends, madam."

"Your relatives…"

"I no longer have any relatives."

"Then I feel for you, Mr. Fogg, for isolation is a grievous thing. What! Is there not a single heart into which you can pour your sorrows? And yet it is said that two together can face the cruellest miseries."

"So they say, madam."

"Mr. Fogg," said Mrs. Aouda then, rising and extending her hand to the gentleman, "would it please you to have, in me, both a relative and a friend? Will you have me as your wife?"

At these words, Mr. Fogg, too, rose from his chair. His eyes, it almost seemed, were shining. It almost seemed as though his lips were trembling. Mrs. Aouda looked at him. He was first surprised — and then pierced — by the sincerity, the uprightness, the firmness and the sweetness of that fair gaze, the gaze of a woman who risks all to save the one to whom all is owed. He closed his eyes for a moment, to stop that gaze from piercing

Mr Fogg, would it please you to have, in me, both a relative and a friend?

more deeply...

Then he opened them again. "I love you!" he said simply. "Yes, in truth, by all that is held sacred in the world, I love you, and I am entirely yours!"

"Ah...!" cried Mrs. Aouda, placing her hand on her heart.

They rang for Passepartout. He immediately entered. Mr. Fogg still held Mrs. Aouda's hand in his own. Passepartout understood, and his broad face shone like the noon-day sun above the tropics.

Mr. Fogg asked him if it would not be too late to notify the Reverend Samuel Wilson, of the parish of Marylebone.

Passepartout smiled his very happiest smile.

"Never too late," he said.

It was just five past eight in the evening.

"So it'll be for tomorrow, Monday!" he said.

"For tomorrow, Monday?" asked Mr. Fogg, turning to the young woman.

"For tomorrow, Monday!" replied Mrs. Aouda.

Passepartout left the room and set off at a run.

CHAPTER XXXVI

IN WHICH PHILEAS FOGG IS ONCE AGAIN
IN DEMAND ON THE EXCHANGE

It is now time to describe the reversal of opinion which took place in the United Kingdom when it was learned that the true culprit of the theft at the Bank of England – a certain James Strand – had been arrested on the 17th of December, in Edinburgh.

Three days before, Phileas Fogg had been a criminal whom the police were pursuing at all costs. Now he was the most honorable of gentlemen, who was mathematically pursuing his eccentric journey around the world.

What an effect – what a commotion this made in the

newspapers! All those betting for or against Mr. Fogg, most of whom had already forgotten the entire affair, felt their interest revived as if by magic. All their positions suddenly had value once again. Their transactions were suddenly brought back to life and, it must be said, the betting resumed with additional vigor. The name Phileas Fogg was once again sold at a premium on the Exchange.

The gentleman's five colleagues at the Reform Club spent those three days in a state of apprehension. That man Phileas Fogg, who had so conveniently disappeared from view, was now threatening to reappear before their eyes! Where was he at that very moment? On the 17th of December – the day James Strand was arrested – he had been gone for seventy-six days, and they had not received a single report of his progress! Had he given up? Had he renounced the struggle, or was he continuing his campaign according to the agreed itinerary? And would he reappear, on that Saturday, the 21st of December, at eight forty-five in the evening, like some patron deity of precision, at the entrance of the salon at the Reform Club?

One cannot hope to depict the anxiety which, for three days, gripped all of that great circle of English society. Dispatches were sent to America, to Asia, in hopes of some news of Phileas Fogg. Observers were sent every morning and evening to the

house on Savile Row…

In vain. Even the police themselves no longer knew what had become of the detective Fix, who had so rashly thrown himself upon a false trail. None of this, however, prevented the resumption of betting – now on an even vaster scale. Phileas Fogg, like a race horse, was coming to the final turn. He was no longer sold by the hundred, but by twenties – then by tens – then by fives, and the aged paralytic, Lord Albermale, bought him at even odds.

That is why, on Saturday evening, crowds gathered in Pall Mall and filled the neighboring streets. The people resembled an immense troupe of courtiers, permanently attending the court of the Reform Club. Traffic was disrupted. There were discussions and arguments, and changes in the value of 'Phileas Fogg' were announced to the crowd, like those of the great English funds. It was with considerable difficulty that the policemen maintained order in the crowd, and as the hour drew nearer at which Phileas Fogg was expected to arrive, passions rose to an unimaginable degree.

That evening, the gentleman's five colleagues had gathered in the grand salon of the Reform Club. The two bankers, John Sullivan and Samuel Fallentin, the engineer Andrew Stuart, Gauthier Ralph, administrator of the Bank of England, the

brewer Thomas Flanagan, all waited anxiously.

When the hands of the clock in the grand salon stood at twenty-five past eight, Andrew Stuart rose.

"Gentlemen," he said, "in twenty minutes the period agreed by Mr. Phileas Fogg and ourselves will have expired."

"At what time did the last train from Liverpool arrive?" asked Thomas Flanagan.

"At twenty-three past seven," replied Gauthier Ralph, "and the next train will only arrive at ten past midnight."

"Well then, gentlemen," continued Andrew Stuart, "if Phileas Fogg had arrived by the seven-twenty-three train, he would already be here. We can therefore consider the wager to be won."

"Wait — let's not get ahead of ourselves," countered Samuel Fallentin. "You know that our colleague is an eccentric of the first order. His exactitude in all matters is well known. He never arrives too late or too early, and it would not surprise me in the least if he appeared tonight at the very last minute."

"As for me," said Andrew Stuart, who was, as always, very nervous, "even if I saw it with my own eyes, I couldn't believe it."

"That's right," agreed Thomas Flanagan. "Phileas Fogg's project always was absurd. However exact he may be, he cannot prevent inevitable delays from occurring, and even a setback of

two or three days would be enough to compromise his entire journey."

"You will note, moreover," added John Sullivan, "that we have received no news of our colleague – and this despite the fact that telegraphic cables can be found everywhere along his route."

"He has lost, gentlemen," insisted Andrew Stuart, "he has lost a hundred times over! You know, at any rate, that the *China* – the only steamer from New York on which he could have sailed to reach Liverpool in time – arrived yesterday. Well, here is the list of passengers, published by the Shipping Gazette, and the name Phileas Fogg does not feature in it. Even with the best of luck, our colleague can only just have arrived in America! I estimate that he will reach his destination twenty days, at least, after the date we have agreed upon, and that old Lord Albermale will have lost his five thousand pounds!"

"It's perfectly obvious," replied Gauthier Ralph, "and tomorrow we have only to present Mr. Fogg's check to Baring Brothers."

At that moment, the hands of the clock in the salon stood at eight forty.

"Five more minutes," said Andrew Stuart.

The five colleagues looked at one another. The beating of their hearts had somewhat accelerated – as is understandable, for

this was a nerve-wracking finish, even for experienced gamesmen such as themselves! But they clearly did not wish to betray their anxiety, for, at Samuel Fallentin's urging, they all took their places at a card table.

"I wouldn't give up my share of four thousand pounds in this wager," said Andrew Stewart as he sat down, "even if you offered me three thousand, nine hundred and ninety-nine!"

The hands of the clock had moved to forty-two minutes past eight.

The players had taken up their cards, but their eyes returned constantly to the face of the clock. It must be said that, however confident they might be, no minutes had ever seemed to pass more slowly!

"Eight forty-three," said Thomas Flanagan, cutting the deck presented to him by Gauthier Ralph.

There was a moment of silence. The club's vast salon was quiet, but they could hear, outside, the noise of the crowd, punctuated from time to time by sharp cries. The pendulum of the clock swung once every second with mathematical regularity. Each player could count for himself the sexagesimal divisions ringing in his ears.

"Eight forty-four!" said John Sullivan, in whose voice could now be detected an involuntary thrill.

Just one more minute, and the wager would be won. Andrew Stuart and his colleagues had stopped playing. They had dropped their cards! They were counting the seconds!

At the fortieth second – nothing. At the fiftieth – still nothing!

At the fifty-fifth, they heard outside a sound like thunder, applause, cheers, and curses as well, which built into a continuous, reverberating roar.

The players rose from their seats.

At the fifty-seventh second, the door to the salon opened, and the pendulum had not yet swung the sixtieth second of the minute, when Phileas Fogg appeared, followed by a delirious crowd which had forced its way into the club.

"Gentlemen, here I am," he said calmly.

CHAPTER XXXVII

IN WHICH IT IS PROVEN THAT PHILEAS FOGG GAINED NOTHING FROM HIS JOURNEY AROUND THE WORLD, ASIDE FROM HAPPINESS

Yes! It was Phileas Fogg in person.

It will be recalled that, at five past eight in the evening – some twenty-five hours after the arrival of the travelers in London – Passepartout had been charged by his master with notifying the Reverend Samuel Wilson that a certain marriage was due to take place the very next day.

Passepartout, delighted, had immediately set off. He had rushed to the home of the Reverend Samuel Wilson, who was not yet in. Naturally, Passepartout waited – and waited a good twenty minutes, at least.

In short, it was eight thirty-five when he left the reverend's home. But in what a state did he leave it! Disheveled, hatless, running – running as no man has ever been seen to run, shoving pedestrians aside and flying along the pavements like a whirlwind!

Within three minutes, he had returned to the house on Savile Row, and he collapsed, out of breath and unable to speak, in his master's room.

"What is it?" asked Mr. Fogg.

"My master –" gasped Passepartout, "marriage – impossible."

"Impossible?"

"Not possible – for tomorrow."

"Why is that?"

"Because tomorrow – is Sunday!"

"Monday," corrected Mr. Fogg.

"No – today – Saturday."

"Saturday? Impossible!"

"Yes, yes, yes, yes!" cried Passepartout. "You miscalculated – by one day! We arrived twenty-four hours ahead of schedule… But we have only ten minutes to spare…!"

Passepartout seized his master by the collar, and he dragged him along with irresistible force!

Phileas Fogg, thus propelled, without having the time to think, exited his room, exited his house, vaulted into a cab, promised a

Phileas Fogg, thus propelled, without having the time to think,
exited his room, exited his house, and vaulted into a cab.

hundred pounds to the coachman and, having run over two dogs and struck five other carriages, he arrived at the Reform Club.

The hands of the clock stood at eight forty-five when he appeared in the grand salon...

Phileas Fogg had completed his journey around the world in eighty days...! He had won his wager of twenty thousand pounds!

And now – how is it possible that a man so exact, so meticulous, could have made an error in his calculations of an entire day? How is it possible that he had believed, when he stepped from the train in London, that it was Saturday evening, the 21st of December, when in reality it was Friday the 20th of December, and only seventy-nine days after his departure?

Here is the reason for his error, and it is quite simple.

Phileas Fogg had unsuspectingly gained a day on his itinerary – and this was purely because he had made his journey around the world by going east. If, on the contrary, he had traveled in the other direction, towards the west, he would have lost a day.

Indeed, by going east, Phileas Fogg was traveling towards the sun – and, in consequence, the days were shortened by four minutes for every degree of longitude that he traversed along his route. Now, the total number of degrees on the circumference of the Earth is three hundred and sixty, and those three hundred

and sixty degrees multiplied by four minutes yield precisely twenty-four hours – which is to say, they yield the one day which Phileas Fogg had unwittingly gained. In other words, while the gentleman, traveling eastwards, saw the sun pass overhead eighty times, his colleagues in London had only seen it pass seventy-nine times. This is why, on that fateful day, which was the Saturday and not the Sunday as Mr. Fogg believed, those colleagues were waiting for him in the salon of the Reform Club.

And this is precisely what Passepartout's infamous watch – which had remained set to London time – would have shown if only, in addition to the minutes and the hours, it had displayed the days!

So Phileas Fogg had won the twenty thousand pounds. However, because he had spent roughly nineteen thousand pounds in the process, the pecuniary result was negligible. After all, as we have said, the eccentric gentleman had made his wager for the sake of the endeavor, not for the sake of fortune. And in fact, the thousand pounds which remained of his winnings, he divided between the honest Passepartout and the unhappy Fix – against whom he was unable to bear a grudge. Naturally, for the sake of consistency, he deducted from his servant's share the price of the nineteen hundred and twenty hours of gas burned on his account.

That very evening Mr. Fogg, as impassive and phlegmatic as ever, said to Mrs. Aouda: "Madam, is this marriage still agreeable to you?"

"Mr. Fogg," replied Mrs. Aouda, "it is for me to ask you that question. Before, you were ruined, now you are rich…"

"Pardon me, madam, but this fortune belongs to you. If you had not proposed this marriage, my servant would not have visited the Reverend Samuel Wilson, and I would not have been alerted to my error, and…"

"Dear Mr. Fogg…" said the young woman.

"Dear Aouda…" replied Phileas Fogg.

To the satisfaction of all, the marriage took place forty-eight hours later. Passepartout – superb, resplendent, dazzling – took part as the young woman's witness. Was it not he who had saved her, and was that honor not rightfully his?

The following morning, however, at dawn, it was this same Passepartout who hammered noisily at his master's bedroom door.

The door opened, and the impassive gentleman appeared.

"What is it, Passepartout?"

"Monsieur! It's… It's that I've found out, only this instant…"

"Well, what?"

"That we could have made our journey around the world in just seventy-nine days."

"Yes, without a doubt," replied Mr. Fogg, "by choosing not to cross India by land. But if I had not crossed India, I should not have saved Mrs. Aouda, she would not be my wife, and..."

And Mr. Fogg calmly shut the bedroom door.

So Phileas Fogg had won his wager. He had completed within eighty days a journey around the world! To do so, he had used every means of transportation available: steamship, train, sailing yacht, carriage, merchant vessel, sledge, elephant... And throughout this affair, the eccentric gentleman had deployed his marvelous qualities of composure and exactitude. But what then? What had he gained by this expedition? What had he brought home from this voyage?

Nothing, one might say. Nothing, indeed, unless it were a charming wife who – as incredible as it may seem – made him the very happiest of men!

And truly, who would not, for less than that, embark on a journey around the world?

ABOUT *AROUND THE WORLD IN EIGHTY DAYS*

"I wager twenty thousand pounds that I will travel around the world in eighty days or less – that is, in nineteen hundred and twenty hours, or one hundred and fifteen thousand and two hundred minutes."

With this precisely stated challenge, Phileas Fogg sets out on his famous journey around the world. Along the way, he will travel by sea and land, train and steamboat, through jungles, over mountains, and across snowy plains. The journey will cost him half of his fortune, and put the other half at risk. It will spark an international manhunt. It will see him risk his life several times

over — for his honor, for his friends, and for the sake of a woman he has never met before.

None of this is particularly unusual: such hazards and adventures were to be expected from a journey around the world. What makes Phileas Fogg's wager so extraordinary is his calm division of the eighty-day time limit into hours — and even minutes. It is this audacious punctuality that drives the pace of the story that follows, and makes Phileas Fogg such a heroic figure (despite his cold demeanor). It also changes a seemingly ordinary travel narrative into a story about technology and the way in which it can transform the world.

Around the World in Eighty Days was first published in 1873, and the fictional events it describes take place in 1872. At that time, it would have seemed slightly absurd to predict the duration of a journey around the world. For almost all of human memory, long-distance travelers had been at the mercy of wind, weather and circumstance. New technologies such as trains and steam-powered ships were starting to change this, and were indeed improving the speed, comfort, and reliability of travel. However, as Phileas Fogg's Reform Club colleagues point out to him, these modes of transportation were still vulnerable to mechanical failure and other unforeseeable delays. And Fogg's eighty-day journey would depend on near-perfect coordination

between at least a dozen different travel networks — between the arrival of steamers and the departure of trains.

In fact, in the early 1870s, several real-life developments had combined to make Phileas Fogg's project slightly less preposterous. In 1869, the Suez Canal opened in Egypt, making it possible for ships to sail from the Mediterranean to the Red Sea, rather than having to sail around the whole of Africa. In the same year, a transcontinental railway line was completed in the United States, connecting San Francisco to New York. And in 1870, in India, a railway line opened between Bombay, Allahabad and Calcutta. These feats of engineering shortened and simplified the route Phileas Fogg would take. They made it possible to imagine a case in which a human machine such as Fogg might, with perfect regularity and a minimum of exertion, almost make his orbit around the Earth.

Almost. Ultimately, *Around the World in Eighty Days* reveals that Phileas Fogg is in the wrong. His vision of a world in which travel can be calculated down to the minute is premature. The world is indeed changing — is 'getting smaller', as Fogg and his colleagues put it — but it has not yet shrunk far enough to dispense with drama and adventure. If Fogg wins his wager, it is due not to his meticulous, unperturbable regularity, but to his willingness to stop the gaps in his global itinerary with acts

of personal heroism — such as pirating a vessel and burning it down to the waterline. And even then, Fogg must rely on the navigational quirk of an unexpected extra day to nip in under the wire.

In this sense, Verne's novel is less about geography and technology than it is about character. Phileas Fogg, who aspires to be an automaton, is forced by his journey around the world to become human. He is forced to make accommodations in his character and his actions — and in his itinerary — for friendship and romance, for disappointment and even for surprise. It is partly this exploration of Fogg's character, rather than Verne's survey of his route across the globe, which makes *Around the World in Eighty Days* so compelling.

As far as Verne's literary world tour is concerned, the author does make some missteps. It appears, for example, that Verne got mixed up in his American geography more than once, misplacing towns and even a river. Perhaps this is all to be expected. Jules Verne had never traveled to Bombay or to Yokohama; he never wandered through the Suez bazaar, or waited for a herd of buffalo to clear the way across the prairie. He sought to depict these places and scenes accurately, but his sources of information were, by modern standards, limited.

Verne devoted many hours to research in the French National

Library, in Paris, where he read books and articles about travel, consulted periodicals and pored over technical manuals. He took extensive notes, collecting them on cards which he would categorize for future use. But despite this, he seems to have made errors from time to time. And he was further limited by his reliance on other writers: he added their errors, exaggerations and prejudices to his own.

For many readers today, it is Verne's prejudices, rather than his errors, that jar them most. The descriptions of other cultures, races and religions in *Around the World in Eighty Days* are frequently offensive. The casual, offhand racism of Verne's comments about the inhabitants of the Andaman Islands, for example, or about the Japanese, cannot easily be explained away. Such comments are, partly, a symptom of the era of empire and colonialism to which Phileas Fogg and his creator both belong, and which they cannot escape. And yet, to say that Verne was a product of his time – which undoubtedly he was – does not excuse him.

Still, Verne does succeed in undermining – or at least complicating – some of the contemporary views about the roles of women. When Mrs. Aouda first appears in the narrative, she seems set to play a conventional part: that of a helpless, beautiful heroine in need of rescue. But once she has shaken off the opium

haze imposed on her by her captors, she reveals a rather different character. She is as tough and uncomplaining a traveler as Phileas Fogg himself. She shows courage under fire, and is perfectly comfortable with a six-shooter in her hands. And, when her rescuer is plunged into defeat and despair, she takes charge, rescuing him in turn with her proposal of marriage.

Perhaps *Around the World in Eighty Days* is a novel that's perpetually ahead of and behind the times. It is a book that feels both antiquated and visionary, frustratingly conventional and daringly new. Today, technological changes and engineering achievements continue to transform the globe. But Fogg's vision of a world in which our course can be determined, eighty days in advance, down to the hour and the minute, still feels like science fiction.

ABOUT JULES VERNE

Jules Verne was born on the 8th of February, 1828, in the French port city of Nantes. He was the first of five siblings. His mother, Sophie, came from a family of ship-owners and navigators, and his father, Pierre, was a lawyer.

From his earliest days, the young Jules Verne was fascinated by literature and geography. He loved reading adventure stories set in far-flung, exotic locations. Two of his favorite authors were James Fenimore Cooper, who wrote novels about pirates and naval battles, and Johann David Wyss, who wrote *The Swiss Family Robinson*, about a family shipwrecked on a desert island.

Verne was enchanted by these tales, and the worlds they described seemed almost within his reach. The Loire River, passing through his home city, was crowded with ships setting out or returning from distant ports. Sailing vessels were moored in ranks three deep along the quays. Verne would later recall how, one night, he slipped aboard a three-masted merchant ship and wandered the decks, running his hands along the ropes and cables, breathing the aroma of spices and tar from the cargo hold, and dreaming of sailing to distant ports.

Sadly, it was not to be. The boy was expected to follow in his father's footsteps, and in 1847, at the age of 19, he went to Paris to study law.

LAWYER, AUTHOR OR STOCKBROKER?

In Paris, Verne studied diligently – but he also became increasingly interested in writing. He composed poetry and plays. He began attending literary salons – parties hosted by well-known members of society, at which writers discussed their craft. Verne made friends with playwrights and musicians and other members of the Parisian theater community. And, in 1850, his comic play *The Broken Straws* was staged at the French capital's Théâtre Historique.

One year later, Verne completed his law degree – but he resisted pressure from his father to begin a career as a lawyer. By now he was writing more plays and comic operas, and publishing stories in popular magazines. He had also taken on a job (more or less unpaid) as the secretary of a theater. He still wasn't sure that he could support himself by writing. Becoming a writer was much riskier than taking over the family law practice. But Verne believed in his own potential, and he persisted.

It was during this period that Verne began to explore the idea of writing a new kind of novel: what he came to call a 'novel of science'. It would blend adventure stories with carefully researched information and scientific facts. Verne's first attempt at such a book depicts a journey, made in a hydrogen-filled balloon, across Africa – a continent that was then largely unfamiliar to many European readers. To write the book, Verne did extensive research in the Paris libraries, poring over maps and explorers' accounts of their travels. The resulting story was filled with technical, historical, and geographical detail – as well as feats of daring and narrow escapes.

While he continued to work on his scientific novels, Verne came to an important turning point. In 1856, he met a young widow named Honorine de Viane Morel. The two fell in love and, less than a year later, they married. Honorine had two children

from her previous marriage, which meant Verne suddenly had a family to support. He gave up his unpaid work in the Paris theater, and instead, he became a stockbroker. He would rise early in the morning to write, and then proceeded to the Bourse de Paris, the Paris Stock Exchange, where he spent the rest of the day trading stocks. He was not, by all accounts, a financial wizard – but he was earning enough to get by, even after the birth of his son, Michel, in 1861.

HETZEL AND THE *VOYAGES EXTRAORDINAIRES*

In 1862, Verne met a man who would truly change the course of his life: the publisher Pierre-Jules Hetzel. Hetzel was putting together a new family magazine, called the 'Magazine of Education and Recreation'. It was to feature illustrated adventure stories and articles with a modern, scientific angle. Verne's 'novels of science' were a perfect fit. Verne showed Hetzel his story of the balloon journey across Africa and, in January of 1863, this first novel was published in the new magazine under the title *Five Weeks in a Balloon*.

From this point on, Hetzel published nearly all of Verne's novels. The publisher offered him a long-term contract for three new books per year, which provided him with a reliable and

respectable income. He left his job at the Stock Exchange and wrote full time. Each of his novels was serialized in Hetzel's magazine – they appeared chapter by chapter in successive issues. At the end of the year, when the last instalment had appeared in the magazine, the novels were elegantly reprinted, bound and issued in book form, so that children might receive them as Christmas presents.

This approach was hugely successful, and Verne went on to publish more than 50 novels with Hetzel. Together, the books formed a series known as the *Voyages Extraordinaires*, or the 'Extraordinary Voyages'. Some of the most famous of these stories include *20,000 Leagues Under the Sea*, which features a submarine piloted by a mysterious outlaw, *From the Earth to the Moon*, which describes a project to reach the moon by firing a spaceship out of an enormous gun, and *Journey to the Center of the Earth*, which imagines a hidden world beneath the Earth's crust.

The Extraordinary Voyages earned Verne an international reputation, as well as financial success. His best-selling book, appearing in 1872, was *Around the World in Eighty Days*. It would sell over 100,000 copies in his lifetime – and an adaptation for the stage, co-written by Verne himself, proved wildly successful, running for some 68 years.

SETTING SAIL

Verne was now able to fulfil some of his childhood dreams. He traveled to America, where he visited New York and Niagara Falls. He made a short flight in a balloon – an experience he could only imagine when he had described it in his first novel. And he was able to buy a sailing boat of his own, the *Saint-Michel*. Aboard this vessel (and its larger successors, the *Saint-Michel II* and *Saint-Michel III*) Verne went on long cruises around Europe, from the Mediterranean to the North Sea. The boy who had yearned for a life of adventure and travel was now a seasoned mariner, and had seen the world.

In his later years, Verne dabbled in politics, collected accolades, and continued to write steadily, producing new novels every year. When he died in 1905, he left behind manuscripts for a last handful of books which his son, Michel, revised and edited for publication.

VERNE'S LEGACY

Today, Jules Verne's novels are read by children and adults alike, and are routinely adapted for the stage and screen. Verne is celebrated as an artist and innovator, and described by some as a

pioneer of the science fiction genre.

Indeed, technology – whether real or imagined – often plays a central role in Verne's novels. He himself claimed that he had not invented or predicted anything – but his willingness to build upon what was technically possible, his confidence in human scientific ability, and the sheer scale of his imagination made his stories truly remarkable. In a time when the streets of Europe were still lit with gas lanterns and crowded with horse-drawn carriages, Verne wrote about vast underground cities, floating islands, airborne fleets, and ambling, steam-powered houses.

Even if Jules Verne never invented new technologies himself, it is certain that he influenced many of those who did invent them, or who used them to expand human horizons. Many scientists, engineers and adventurers – from the rocket designer Wernher von Braun to the polar explorer Fridtjof Nansen – have spoken of Verne as someone who first inspired them.

In 1969, when the Apollo 11 space mission returned from the moon, and the crew prepared to splash down in the Pacific Ocean, Commander Neil Armstrong addressed the world by radio. "A hundred years ago, Jules Verne wrote a book about a voyage to the moon," the astronaut said, noting that Verne

had even seemed to predict their launch from Florida and their water landing in the Pacific. In that moment of triumph for the scientific community, the improbable fictions of Jules Verne had sprung from the pages of a book and become historical fact.

It was not the first time that this had happened, nor would it be the last.

WHO, WHAT AND WHERE

Note: All words appearing in capital letters have their own entry in this glossary.

A

ALABAMA, THE • a warship constructed by English ship builders for the Confederate States of America during the American Civil War

ALABAMA AFFAIR, THE • a legal and diplomatic controversy in which the American government sought payment from the British government to make up for the loss of Union ships to Confederate Navy warships (such as the *ALABAMA*) which had been constructed in the United Kingdom

AMPHION • a character from Greek mythology who built a city with his musical skill: he played a lyre – a kind of harp – to enchant the building stones so that they leaped into place

ANNAM • the former name of the central coastal region of Vietnam

ASPHALTITES, LAKE • the Greek name for the Dead Sea

ATHENS • a Greek city, one of the oldest European centers of art and culture

B

BANIYA • a class or group of people in India who worked as merchants, bankers, and moneylenders

BANK, THE • short for 'the Bank of England', the United Kingdom's central bank

BARNUM • general term for a circus proprietor, after the famous American showman P. T. Barnum (1810 - 1891), who founded the Barnum & Bailey Circus

BLONDIN, CHARLES • (1824 - 1897), a French tightrope walker and circus performer, who crossed the Niagara gorge on a tightrope, blindfolded

BOMBAY • the former name of the Indian city Mumbai

BRAHMA • a HINDU god, often depicted with four faces and four arms

BRAHMIN • a HINDU social class, composed primarily of teachers and priests

BUDDHIST • relating to Buddhism, a religion and philosophy originating in India 2,500 years ago

BYRON, GEORGE GORDON (LORD BYRON) • (1788 - 1824) an English poet, famed for his good looks, dashing exploits, and scandalous behavior as well as for his verse

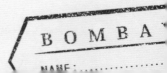

C

CANTON RIVER, THE • a river in Southern China, today known as the Pearl River

CELESTIAL EMPIRE, THE • a former name for China

CEYLON • the former name of the island of Sri Lanka

CEYLANIANS • the inhabitants of **CEYLON**

CITY, THE • the City of London, a small part of central London which was historically its financial and business center

CHURCH OF JESUS CHRIST OF LATTER-DAY SAINTS, THE • a Christian sect originating in the US in the 1820s and headquartered in Salt Lake City, Utah

COCHINCHINA • the former name of a region in southern Vietnam

COLORADO RIVER, THE • a major river running through the southwestern United States and Mexico

COLT • a manufacturer of firearms, founded in 1855

CONFUCIUS • (551 BCE - 479 BCE) a Chinese philosopher whose ideas developed into a system of thought known as Confucianism

CORNWALLIS, LORD CHARLES • (1738 - 1805) a British nobleman and army officer who served as Governor-General of India

D

DE LESSEPS, FERDINAND • (1805 - 1894) a French diplomat and the developer of the Suez Canal, which was completed in 1869

E

EAST INDIA COMPANY • a vast British trading company, founded in 1600 and dissolved in 1874. At the height of its power, it maintained its own military forces and ruled over vast territories

ELEPHANTA • an island in the harbor of **BOMBAY**, renowned for a system of caves containing magnificent **HINDU** and **BUDDHIST** carvings in stone

EMPIRE OF THE SUN, THE • a name for the Empire of Japan (1868 - 1947)

ENFIELD • an English town, home to the firearms manufacturer the Royal Small Arms Factory, founded in 1816

ESQUIRE • a title referring to a rank just below knight, formerly accorded to gentlemen of a certain social standing

EXCHANGE, THE • refers to the London Stock Exchange, the place where stocks and bonds are bought and sold

F

FARMER & CO. • a department store once located in Regent Street, London

FASTNET LIGHT, THE • a lighthouse which warns ships away from a dangerous rocky islet in the Atlantic, off the southwest coast of Ireland

FIGARO • general term for a barber, after the lead character in an opera by Gioachino Rossini, *The Barber of Seville*

FORMOSA • the former name for the island of Taiwan

G

GIBRALTAR • a tiny, well-defended and strategically important British territory located at the western end of the Mediterranean Sea

GOLCONDA • a region of India known for its diamond mines

GRAND BANKS OF NEWFOUNDLAND, THE • a series of underwater plateaus found off the coast of Newfoundland, whose shallow waters are a danger to shipping

GUEBRE • see PARSEE

H

HINDU • relating to Hinduism, a religion originating, and primarily practiced, in India and Nepal

HOTTENTOT • (outdated, offensive) a term used to refer to the Khoikhoi peoples of southwestern Africa

HUGO, VICTOR • (1802 - 1885) a French poet, novelist and playwright

JOHN BULL • a figure representing England, who appeared frequently in political cartoons in the 18th and 19th centuries

J

JORDAN RIVER, THE • there are several Jordan Rivers: one, in the Middle East, flows into the Dead Sea; another, in the US, flows into the Great Salt Lake

JUGGERNAUT, THE CAR OF • a towering, heavy chariot bearing a HINDU idol; some European writers claimed that fanatical worshippers would throw themselves before its unstoppable wheels and be crushed to death

K

KALI • a HINDU goddess, often shown wearing a necklace of human heads and a skirt of human arms

KAMA OR KAMADEVA • the HINDU god of love and desire

KANHERI CAVES • a group of caves outside Mumbai containing BUDDHIST sculptures, stone carvings and other artworks

KAUFFMANN, ANGELICA • (1741 - 1807) a Swiss painter who worked for many years in Great Britain

L

LATTER-DAY SAINTS • the name by which the MORMONS refer to themselves

LÉOTARD, JULES • (1838 - 1870) a French acrobat known for performing on a trapeze

M

MEACO • one of the names of the former Japanese capital city, Kyoto

MIDDLE KINGDOM, THE • a name for China, often used in the 19th century

MIKADO • a former name for the Emperor of Japan

MINERVA • the Roman name for the goddess of wisdom and strategy; known by the Greeks as Athena

MOHAMMED • (570 - 632) prophet and the founder of the Muslim faith

MOLIÈRE • (1622 - 1673) the stage name of Jean-Baptiste Poquelin, a French comic playwright

MORMON • a member of the CHURCH OF JESUS CHRIST OF LATTER-DAY SAINTS, a Christian sect originating in the US in the 1820s

N

NEW HOLLAND • (outdated) a name for the continent of Australia, first used by a Dutch navigator in 1644

P

PARSEE (OR GUEBRE) • a member of the cultural and ethnic group linked to the Zoroastrian faith, originally from Persia and now based primarily in India

PAWNEE • a Native American tribe historically based on the Great Plains, between the Rocky Mountains and the Mississippi River

R

RAMAYANA, THE • an epic poem, originally composed in Sanskrit, which depicts events and characters central to the teachings of the HINDU religion

REFORM CLUB, THE • a private club, founded in 1836, and located in Pall Mall, London

S

SANDWICH MEN • men employed to carry large advertising posters, often with one hanging on their chest and one on their back – giving them the appearance of a sandwich

SCOTLAND YARD • the headquarters of the Metropolitan Police Service; often used to refer to the service itself

SEPOY MUTINY • a violent uprising which took place in India, in 1857, against the BRITISH EAST INDIA COMPANY and the British more generally; it began with a mutiny of the sepoys (Indian troops) serving in the Company's army

SHEPPARD, JACK • (1702 - 1724) a notorious English thief who escaped from prison four times before he was finally captured and publicly hanged; he was idolized by the poor and celebrated in songs, plays and novels

SHERIDAN, RICHARD BRINSLEY BUTLER • (1751 - 1816) an Irish satirist, playwright, poet and politician

SINDHIS • members of a community and culture originating in the Sindh region in modern-day Pakistan

SIOUX • refers to a group of Native American tribes historically based on the Great Plains, between the Rocky Mountains and the Mississippi River

SMITH, HYRUM • (1800 - 1844) the older brother of JOSEPH SMITH, and a leader of the CHURCH OF JESUS CHRIST OF LATTER DAY SAINTS

SMITH, JOSEPH • (1805 - 1844) an American prophet and religious leader; founder of the CHURCH OF JESUS CHRIST OF LATTER-DAY SAINTS

SOLOMON • (1010 BCE - 931 BCE) a famously wise king of Israel, mentioned in the Bible

STEPHENSON, ROBERT • (1803 - 1859) an English engineer specializing in railways and railway bridges, who incorrectly predicted that the Suez Canal project was not feasible, because the canal would rapidly fill up with sand

T

TAIKUN • a diplomatic title, meaning 'Great Lord', given to the military ruler (Shogun) of Japan in the 19th century

THUGS, THE • an association of thieves and murderers operating in India until the mid-19th century, known for strangling their victims

TREATY POINT • a small cape outside the Bay of Yokohama

TROPIC OF CANCER, THE • a line of latitude running around the Northern Hemisphere, marking the northern-most latitude at which the sun can be seen directly overhead

TUSSAUD, MADAME ANNA MARIE • (1761 - 1850) a French artist and entrepreneur who established a museum of startlingly lifelike wax sculptures in London

V

VISHWAKARMA • a HINDU creator deity; architect of the world

Y

YEDDO • one of several names given by the English to the Japanese port city of Edo (modern-day Tokyo) in the 19th century

YOUNG, BRIGHAM • (1801 - 1877) the second President of the CHURCH OF JESUS CHRIST OF LATTER-DAY SAINTS; led his MORMON followers in a migration to Utah; founder of Salt Lake City

Z

ZOROASTER • an ancient Iranian prophet whose teachings gave rise to the Zoroastrian religion; see PARSEE, GUEBRE

GLOSSARY

Note: All words appearing in capital letters have their own entry in this glossary.

A

ABEAM • (nautical) located at a right angle to the side of a vessel

ABLUTIONS • bathing or washing as part of a religious ritual

AERIALIST • an acrobat specializing in trapeze or tightrope

AFICIONADO • one who knows about and appreciates a certain activity

ANTIPODES • a location on the exact opposite side of the globe

B

BABOUCHE • a type of footwear, common in North Africa and the Middle East, resembling a slipper, often without a heel

BALLAST • (nautical) a heavy substance such as stone, sand, or iron, carried in a vessel's hold to help maintain its stability in the water

BAROMETER • an instrument used to track changes in atmospheric pressure, which can help to predict the weather

BATTEN • (nautical) to secure a HATCH, using tarpaulins and long, flat strips of wood called battens, in preparation for a heavy storm

BAZAAR • a market, usually with rows of stalls

BETEL • a plant, whose Latin name is *Piper betle*, and whose leaves are chewed as a stimulant; found primarily in South and Southeast Asia

BOND • (financial) a financial product: a type of loan, which can be bought and sold on the bond market, and which changes in value according to people's confidence in its future repayment

BONZE • another name for a Buddhist monk

BOW • (nautical) the front part of a vessel

BOWSPRIT • (nautical) a SPAR extending forward from the BOW of a vessel; provides an anchor point for STAYS and JIBS

BRIDGE • (nautical) the station, often an elevated platform such as the QUARTERDECK, from which a vessel is commanded

BULKHEAD • (nautical) a wall or partition used to divide the space inside a vessel

BULWARK • (nautical) a raised barrier surrounding the decks of a vessel, which offers some shelter and protection from the waves

C

CABLE • (nautical) a measure of length roughly equivalent to 185m (608 ft)

CACOLET • a seat or litter, usually one of a pair slung across the back of a pack animal, permitting passengers to ride on either side of the animal

CALICO • a type of cheap fabric, often dyed or printed with bright colors

CAPARISON • a decorative or protective covering made for an animal, such as a horse or elephant

CARBURETTED HYDROGEN • (now obsolete) term for the flammable gas methane

CAST OFF • (nautical) to release the ropes or cables attaching a vessel to a dock or mooring buoy, enabling the vessel to set sail

CENTERFIRE CARTRIDGE • a type of ammunition used in pistols, rifles and shotguns which came into widespread use in the mid-19th century

CHARTER • the process of hiring a vessel or a train for a journey

CHROMATIC SCALE • a twelve-note musical scale

CHRONOMETER • a particularly accurate watch or clock; ships' chronometers were an essential navigational tool and needed to be very accurate

CLIPPER • (nautical) a fast, three-masted, square-rigged sailing vessel

CLOSE-REEFED • (nautical) describes sails which have been set to expose a minimum of surface area, thereby lessening the risk of capsizing in high winds

COMPANIONWAY • (nautical) a ladder or set of steps leading from the deck of a vessel to the cabin or deck below; often sheltered by a raised HATCH

COOLIE • name for unskilled laborers, mainly from India, China, and other Asian countries, who worked in conditions similar to slavery; today this word is rarely used and is considered offensive

COURSE • (nautical) the lowest square sail on a mast

COWCATCHER • (railway) an angled metal structure, projecting from the front of a locomotive, designed to push livestock and other obstacles out of the way

CULVERT • (railway) a channel or tunnel allowing water to pass beneath a railway or road

CUSTOMS HOUSE • a building, usually located in a port, used by government officials who enforce laws concerning the import and export of goods

CUTTER • (nautical) a small, usually one-masted sailing vessel built for speed

D

DAMASCENED • ornately decorated with inlaid metals such as gold or silver

DIABLE • a French interjection meaning, literally, 'devil'

DILETTANTE • a dabbler; one who engages in a pursuit without much conviction, application, or understanding

DISPLACEMENT • (nautical) the weight of the water pushed aside by the hull of a floating vessel, which is exactly equal to the weight of the vessel itself

DIURNAL • relating to the daytime

DRAFT • (nautical) the distance from a vessel's KEEL to its waterline

DRAWBAR • (railway) a bar coupling one train carriage to the next

DRAW, TO • (nautical) referring to sails: to fill with wind and propel the vessel

DRAWING OFFICE • the bank office responsible for processing the deposits and withdrawals of private customers

DUMMY • the imaginary holder of the fourth hand of cards in a three-player variation of **WHIST** (a card game)

E

EQUILIBRIST • an acrobat specializing in feats of balance

EQUINOX • the time, or day – which comes twice every year – when the length of the day and night are equal

EXTRADITION • a process by which a suspected or convicted criminal is transferred from one country to another to stand trial or serve a sentence

F

FAKIR • term referring to a Hindu or Muslim holy man; usually one who lives a life of poverty

FELLAH • an Egyptian peasant

FIREMAN (railway) • member of a train crew responsible for tending the engine's furnace

438

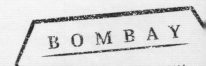

FOREDECK • (nautical) the deck at the front of a vessel

FORESTAY • (nautical) see 'STAY'

FOUNDER • (nautical) to fill with water and sink

G

GANGWAY • (nautical/railway) a walkway leading from the land to the deck of a ship, or from one train carriage to another

GIMBAL LAMP • (nautical) a lamp mounted in such a way that it remains upright even on board a vessel that is pitching and rolling

GRAND SLAM • when a team of two players wins all of the thirteen TRICKS in a hand of WHIST (a card game)

GUINEA • a British gold coin whose value was equal to just over one pound sterling; although the coin fell out of circulation in the early 19th century, the term continued to be used to indicate an amount of twenty-one shillings

H

HALYARD • (nautical) a line or rope used to raise a sail

HATCH • (nautical) a wooden covering for a HATCHWAY

HATCHWAY • (nautical) an opening in the deck of a vessel

HELM • (nautical) a vessel's steering equipment, such as a wheel or tiller

HEMP • a plant, whose Latin name is *Cannabis sativa*, which contains chemical compounds that produce an intoxicating effect

HENNA • a plant, whose Latin name is *Lawsonia inermis*, which can be ground into a powder used in cosmetics, for example, to stain the skin or hair

HONORS • extra points which may be won for the possession of certain cards in WHIST (a card game)

HOROLOGY • the study or manufacture of watches and clocks

HYDROGRAPHICAL • concerning the scientific study of oceans, seas, lakes, rivers and other bodies of water

HYPOGEA • an underground building, such as a temple or tomb

I

INSOUCIANCE • a lack of concern

IONIC • a style of classical architecture; used especially to describe a particular type of column

J

JETTY • a man-made structure projecting out from the land into the water

JIB • (nautical) a triangular sail carried at the front of a vessel

JUNK • (nautical) a type of Chinese sailing ship, whose sails are braced by horizontal rows of thin wooden battens

K

KAGO • a type of LITTER used for transportation in Japan

KEEL • (nautical) the long timber running along the bottom of a vessel and supporting the hull

KIMONO • a T-shaped robe with long, wide sleeves, secured around the waist by a sash, traditionally worn by both Japanese men and women

KNOT • (nautical) a unit of speed, used primarily at sea, equivalent to 1.85 km per hour (1.15 miles per hour)

L

LIGHTSHIP • (nautical) a ship, equipped with a bright light, which can be moored in dangerous waters to act as a lighthouse

LILLIPUTIAN • tiny

LITTER • a means of transportation consisting of a bed-like platform, mounted on poles, carried by two or more bearers

LOG • (nautical) an instrument used to determine the speed of a vessel through water; consists of a piece of wood attached to a rope marked off by evenly spaced knots

LOST-MOLD CRYSTAL • crystal cast using a technique in which the mold is destroyed, and so can be used only once

M

MASTHEAD • (nautical) the very top of a mast

MERIDIAN • an imaginary line running across the Earth's surface from pole to pole and perpendicular to the equator, used in navigation and geography; also known as a line of longitude

MINARET • a tall, slender tower, usually associated with a mosque, and often featuring a balcony from which the Muslim call to prayer is given

MISDEAL • an error made during the distribution of cards to the players of a card game

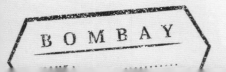

440

MITER • a type of tall headgear, resembling that worn by a Christian bishop

MONSIEUR • a French word meaning 'sir'

MOLDED DEPTH • (nautical) the height of the space enclosed between a vessel's KEEL and its deck

N

NADIR • the lowest point

NOON SIGHT / SIGHTING • (nautical) at noon, a navigator uses an instrument called a sextant to measure the height of the sun above the horizon; this can be used to determine a ship's longitude

NORIMON • a type of covered LITTER used in Japan

O

OMNIBUS • an enclosed, horse-drawn vehicle for the transport of passengers

OPIUM • a drug derived from the poppy plant, whose Latin name is *Papaver somniferum*

P

PAGODA • a building, often a temple, usually in the form of a tower, with several eaves or roofs stacked one above the other

PALANQUIN • a mode of transportation consisting of a chair or LITTER, open or enclosed, mounted on poles and carried by two or more bearers

PALKI-GHARRY • a type of enclosed carriage commonly used in India

PAR, AT • (financial) at a price equal to its stated value

PARALLEL • one of the circles of latitude: imaginary lines, running parallel to the equator around the surface of the Earth; used in navigation and geography

PARBLEU • a mild French interjection which can mean 'Certainly!' or 'By Jove!'

PELISSE • a type of women's cloak, often trimmed with animal fur

PERISTYLE • a walkway or porch with a roof supported by rows of columns, constructed along the edge of a building or around a courtyard

PERSPICACITY • discernment; shrewdness; insightfulness

PHLEGMATIC • calm; expressionless; displaying little or no emotion

PHYSIOGNOMY • term referring to physical features, especially of the face and skull

PHYSIOGNOMIST • one who studies PHYSIOGNOMY, especially in the belief that the features may reflect aspects of a subject's character; theories about PHYSIOGNOMY were popular in the 19th century

PILOT • (nautical) a professional navigator with specialized local knowledge who can guide vessels safely into and out of ports – avoiding hidden reefs, dangerous currents, etc.

POLYGAMY • the practice of having more than one wife at the same time

PONTOON • (nautical) a flotation device that can bear a heavy load; often incorporated in floating docks or rafts

PORPHYRY • a type of igneous (volcanic) rock, often of a purple or reddish color, and containing large crystals

PORT • (nautical) of or relating to the left side of a vessel when facing forward (see also 'STARBOARD')

PORTICO • a porch-like entrance to a building, often supported by columns

PREMIUM, AT A • (financial) at a price above its stated value

PRESTIDIGITATION • a term for stage magic and sleight-of-hand tricks

PROBOSCIS • a term referring to the nose of an animal – particularly one which is elongated and movable

PROSELYTISM • the practice of seeking converts to one's religious beliefs

PUGILISM • the art of boxing

PURSER • (nautical) an officer responsible for the keeping of financial accounts, and for the purchasing and distribution of supplies

Q

QUARTER • (nautical) of or relating to the side of a vessel near the STERN

QUARTERDECK • (nautical) the deck or part of the deck near the STERN of a vessel; traditionally the station of the captain and other officers

R

RAJAH • an Indian monarch or ruler

REACH • (nautical) the act of sailing with the wind coming from the side

REEF • (nautical) to reduce the area of a sail exposed to the wind – for example, to reduce the risk of capsizing in heavy winds

RELIQUARY • a container, often highly decorated and made from precious materials, intended for the storage of holy objects, particularly the remains of saints

RIGGING • (nautical) a vessel's ropes, **SPARS** and masts

RIO • the Spanish word for 'river'; widely used in the western US to refer to rivers and creeks

ROADSTEAD • (nautical) the sheltered waters outside a port, where a vessel may safely anchor

RUBBER • the best of three games of **WHIST** (a card game)

RUNNING LIGHTS • (nautical) red, green and white lights borne by a vessel to indicate its position and orientation in the dark

S

SAKE • a Japanese rice wine

SALON • a large reception room, often lavishly decorated

SAMPAN • (nautical) a small, flat-bottomed Chinese boat

SCHOONER • (nautical) a two-masted sailing vessel whose foremast is shorter than or equal in height to its mainmast

SCUD • (nautical) to move swiftly in a straight line, especially when blown before the wind

SECOND • the assistant to one of the principal participants in a duel; usually expected to act as a go-between and to help make arrangements before the combat

SEXAGESIMAL • of or relating to a division into sixty parts

SHARE • (financial) a financial product representing a small ownership stake in a particular company

SHEET • (nautical) a rope controlling the orientation of a sail relative to the direction of the wind

SHROUD • (nautical) a rope or cable extending from the top of a mast to the sides of a vessel, which help keep the mast upright

SLOOP • (nautical) a single-masted sailing vessel

SOMBRERO • a wide-brimmed Mexican hat

SPAR • (nautical) any pole, boom, mast, gaff or other piece of wood used to spread or carry a sail

SPAR DECK • (nautical) a vessel's upper deck

SPECIFIC GRAVITY • relative density

SPINDRIFT • the spray blown by the wind from the crests of waves

STARBOARD • (nautical) of or relating to the right side of a vessel when facing forward (see also 'PORT')

STAY • (nautical) a rope or cable running fore and aft from a vessel's deck to the tops of the masts and back down to the bow, which helps keep the masts upright; the stay attached to the stern is called a 'backstay'; the stay attached to the bow is called a 'FORESTAY'

STEM • (nautical) the timber at the very front of a vessel, extending from the forward end of the KEEL to the deck

STERN • (nautical) the rear part of a vessel

STRIKE • (nautical) to bring down onto the deck – for example, a flag or SPAR

SUPERSTRUCTURE • (nautical) the parts of a vessel built above the deck, such as cabins and deckhouses, but not including masts

SUTTEE • an outdated custom in which some Hindu widows would throw themselves upon their husbands' funeral pyres and be burned to death

SYENITE • a type of igneous (volcanic) rock similar to granite

T

TELEGRAM • a message sent via telegraph, and usually delivered in written form

TELEGRAPHIC CABLE • a cable carrying an electric charge, used for sending messages across long distances

TOPOGRAPHY • the particular arrangement of features in a landscape

TOPSAIL • (nautical) a sail set high on a mast, above the mainsail or COURSE

TOUCH HOLE • a small hole at the back of a gun or cannon, through which the charge is ignited to fire the weapon

TRACTION • a continuous pulling force

TRAPP • a type of dark-colored igneous (volcanic) rock with a fine grain

TRUCK • (railway) a structure found beneath a railway carriage, to which wheels and axles are attached; most carriages have one truck at either end, and most trucks feature two or more pairs of wheels

TRUCK • (nautical) a spherical or disk-like cap found at the very tip of a mast

TRUMP • the suit which, in a given game of WHIST, beats all others

U

UPPERWORKS • (nautical) the various parts of a vessel above the waterline

V

VIHARA • a Buddhist monastery, often used by wandering monks

W

WATERSHED • high ground from which water flows down into streams, creeks and rivers

WATTLE-AND-DAUB • a building material, used to make walls, consisting of woven sticks plastered with a combination of mud, clay, straw and dung

WEIGH ANCHOR • (nautical) the act of raising the anchor from the seabed in order to set sail

WHIST • a trick-taking card game, somewhat similar to bridge, usually played by four people, and popular in the 18th and 19th centuries

WING AND WING • (nautical) an arrangement of the sails, when sailing before the wind, in which the JIB is set to windward; this may give a vessel the appearance of having a pair of wings, one on either side

WITHERS • the part of a four-legged animal's back above the shoulders and at the base of the neck

Y

YAKUNIN • a Japanese official

YARD • (nautical) a horizontal SPAR, on a mast, used to carry a sail, especially a square sail

Z

ZEBU • a species of cattle, found mainly in South Asia, which have a large hump and a pronounced dewlap

ZENITH • the highest point

USBORNE QUICKLINKS

For links to websites where you can find out more about Jules Verne and the stories he wrote, go to the Usborne Quicklinks website at Usborne.com/quicklinks and type in the keywords 'Around the World in Eighty Days'.

The recommended websites are regularly reviewed and updated but, please note, Usborne Publishing is not responsible for the content of any website other than its own. We recommend that children are supervised while using the internet.

ACKNOWLEDGEMENTS

Designed by Brenda Cole and Vickie Robinson
Digital manipulation by Nick Wakeford
Design Manager: Nicola Butler

Every effort has been made to trace the copyright holders of material in this book. If any rights have been omitted, the publishers offer to rectify this in any subsequent editions following notification.

p.415 © World History Archive/Alamy Stock Photo